BUTTERFLIES DANCE

# Butterflies Dance in the Dark

Beatrice MacNeil

KEY PORTER BOOKS

National Library of Canada Cataloguing in Publication Data

MacNeil, Beatrice, 1945-
    Butterflies dance in the dark/Beatrice MacNeil.

ISBN 978-1-55263-474-5

I. Title.

PS8575.N43B88 2002        C813'.54        C2002-903525-2
PR9199.3.M3355B88 2002

THE CANADA COUNCIL | LE CONSEIL DES ARTS
FOR THE ARTS | DU CANADA
SINCE 1957 | DEPUIS 1957

ONTARIO ARTS COUNCIL
CONSEIL DES ARTS DE L'ONTARIO

The publisher gratefully acknowledges the support of the Canada Council for the Arts and the Ontario Arts Council for its publishing program.

We acknowledge the financial support of the Government of Canada through the Book Publishing Industry Development Program (BPIDP) for our publishing activities.

Key Porter Books Limited
Six Adelaide Street East, Tenth Floor
Toronto, Ontario
Canada M5C 1H6

www.keyporter.com

Text design: Peter Maher
Electronic formatting: Heidi Palfrey

Printed and bound in Canada

09 10 11 12 13  6 5 4 3 2

**Mixed Sources**
Product group from well-managed forests, controlled sources and recycled wood or fiber
www.fsc.org  Cert no. SW-COC-002358
© 1996 Forest Stewardship Council
FSC

*Dedicated to playwright*
*JOHN HERBERT*
*who listened to my words and gave them wings.*

ACKNOWLEDGEMENTS
Many thanks to Michael for standing by my words, my friend Penny for countless hours of typing them and to Clare McKeon, who guided them gently between the covers. And to all who lent a hand in the process of this novel, especially Alistair MacLeod, I greet you kindly from the printed word.

# one

When I was five years old I did not have a birthday cake. It was because of the storm that streaked the afternoon sky early in October of 1953 and took from me a wish for one hundred crayons to colour my world. I had a backup wish. A father for me and my twin brothers, Alfred and Albert.

My world of storms and wishes was located on the rim of a paper map in the Acadian village of Ste. Noire, on Cape Breton Island.

The storm came without warning. Sudden rumblings and veins of gold lightning panicked my mother. She had little time to gather her defences—holy water and palm and rubber boots. The relics of fear and salvation.

She shouted to Alfred to throw water in the stove to choke the flames. He poured two dippers of water on the burning wood. Albert put on his boots and ran out the back door to get our neighbour, old Mrs. Landry. She lived across the road from us with her three tomcats and a faded picture of her dead husband, Zeppie.

They got to our house just as the rain fell as hard as nails on the roof and the grass in the fields shone like green frost.

Mrs. Landry was praying when she came in the door. "My God," she shouted to my mother, who was sprinkling holy water on the stove, "we are going to get hell today—the world is on fire. It's rotten with sin."

Mama opened another bottle of holy water and squirted the flue. They started saying the rosary together in French and breathing hard like two dogs running up a hill.

I hated for hell to be so close to me on my birthday.

"How close is it?" I sobbed.

Mrs. Landry answered. "The storm is over the Co-op Hall."

"The Co-op is two miles from here," said Alfred.

I ran upstairs to get my rag doll Lizzie and stuffed her, head and all, into an old rubber boot. I carried the boot under my arm and ran down the stairs to wait for hell to come.

Alfred and Albert were sitting on the kitchen floor. They were counting the distance between a clap of thunder and a flash of lightning.

"It's getting closer," said Albert. Mrs. Landry screamed. Mama threw a boot at my brothers and made them pray. I pulled Lizzie out of the boot and cried for the sun.

"Youse two might as well be Presbyterians for all the rosaries youse say," Mama screamed at Alfred and Albert in French.

Mrs. Landry sat on the couch. She was seventy years old and full of blue veins and bobby pins. Mama soaked a face cloth in holy water. She tried to wash Mrs. Landry's face, as if she could wash the fear out of our neighbour, who threw her head against the back of the couch and moaned.

"It's okay, Tori." Mama's voice trembled. "God knows, it is October, this is His last storm until spring, we pray." My brothers laughed out loud.

8

"Go to hell upstairs," Mama shouted, "so youse will be closer to the roof in case it caves in."

I sat at the bottom of the stairs with Lizzie. I could hear the rain falling on the roof as if it were washing it with a heavy steel brush.

Alfred and Albert were at the top of the stairs looking out the window. They dragged their tongues down the window pane. They were trying to race the raindrops that were crawling down like slow bugs on a mound.

My brothers' birthday was in May. They were eight years old when I was five. They got a birthday cake because there were no clouds to threaten our souls with thunder that day. God kept the skies clear on their birthday and afterwards they chased each other around the woodpile with an axe.

We were not allowed to go outside in a thunderstorm. Mama said God knew what He was doing. And on my birthday He was warning us that we had sinned too much and He could burn us up at any minute for punishment.

"Thunder is God's voice," Mama warned. "His angry voice, the one He uses when people are breaking too many of His laws. God knows it was youse who put the turpentine under the tails of Mrs. Landry's tomcats."

Please God, I prayed to myself, I didn't soak the tomcats, it was Alfred and Albert. I just borrowed the turpentine from Mrs. Landry. Please don't burn me up on my birthday—or my brothers either.

Mrs. Landry began to cry for her dead husband, Zeppie.

My brothers sneaked down the stairs and sat beside me and Lizzie.

"She is going foolish," Alfred said. "The holy water is not working on her."

The three of us stuck out our necks to get a better look at Mrs. Landry. Her face was pale. She kept mumbling something about her dead husband.

"He had the prayer, Adele," she said to Mama in French. "He had the prayer that could stop storms in mid-air, but the fool took it with him when he went."

"Where did Zeppie take the prayer?" I asked.

"He must have taken it to Halifax," whispered Alfred, "when he worked on the docks."

"He was a stevedore," Albert said. "The prayer might have drowned in the harbour."

Mrs. Landry and her husband lived six puddles from our house when it rained. I counted them one day when my mother sent me over to borrow a turnip. Zeppie was very kind. He gave me a picture of three dancing girls staring in a mirror. Their ponytails were tied with pretty rainbow ribbons that matched their dresses. On their feet were soft slippers. They looked like they were painted there forever and the girls smiled as if they knew they would never have to wash their feet again.

"See the girl in the middle?" Zeppie had said. "She looks like you, Mari-Jen. She has your fiery red hair."

Mrs. Landry put the picture in a paper bag with the turnip.

"Don't let your brothers near the picture," Zeppie warned, "or they will take the axe to it because I didn't have something for them!"

I was closing the latch on the back door when Zeppie said to his wife, "That poor kid—a Scotchman got in on that one for sure, with that colouring and all. God knows who owns her and them twins, with their black curly hair and blue eyes. They are all real good-looking like their mother."

I ran home with my picture and the turnip. I was happy that God knew for sure who owned me and my brothers. I remember asking Mama for a father for me and Alfred and Albert. "I want a kind father, one like old Zeppie, who will give me pictures."

Mama got very cross. "They'll give you more trouble than pictures, Mari-Jen. Don't ask me that again." She spoke French to us when she was sad or scared.

She cried then and I did not know why. She was scrubbing the kitchen floor. I watched as she wiped her tears with the scrubbing rag and then soaked them in the bucket.

Alfred and Albert climbed back upstairs and started to drag their tongues on the window pane again.

"Come and play, Mari-Jen," they coaxed.

"No, I'm too scared."

"It's only a storm," Alfred said.

"They scare me."

"You're scared of everything," Albert said, "and besides, you'd be deader than a nit if it hit ya, so come on up."

"No, I don't want to be dead."

The lightning was blazing like a bonfire burning up all the clouds in its way.

Alfred said to Albert, "Let's open the window and collect a handful of rain. We can soak her head."

I told Mama what they were doing. I was scared that a piece of thunder might be in the rain.

Mama went upstairs after them. I tried to squeeze out the sound of the beatings. I put my fingers in my ears, but I could still hear.

"We were only fooling," Albert's voice cried.

"You can't fool God in a thunderstorm," Mama yelled. "He knows who's possessed. I'm going to drag the two of youse to Father Benoit and have him bless the devil out of you at mass on Sunday."

Mama came down the stairs with her beads in her hand. I didn't know how the devil got in the house and possessed my brothers. I figured it must have been when they opened the window.

I didn't hear my brothers moving again until Albert whispered to me to look up. They were standing at the top of the stairs with their pants down and wearing their cowboy hats. They had tied rags around their necks. They did this when they wanted to be brave. They would put empty Carnation Milk cans on their feet to make the sound of horse hoofs. They warned me to speak English to them when they were cowboys. They said they didn't know a cowboy or a horse that understood French. I didn't tell Mama. There were enough welts on them to scare the devil for a long while.

I heard Mama telling Mrs. Landry, "You're so lucky, Tori, you have no kids to torture you in storms."

I could hear Alfred and Albert's laughing voices leaking out from under their quilt.

I did not want Mama to drag them to the priest for a blessing. Father Benoit shouted to the parishioners on Sunday, "You are all spotted with sins, each and every one of you. You had better start erasing them before it's too late."

I saw a man sitting two rows from us scratch his head and then his ear. He's starting to erase before anyone else, I thought to myself. The priest looked at everyone. Row by row. I did not like the sound of his voice. It went up and down, up and down. "I am warning you," the voice said.

Alfred and Albert grabbed each other by the ears until they turned blood red. "I got yours," Albert whispered to Alfred, and then they laughed.

We rode the seven miles to church in the back of the old Co-op truck. It was filled with wooden benches on Sunday. I sat on Mama's lap to make more room for older people to sit down.

"Stand in front of me," Mama ordered my brothers. "I can keep an eye on you so youse don't try anything smart, like jumping out of the truck."

When we got to church the skinny Co-op man came around the back and unhooked the rope. Mama gave him ten cents for taking us to church to erase our sins.

When our neighbour Zeppie died that spring, we did not go to church in the Co-op truck. Someone gave us a ride in a blue car. We followed behind the truck that carried Zeppie and the pallbearers in the back. Mrs. Landry sat in the front seat. She didn't take her nose from her handkerchief until we reached the church. Me and my brothers sat in the back seat with our mother. The man opened the car door for us and then he opened the front door for Mrs. Landry. She let out a squeal.

"Zeppie, Zeppie, you're really dead, my poor Zeppie."

The man and Mama helped her out of the car. She wobbled back and forth like a strip of raw wind.

Alfred and Albert ran into the graveyard next to the church. They wanted to see the hole that was dug for Zeppie. They climbed on the blanket of dirt that was waiting to cover him.

The six pallbearers, with black ribbons tied around their arms, unloaded Zeppie from the truck and carried him into the church. We followed behind. Father Benoit sprinkled the coffin with holy water and then circled Zeppie with smoke hanging from a chain.

"Zeppie is on his way home," he said in a sombre voice. Mrs. Landry blew her nose loudly. Father Benoit looked around and then continued to speak. "When you cry for the dead, it means you are crying for yourself."

Mrs. Landry cried for herself all spring and summer and into the October storm.

Mama told us that Zeppie's heart fell out from hard work. He had been cutting kindling for the morning fire when he died. Mrs. Landry had found him at the woodpile. We were not allowed to their house until Zeppie was ready for his wake. Some men came to the house and washed the balsam from his hands and shaved the whiskers from his face. Alfred and Albert said they stuck Zeppie in the washtub and cleaned him with the scrubbing brush. They cut his hair and trimmed his moustache and closed his gentle blue eyes forever from the world with two brown coppers.

Mama took me by the hand over to Mrs. Landry's. Old Zeppie was lying on his bed in his dark suit. His stocking feet were pinned together with a rusty safety pin. His beads were wrapped in his still hands. His black coffin was sitting on two wooden barrels. The men lifted Zeppie and put him in the coffin so people could get a look at his clean face.

I looked at his face for a long time. I had never seen a dead person. I was sure I could see the smile on his face. The one that was there when he gave me the picture.

At the wake, Mama made me and my brothers touch Zeppie's hands. "You have to touch the dead or you will dream about them," she said. I did not like the feel of the dead in my hands. People got too cold with no heart, even kind Zeppie.

My brothers grabbed his hand and shook it hard, as if they were meeting him for the first time. Mama grabbed them by the hair.

"Do that again," she warned, "and Zeppie will come back and rip the tongues right out of your heads."

She chased them outside. I went out behind them. They ran home with their lips sealed tight until they reached our doorstep and stuck out their tongues.

A few weeks later they said they had had the same dream. "Zeppie was in our porch, in his dark suit, stealing flour and potatoes. He was covered with flour because he had nothing to put it in, so he just filled his pockets. He then opened the bag of potatoes and helped himself. He put as many potatoes as he could in his pockets that were overflowing with flour. When he couldn't steal any more," they said, "Zeppie jumped clean through the storm door without breaking it. He just went through the crack in the door because he couldn't walk straight with his socks pinned together with a rusty safety pin."

Mama said the dream was a sign that Zeppie was still hungry for heaven.

"He has to wait in a place called purgatory, until he is ready for heaven. Sometimes it takes years," she said, "and a lot of masses and prayers to clean a soul for heaven. Only priests and nuns and little baptized kids get straight through—after death. They don't have to detour like the rest of us, who have to wait and have our sins peeled away prayer by prayer."

My brothers said they wanted to get to purgatory when they died. "It's near Alaska, Mari-Jen," Alfred said, "where the snow is shimmering blue and you can slide off igloos all day. I found the place on the map at school. The one that rolls down over the blackboard."

Mama warned Alfred and Albert not to tell Mrs. Landry where Zeppie had landed. "It will only make her cry more, and her knees are weak. It's hard for her to kneel and get going on her beads."

They didn't. But they asked her if she knew where Alaska was.

"No, I don't," she snarled, "and I don't care if I ever do."

I believed that she said that because she didn't know that's where Zeppie was eating our potatoes and flour, while waiting to get to heaven. My brothers asked about the place called hell.

"Hell is for people who leave the church," Mama said, "and start sinning before they're off the step. These people die with cancer in their souls and there is no cure for them. No prayers enter there, nothing can put out the flames of hell once you're there."

Albert said it was nowhere near Alaska on the school map. I was glad. I didn't want them to take a notion to go there if purgatory got too cold.

When the storm passed, Mama told me and Alfred and Albert to look up at the sky. We ran to the porch, where she was looking out the door.

"Look at this. Do you know what this means?" She smiled.

The sun was peering out from behind a cloud and the rain was still falling. Her voice was excited. "When the sun shines and the rain falls, it means only one thing." She hurried on. "The blessed mother and the devil are fighting together. A soul is on its way to heaven and the devil is trying to stop it, so the blessed mother came to meet it and the devil started the fight."

She made us make the sign of the cross. "It could be Zeppie," she said. "He could be on his way."

We went back into the house. Mrs. Landry was snoring on the couch. Mama made a fire. She burned the old boot that saved me and Lizzie. We had pea soup for supper. After supper, she made me some fudge for my birthday. It was too late to make a cake. When Mrs. Landry woke up, my brothers walked her home in the dark. They said they never told her that Zeppie had floated over our porch, between the mother of God and the devil, when she was snoring.

# two

The brown dress Mama made for me used to be her skirt. She wrapped it around my body and pinned it, like Zeppie did to dress his scarecrows. When she cut it out and sewed it up, I had a new dress for my first day at school.

She bought new scribblers and pencils for me and my brothers. Their scribblers were orange with a beaver on the front cover and the times table on the back.

"Scribble on them," Mama warned my brothers, "and youse can write on your ears until next year."

Alfred and Albert didn't like to go to school. "Mother Superior looks like the beaver on the cover," said Alfred, "and she has a moustache."

We waited for the school bus at the end of our road.

"You better be careful," they warned, "because Mother Superior bites kids with her long teeth right through their clothes." They took their slingshots to school for protection from bites, they said.

When we got to school, Mother Superior was standing at the gate. She wore a long black robe and veil. White cloth covered her forehead. Two starched strips of material trimmed the veil on each side of her face. A long rosary was draped on the robe; its cross dangled near her feet. I watched the cross swaying as she walked around the schoolyard. It was wooden. The crucified Christ ducked in and out of the folds of her robe, as if He were playing a game of hide and seek. She ordered the kids to form a straight line.

"The beginners," she shouted, "form a line on the left-hand side." I didn't know what the word "beginners" meant. I didn't move. A group of kids went to the left. Another Sister was talking to them and smiling. Mother Superior walked up to me. Her eyes were black and bare, yet full of everything; her teeth came down over her bottom lip as if she were trying deliberately to bite her chin.

"Do you have clean ears?" she asked.

"Yes."

"Then why didn't you move to the left with the others?" I didn't answer.

"Get going!" she said as she grabbed me by the shoulder.

I walked towards the group of smaller kids and the smiling Sister.

Sister Thérèse took my hand and put me at the front of the line. We followed her into the school and down a long hall. She stopped at a door with angels and clouds painted on it, and we went inside.

"I would like to welcome all my new children," said Sister Thérèse, "and my group of grade ones and twos."

Everyone got a little wooden desk to sit in. Sister Thérèse wrote our names on a paper and put them on our desks. I looked at the letters in my name but I didn't know what they were. They looked crooked and jumped from side to side, like a rabbit caught in a snare.

"You, petite Mari-Jen, can sit at the front, next to my desk," she said to me.

When everyone was seated, Sister asked us to stand and say morning prayers. "Dear Jesus, let the road of knowledge lead us to your door."

"Amen."

Mother Superior came into our class then. Everyone stood up and said, "Good morning, Mother," all together in French.

I was scared of her, scared of her black eyes and her hide-and-seek Christ. The same kind of fear that came with storms and Zeppie's hands crawled through me. Mother Superior walked up and down the aisles. She was reading the names. She stopped at my desk and read my name out loud.

"Mari-Jen Delene, when I speak to you, stand up immediately." She grabbed my shoulder and pulled me from my desk. "I know who you are," she said. "I know your brothers. I know all about your family."

I started to cry then. Sister Thérèse was not smiling any more. I remained standing until Mother Superior left our class.

Sister Thérèse told me to sit down. "Look, Mari-Jen, you have the world in front of you." She pulled down a paper map over the blackboard.

"See where Canada is, children," she said softly. She pointed her ruler to the Atlantic Ocean and to the rivers that caught up with it. She pointed to our province of Nova Scotia. "Here we are," she said, "right here in the corner of Cape Breton."

The bell rang for recess. My brothers were waiting for me by the side of the school.

"Did you see Mother Superior, the beaver?" Alfred asked. "Yes," I said. They ran behind the school and loaded their slingshots. When we got home I told Mama that Mother Superior knew all our family, even Aunt Clara and Uncle Jule.

"Nuns know almost as much as a priest, Mari-Jen. They can spot sins up close if they have to."

"She talks to the devil," said Albert. "I know 'cause I heard her one day when nobody was around."

"Your head is cracked," Mama's voice scolded.

"She does so," Alfred said. "We heard her at the cloak-room door. She was screaming, 'If you're in there, Lucifer, come out and face me.'" They didn't remember which cloakroom it was. There were a number of them in our school where you kept your coats and boots and lunch cans out of the way.

The fresh smell of Monday mornings at school stayed with me. I watched the janitor cleaning the floors with the green dust—it looked like dust. He'd reach in the container and throw it out by the handful over the floors. I loved the smell.

Mother Superior came into our class around ten o'clock on Monday mornings. She asked questions about the mass on Sunday. "What feast did we celebrate? Who remembers the message in the gospel? What colour was Father Benoit's robe?"

She asked me that question. I stood up by my seat. I knew the answer. It was green. But the colour would not come out of my mouth.

"Sit down, you stupid girl. I should have known better than to ask you."

A girl named Lucy gave the correct answer. Mother Superior made me stand by my seat again. She told Lucy to stand beside me.

"Remember, class," she announced, pointing to us, "the opposite of stupid is smart. Take a look at smart and stupid. The word for opposites is antonyms."

I asked my brothers if they had heard the word before.

"Yes," said Albert, "it's a word the devil gave her to get her away from the cloakroom."

We made letters between the lines in our scribblers. Sister Thérèse put the letters on the blackboard and we copied them. Small a's and big A's, small b's and big B's, until we got to the letter Z. She put stars in our scribblers that looked like they had fallen from a midnight sky and Sister Thérèse had collected them in a jar.

I learned to put letters together and form a word. "C" and "a" and "t" made a cat. I didn't realize that my cat was crooked and falling out of the lines.

Mother Superior came to our class on Fridays and checked our scribblers. She opened my scribbler with her ruler. "You're too messy, girl," she said out loud. "A hen could scribble more clearly."

She ripped the page from my scribbler and threw it in the wastepaper basket beside Sister Thérèse's desk. The edge of the paper stood up. I could see my blue star.

"Do that work over again," she ordered.

C-a-t—I printed again. There was no way I could explain what I saw. She would never understand that my letters were jumping in front of me and would not stay still.

She didn't tell me what I had done wrong. "It's something she spotted up close," I said to myself, "some kind of sin that I scrawled there on the page."

Mother Superior walked to the front of the class and demanded attention.

"Class, I want to tell you that we are the Sisters of the order called 'Les Soeurs de Jésus.'" She continued to speak. "We've dedicated our lives to Jesus to do this work here on earth. We help people, especially children."

I kept looking at my blue star in the basket. The corner of the page curled up and fell over. Mother Superior hit my desk with her ruler.

"Have you heard a word I've said?" she screamed.

I stood up.

"Speak up!"

I couldn't move.

"Did you hear my question?"

"Yes," I sobbed.

"Then answer me."

No voice. Her face was very angry.

"Sit down!"

I heard the swishing of her robe as she went out the door. Sister Thérèse read us a story in a trembling voice.

I told Mama what Mother Superior had said.

"Nuns are saints," she said. "You have to listen to them or your tongue will turn black and fall out of your head."

My brothers laughed.

"We are not scared of her," said Albert. "She's made of sawdust and sins, the only flesh she has is on her face and hands."

"That's to make her look real," said Alfred.

Sister Thérèse taught the class how to do sums. Two moons and one more moon made three moons. I liked to add up the moons. I didn't like the take-aways. I got mixed up. I made a hole in my scribbler from erasing them.

Mother Superior noticed it. She was standing by my desk.

"How old are you, girl?"

I stood up by my desk. "I am six."

"You should be able to do that simple arithmetic. Sit down, you stupid girl!"

She walked over to Sister Thérèse and said something to her. I couldn't hear what they were saying.

After school I asked my brothers to help me do take-aways. They said they were easy. Alfred drew six nuns on six pieces of paper, and then Albert set five of them on fire.

"Now how many are left?" he asked.

"One," I answered.

I learned to do take-aways at the kitchen table with fire and nuns while Mama was visiting at Mrs. Landry's.

A month later Mother Superior gave me a letter to take to my mother.

"Don't show it to the twins," Mother Superior ordered, "or she'll never see it."

I didn't know what secret was inside the white envelope. I hadn't told anyone that my brothers had set fire to five nuns.

Her message was plain: "Don't expect miracles from Mari-Jen," it read. "She is not learning as fast as the others. There could be a problem like retardation—a slowing of the learning process, causing confusion with numbers and reading. But the good Lord takes care of everyone in His own way." Mama read the letter four or five times and explained it to me.

"It's as simple as that, Mari-Jen," Mama said. "Them nuns know about how your head works. We can't question them."

I went upstairs and took Lizzie from the cubbyhole. Her body was soft and warm. I rocked Lizzie in my arms. Back and forth. Neither one of us knew what retardation meant. But I cried. I knew the word did not belong to me. I took the cracked mirror from under my bed and looked at my face. I looked like everyone else. My head wasn't crooked. My ears were on straight. But something was broken in me. I couldn't reach it with my fingers to fix it.

On Monday morning Sister Thérèse hugged me tightly. "I will help you." She smiled.

At recess I saw a group of kids gathered in a circle. Some of the bigger kids were cheering and laughing. I could hear the voices of my brothers coming from inside the circle.

"She's not retarded, you bastard," Alfred yelled.

Mother Superior walked quickly to the circle. I watched the kids spread away. Alfred and Albert were lying on the ground. She pulled them up by the hair. Blood was trickling down Albert's face.

"They started the fight," a bigger boy said to Mother Superior.

"Into the office!" she screamed at my brothers.

They walked in front of her. The crowd broke away. I watched them go into the school. I knew they were fighting for me—they said I wasn't retarded. Pain clawed at my heart and made me shiver. I stood frozen in one spot. I felt something hot moving down my leg. For a moment, I thought it was blood, spilling from my own heart.

At home they showed me their hands. They were swollen like the dumplings Mama boiled in the stews she made. They soaked their hands in a pan of water and creolin, and then were sent to bed early for torturing Mother Superior.

Their prayers floated down the stairs before they fell asleep.

"Our Father with warts in heaven … who suffered under Punching Pilot, was crucified, died and was buried …"

On Saturday morning we went to visit Aunt Clara and Uncle Jule. They were Mama's sister and brother. He wasn't really their brother. When he was ten, his half-crazy mother had left him behind when she ran off with some man, my mother said. "Your grandfather had to beat him a few times to keep him in line." He was a real handful. "He'd howl like a wolf for his mother," Mama said. "His mother had worked for my grandmother one summer when she was sick. He kept watching the hill for her to return but she never did."

"Aunt Clara might take a queer fit while we're there, so don't get too close to her," Alfred warned me.

"You might catch them," said Albert.

Aunt Clara and Uncle Jule lived in an old house down by the sea. It was Grandmère and Grandpère's house, but they had died before I was born. Mama went down regularly to clean the house and do the baking.

Aunt Clara had long black curly hair. She was tall and skinny with a long nose.

"Let me wash your hair, Clara," Mama said to her. "It's knotted like sheep's wool."

Aunt Clara laughed and swore. "Go to hell!" She ran upstairs and slammed her door, and stayed in her room for a while.

"Leave her alone," Mama sighed wearily. "Her queerness will pass and she'll come back down."

My brothers went down to the shore to visit Uncle Jule. He was mending nets in the fish shed. I went upstairs to see Aunt Clara. She was sitting on her bed with a rag covering her head.

"Come in, Mari-Jen. You're not nosy and bossy like your fat, ugly mother."

"My mother is not fat and she is real pretty," I said. Aunt Clara laughed. "Are you coming downstairs?" I asked.

"No, they can kiss my arse."

"What are you doing, Aunt Clara?"

"I'm looking at my jewellery."

"What jewellery?"

"What jewellery? The jewellery that the new Queen of England sent me in the mail."

"When did you get it?"

"Last week."

She held up a necklace and a brooch.

"Look at this. Isn't it beautiful?"

"Yes. Why did she send it to you, Aunt Clara?"

"Because she likes me, that's why."

"What is her name?"

"It's Elizabeth and she lives in a palace made of jewels in a place called England."

"I will look for England on the globe at school."

Aunt Clara looked at me. "Watch out for those damn nuns, Mari-Jen. They hide kids in their cellar at the convent. And they're only allowed out at Hallowe'en, so the nuns can steal their fudge."

"Sister Thérèse likes kids, Aunt Clara. She wouldn't steal their fudge."

"That's because Sister Thérèse hates fudge, so she doesn't bother to steal kids' herself. Your mother stole you and your brothers. She stole your brothers in Halifax, and you in Cape Breton and hid you under her dress."

"Was she a nun when she stole us?"

"No, Mari-Jen, she just likes to steal. I have to hide all my jewellery because her and Jule will help themselves."

Mama hollered to me to come down and help her.

"Aunt Clara has jewellery that the new Queen of England sent her in the mail," I announced.

"Don't be repeating what Clara has to say. The poor soul is loose in the head. She got that way from scrubbing the old schoolhouse. The water was full of some queer kind of chemicals. They inhaled her senses."

I didn't understand what she meant.

"After that," she went on, "Grandpère and Grandmère just kept her in the house and took her to the hospital when her head got too loose."

Uncle Jule was younger than Mama and Aunt Clara. He was tall and not too fat. His hair was black and grey like his beard. His skin was dark. My brothers said they heard that his father was a pirate who got shipwrecked in Ste. Noire during a gale. He might have been good looking if he didn't frighten you so much.

When he came home from mending his nets, he hollered to Clara. "Get down here!"

She came downstairs immediately. She was wearing her jewellery. Her face was plastered in rouge and her lips were thick with red lipstick.

My brothers laughed, but Uncle Jule shut them up.

"Wash her hair now," he ordered Mama.

She heated water on the stove and poured it in a pan.

"Come into the porch, Clara," Mama said. "Get me a dipper of rain water, Mari-Jen."

The rain barrel was kept on the veranda. She rinsed Clara's hair in it. Uncle Jule passed my mother a pair of scissors.

"Cut it short," he demanded.

Aunt Clara started to cry as her curls fell at my feet.

"Sweep up her hair, Mari-Jen," said Uncle Jule.

Uncle Jule took the dustpan from me and threw her curls into the flames.

"Your hair will be easier to keep now, Clara," Mama told her.

Aunt Clara still cried. Uncle Jule went outside to cut some wood. My brothers followed behind him.

"I am going to tell the saints, Adele. I am going to tell them what Jule made me do," said Aunt Clara. "They will be as mad as hell." I couldn't read the strange look in Mama's eyes.

"It's the war," Mama said. "It's the war that changed Jule. He used to be nice sometimes when he realized his mother wasn't coming back. He got kind of quiet and stayed to himself. Teachers used to say he had a head full of knowledge and mystery. But since the war he's moody and different. And that girlfriend of his running off with that zombie, and getting married. That added to his queerness."

"What did he do in the war?" I asked.

"He got queer—after shooting them Germans and then stealing their chocolate bars just to keep alive. He did what everyone has to do in a war. Thank God we won the war or the place would be crawling with them."

Uncle Jule showed my brothers his war medals and his wounds. "Six bullet holes real close to his heart," they beamed.

"They are just inches from his heart," Alfred said, "just inches from taking his life and making him a dead hero for his country. But the army gave him six medals anyway. One for every bullet that went through him."

Mama made a pot of stew for supper. Aunt Clara didn't want to eat. Uncle Jule made her sit at the table. After supper she ran upstairs. I went up to see her before we left.

"Come and I'll show you where I hide my jewellery!"

"Where is that?"

"Under my bed. Take a look."

I looked under the bed. There was a big white shell and rocks and pieces of driftwood. I took out the shell.

"What is this?" I asked.

"Put it up against your ear and you will hear the sea calling, and then you will hear the Queen walking around the palace."

I listened for footsteps but I couldn't hear any. "I don't hear them."

Aunt Clara took the shell from my hands. "She's hiding on you. She doesn't want you to hear her."

"Maybe she's gone," I said.

"You're crazy, Mari-Jen. She just doesn't want you nosing around."

We went home after Mama washed the dishes.

"You're gonna catch her fits," Alfred said.

"No, I'm not. You only get them from scrubbing a schoolhouse with your head over a bucket."

My brothers laughed and started to race each other home. I watched them run until they were out of sight behind the fish sheds.

"Do you think Alfred and Albert will ever go to war?" I asked Mama.

"Only if they start it," she answered quickly. I didn't want them to go to any war. I didn't want bullets to land close to their hearts. They helped me do take-aways.

"Get your clothes ready for mass in the morning," Mama warned, before we went to bed.

Albert and Alfred wore their white shirts and dress pants. They shined their shoes with lard. Mama wore the same blue dress every Sunday. Mrs. Landry gave her the material to make it. There was enough material left over to make me a dress too. The dresses had white flowers on them and two pockets on the sides. Mama stuffed a rag in her pocket to wipe our runny noses in church.

I went upstairs and took my brown dress down. It was hanging on a nail above my bed. I hugged it in my arms and wondered if it was the dress that she hid me and my brothers under, after she stole us from someone.

# three

My brothers got the mumps before school finished for the year. Their faces were swollen like the belly on the big toad we found in the swamp. Mama told Mrs. Landry that it was the mumps that stopped Uncle Jule from getting a wife. "He got them overseas, of all places," she said.

I asked my brothers if they knew what the mumps did to him.

"Mumps stop you from kissing," Albert said, "and that makes girls mad and so they go looking for a man whose lips are working right."

"You need good lips," said Alfred, "or your wife will never get a baby."

"That's true," said Albert. "It takes almost a year to make a baby. So every week a man has to add new parts to the baby by sleeping close to his wife, so he can kiss her and pass her the fertilizer that is stored under his tongue like a lizard."

I thought my brothers were trying to trick me.

"Did mumps stop Uncle Jule from getting a wife?" I asked Aunt Clara.

"No, Jule has a wife."

"Where is she?"

"She's here, Mari-Jen."

"Did you ever see her?"

"Yes, in the mirror."

"Do you talk to her?"

"No, but I hear her crying when he hurts her, and then she prays."

"Where did Uncle Jule find her?"

"She's a saint."

"How do you know, Aunt Clara?"

Aunt Clara began to laugh. "Because she has wings."

"Can we see her, Aunt Clara?"

"No, we're not allowed. Jule will be mad."

"Why?"

"'Cause I said so. Now frig off and leave me alone."

I told my brothers what Aunt Clara had told me.

"I'm warning you," said Alfred. "You'll soon be taking fits too."

"Yeah," said Albert, "and you won't be allowed to go to school ever again."

When we went back to Aunt Clara's on the weekend, I didn't go up to her room. I stayed by her door and called out to her.

"I know what you're doing out there, Mari-Jen. I know what you're up to," Aunt Clara shouted.

I went back downstairs, but she followed me down.

"Adele," she screamed, "Mari-Jen is stealing my prayers through the keyhole."

"She wouldn't steal your prayers," Mama protested.

"Like hell. They're all gone."

"She has her own prayers, Clara."

Aunt Clara was very angry. "Mari-Jen is stealing my

33

prayers—I know it. She doesn't know how to pray, so she's stealing all of mine." She ran upstairs screaming, "Mari-Jen won't come into my room, God, because she is stealing my prayers through the keyhole."

I was very scared of her when she screamed. She didn't look the same. Spit ran from her mouth like soft cream dripping down the sides of a jar.

"Stay downstairs," Mama warned, "until Clara stops acting up."

"What is she talking about?"

"Pay no mind to her, you'll never know what comes from a loose mind."

"What part of her head is loose?"

"Her whole head. Stop asking so many questions. I got enough to do. God is punishing me for my sins with kids and fools. I'll have to go crazy so I can have a rest."

"Why, Mama?"

"'Cause crazy people don't get tired or have to do anything. Now shut up and leave me alone."

When we got home Albert and Alfred were looking in the mirror to see who had the biggest lumps in their necks.

"Go upstairs to bed," Mama ordered.

"We've been in bed all day," Albert protested.

"Stay down, and your heads will explode," Mama threatened them.

"Why?" asked Alfred.

"'Cause I seen what mumps can do to people; they can keep them short and simple all their life."

"Who told you that?" they wanted to know.

"Nobody had to tell me. I seen kids with my own eyes.

34

They only grew as high as the seat of a chair after a bout with the mumps."

Alfred and Albert ran upstairs and stayed there for four days. I brought their food up to them. Mama took up a small tub of warm water to wash their hair when they were better. They put their heads in the water to see who could stay under the longest. They dried their hair and went back to bed after Mama put medals under their chins to bring on a cure.

I didn't get the mumps so I went to school by myself. Mother Superior asked if my brothers were staying in the house or running wild. She had taken me to her office after our morning prayers.

"Is your mother taking care of your brothers? It's the least she can do for children without a father."

"Yes."

"Does she feed them?"

"Yes."

"Do they have their own beds, Mari-Jen?"

"They sleep together."

"Do you have a bed of your own?"

"Yes, I sleep near my cubbyhole with Lizzie."

Mother Superior looked at me. "Who is Lizzie?"

"She's my doll. I keep her in the cubbyhole so my brothers can't get her."

"Does your mother make you and your brothers pray together?"

"Yes, but more in the storms."

She was looking at me and making me very nervous. I was not sure if my answers were right, 'cause she was copying them down in her notebook.

"Does your mother have a room of her own?"

"Yes, downstairs."

"Does she have visitors over, especially at night?"

"Only Mrs. Landry, but she leaves early to let in her tomcats."

"Mari-Jen, does your Uncle Jule receive communion when Father Benoit goes to visit your Aunt Clara?"

"I don't know."

She kept writing in her notebook. She finally told me to go back to my class. "You will come back to my office again, Mari-Jen."

A week later my brothers came back to school. After school they measured each other upstairs by the chimney. They marked their height with chalk they stole from school, to keep an eye on their growth.

I asked them if they gave Mother Superior answers for her notebook.

"No," said Alfred, "we just give her lies, 'cause we need lies to take to confession."

"How is that?" I asked.

"It's simple," said Albert. "Ya can't lie in confession, it's impossible."

"Why?"

"'Cause once Father Benoit raises his hand they all disappear," Alfred said.

"How do you know that?"

"There's no way a sin can escape in that black confession box; they're trapped in there—but once the priest moves his hand and speaks Latin, all is forgiven," Albert explained.

"Who told you that?"

"I know that," said Albert, "'cause God picks up the signal on something like a two-way radio hidden in the steeple. And Latin is the secret language between God and the priest."

"And besides," said Alfred, "Mother Superior knows better than to question us. She knows we know what goes on in the steeple."

I went downstairs to ask Mama if Alfred and Albert were making these things up. She and Mrs. Landry were in the kitchen. I could hear Mrs. Landry's voice. "Old Poutine didn't have enough wind left in her to make a good confession."

"That's too bad," Mama said.

"What in the hell did she ever do wrong? She never had a man or even looked at one sideways."

"That's true." Mama replied. "She wouldn't even sit next to a man in church."

Mrs. Landry started to talk about her husband, Zeppie. "Sometimes I think he's in bed, snoring, and I even poke the pillow like I used to do in his ribs to get him to stop."

Alfred and Albert were listening on the stairs. They called to me.

"Hold the back door open," Alfred said.

"Why?"

"'Cause me and Albert are going to sneak out by the window and scare Mrs. Landry."

"You better not, or you'll get a good beating."

"No, we won't," Alfred said. "We got it all planned. And if you tell, Mari-Jen, we'll chop Lizzie up on the block."

I held the door open. They sneaked out in the fog and crawled under the kitchen window.

"Tori, is that you, Tori?" called Albert in a rough voice. "Oh, my ribs, my God-damned ribs," he moaned in French. And then Albert started to snore.

Mrs. Landry screamed. "Mon Dieu, Adele, did you hear something?"

"Well, yes, I heard noises."

"Jesus Christ, it was Zeppie, Adele, it was Zeppie begging for mercy with sore ribs."

"He's in need of prayers, Tori," Mama's voice trembled. "Why else would he come back in the fog?"

Alfred and Albert crept back upstairs. I followed behind them. We went straight to bed and fell asleep while Mama and Mrs. Landry were still saying their beads.

On the weekend I went to bring homemade bread to Aunt Clara and Uncle Jule. Mama was sick with one of her bad headaches. She put the bread in a pillowcase.

"Come right back," she said, as she opened the door for me.

When I got to Aunt Clara's I went in the back door. There was nobody around. I put the bread on the kitchen table. It was then that I heard a scream. And then crying. It was Aunt Clara's voice being drowned out by Uncle Jule's loud voice. I went to the bottom of the stairs. She was still crying. I thought she was sick with fever so I went up to tell her that I had brought her some bread. Her bedroom door was half opened. Aunt Clara was lying on her bed. Her white dress was piled on the floor like a soft snowbank. Her arms and legs were flying in the air, like strips of scrub rags on the clothesline. She was screaming, "I'm telling the other saints, Jule, I'm going to tell them what you do to me."

Uncle Jule was on top of her. His voice rattled in his throat, and his words dampened her hair with spit. "Shut your fuckin' mouth, you fool, nobody will believe a word you say."

And then they were both quiet. Aunt Clara's legs and arms stopped flapping, as if stilled by a dead wind. Suddenly Uncle Jule screamed and his whole body shook. Aunt Clara wrapped her arms around him the way I sometimes held Lizzie when I was scared. I heard Aunt Clara's voice as I went down the stairs.

"Hail Holy Queen, Mother of Mercy, our life, our sweetness, and our hope. To thee we cry, poor banished children of Eve." And then she cried as rain fell on the roof and chased the damp saints away from her window.

When I told Mama what I had seen, she wouldn't believe me.

"You saw nothing of the like, Mari-Jen! You're getting more like your brothers every day. Jule was only trying to shake the fit loose from Clara."

I was never asked to go to their house alone again. Mama took me with her a couple of Saturdays later.

"Put these clothes on the line," she ordered, after she did the wash.

I went to hang them up. Aunt Clara's white dress was on top of the pile. It flapped in the wind like a big white bird getting ready to take flight. I heard Uncle Jule's voice in the distance. It got louder and louder. It was loud and hard and using words I had never heard before. "Who in the hell do you think you are, you're nothing more than a tramp."

Mama was crying. I could only make out some of the words she was saying. "Father Benoit...you'll be punished... warning you, Jule."

Mama screamed. I heard the sound of glass breaking, then silence. And then Uncle Jule's voice again. "You don't even know who owns those three bastards who crawled out from your welfare womb."

I heard the sound of more glass breaking. Then Mama's screaming voice. "Don't you ever hit me again, Jule. I'm warning you."

I ran to the back door. Mama was lying on the floor surrounded by broken dishes. I screamed to her that it was time to go home.

Aunt Clara came running down the stairs when she heard my voice. "Youse better stop all this racket right now!" she demanded. "You're scaring the saints. They will only come as far as the window ledge and poke their noses against the glass."

Uncle Jule staggered and went outside. He was cursing and swearing at the saints in French and English.

Mama shouted to me, "Get the broom and dustpan, Mari-Jen. I slipped on the floor and made all this mess."

I helped her sweep up the broken dishes as Aunt Clara ran upstairs to let in the saints.

We left for home. Mama never mentioned what had happened. She walked very slowly, stopping only to blow her nose. She didn't speak. I looked at her a couple of times. She looked straight ahead, as if the road we were walking on was the wrong direction but she had no cause to turn back. I reached up and took her hand. It was cold. I held it all the way along the road to our house. It didn't warm up until we walked near the store.

I knew Uncle Jule didn't like women and saints, but I didn't know why. That night I prayed again to Jesus to send us a father. A strong father with muscles to fight Uncle Jule. But first I asked Jesus if he could send Jule's mother back to Ste. Noire to make him nice again.

I did not tell Uncle Jule that my mother could have had a father for my brothers. I heard her telling Mrs. Landry about the wedding dress that she looked at every evening in a store window in Halifax. It was satin and lace with tiny pearl buttons on the long sleeves and at the back. The tiny pearl buttons turned a pinkish colour in the light, Mama said. They were delicately sewn on the front of the dress and reminded her of a dove. She said the headpiece had the same pearl buttons and was joined to a long flowing lace veil that swept to the floor. "I would have married him," I heard her tell Mrs. Landry. She sounded like she was crying. "I would have married him if he'd stayed grounded and stopped his drinking," I heard Mrs. Landry's voice then. "You would have looked like the Queen herself, Adele, only better looking. Me, I always said the Queen looks like Zador's wife, Zabeth. You couldn't coax a smile on her face with a miracle." Mama laughed then.

I knew what being a tramp meant. My mother was not a tramp. She would not roam the roads in a wedding dress collecting dust, like crazy Wilfred, the tramp, who collected the wind in the hems of his dirty old coats.

Mother Superior took me to her office on Monday morning. I looked for dust on the hem of her robe. There was never any. She made me sit very close to her desk. She took out her notebook and began to write.

"Do you know your prayers, Mari-Jen?" she inquired in her nun's voice.

"Yes."

"Who taught them to you?"

"My mother."

"Does your mother pray often?"

"All the time. She says God knows everything."

"Is that right?"

"Yes, and the saints even come to Aunt Clara's window."

"They do?"

"Yes, they do."

"Do you ever see them, Mari-Jen?"

"No, just Aunt Clara."

"Do you think they are invisible?"

I didn't answer. I didn't know what the word "invisible" meant.

"Do you think your aunt Clara can see them?" she sighed.

"Yes."

"Why is that?"

"She told me she could."

"Do you believe everything you're told?"

"I don't know."

"Do you believe everything your brothers tell you?"

"Sometimes, because they're smart."

"They are smart indeed. Would you like to be as smart as they are?"

"Yes."

"Then why aren't you? Why do you print everything backwards?"

"I don't know."

"Why do you think you can't read?"

"I don't know."

"Can you see the words?"

"Yes."

She wrote a word on a piece of paper and asked me to read it. I looked at the word on the paper. F-A-T-H-E-R ... Father. The letters jumped in front of me like leap frogs.

"Can you tell me what it reads?"

"No."

"It's father, Mari-Jen. Do you know what a father means?"

"It means God. God the Father," I mumbled.

"Or it could mean a father in a family," Mother Superior added.

I didn't answer.

"Would you like to have a father, Mari-Jen?"

"Yes."

"But you don't have a father, do you?"

"No, not yet."

"Are you planning on getting one?"

"I don't know. My mother says they're only trouble."

"Is that right? Well, she troubled them a couple of times, didn't she?"

"I'm not sure."

I wanted to go back to my class. My head was starting to hurt.

"Before you go, Mari-Jen, I want you to take this word with you." She passed me the paper. "The next time you're here, you will read and spell the word for me. Now go back to your class."

I took the paper and left the office.

The following Saturday Mama made me and my brothers go to Aunt Clara and Uncle Jule's with her. Uncle Jule was down at the shore when we arrived. My brothers were not allowed to go and see him.

Aunt Clara came running down the stairs when she heard us come in. "Adele!" she screamed as she came into the kitchen. "Youse really scared the saints away with all that racket. It's only Saint Anne who will show her face to me now."

Alfred and Albert laughed. "What does she look like?" they asked Aunt Clara.

Aunt Clara laughed. "Do youse think I'm going to tell you my secrets? Youse are crazy."

Mama sent Alfred and Albert out to take in some wood. She made Aunt Clara some tea and told her to sit at the table. She asked her if she was feeling all right. Aunt Clara didn't answer. She kept looking into her cup of tea.

"Come over here, Mari-Jen," Aunt Clara said to me. "Do you see what I see?" she asked, as she put her finger into the cup.

"No, I can't see anything."

"Look at them—they're crawling everywhere, Mari-Jen."

"What's crawling?"

"The creatures, you fool."

"What creatures?"

"Bugs, lots of bugs."

"That's tea leaves, Aunt Clara."

"Tea leaves, my arse."

Alfred and Albert came in with their arms loaded with wood.

"Come here, youse two," said Aunt Clara, "and look at this cup."

My brothers looked at the cup.

"Do you see what I see?"

"Yes," said Alfred.

"Bugs," said Albert.

"Mari-Jen is so damn stupid. She doesn't know a bug from tea leaves," Aunt Clara laughed.

My brothers laughed too. Mama made them go out for more wood.

Aunt Clara laughed loudly. "Your mother makes tea with dead bugs, Mari-Jen. She's gonna poison me," she screamed.

"Don't disagree with her," Mama said to me.

Aunt Clara emptied the cup of tea on the floor. "There's only one way to get rid of them bastards," she screamed. She jumped up and down on the floor and then ran upstairs and slammed her door.

Mama scrubbed the floor and then put on herring and potatoes for supper. Aunt Clara hollered to me to come upstairs for a minute.

"Don't go in her room," Mama warned, "just go by her door and see what she wants."

I walked halfway up the stairs. She was standing at the top.

"Do you want to see something, Mari-Jen?"

"What is it?"

"My tits."

She lifted up her sweater. "See these marks." She pointed to the reddish blue marks on her skin. "The hunger babies made them, Mari-Jen. They come through the night and suck all my milk out."

She pulled down her sweater and ran back into her room. I went back into the kitchen.

"Does she want anything?" Mama asked.

"Nothing. She just wanted to show me what the hunger babies did to her through the night."

Mama shook her head and continued her work.

Before school ended in June, Mother Superior came into our class to test the kids before grading day. She went up and down the aisles asking questions. She looked at me with a hard smile sewn on her face.

"Surprise us, Mari-Jen, and get one right."

I knew the answers. I knew that five taken from six left one. I knew that we lived in the province of Nova Scotia. I knew that it was the Atlantic Ocean that washed up on our shore. I knew what hunger babies did through the night. And that Queen Elizabeth lived in a place called England, in a palace made of jewels. And I knew about a place called purgatory. But I could not give her my answers.

I heard her call my name. "Mari-Jen, stand in front of the class now."

I got up from my seat and stood and faced the class.

"Spell the word 'father'," she ordered.

I could see everyone looking at me. Sister Thérèse looked sad. Her lip was trembling.

"Sit down," I finally heard the beast say.

I walked slowly to my seat with all my answers still in my head.

On grading day Sister Thérèse held a party for the class. Mother Superior came and took me and a girl named Sophie and a boy named Marcel to her office. She told us that we did not grade and therefore we had nothing to celebrate. They were both older than me. She said that both she and Jesus did not like sissy children who would rather cry than try. The boy Marcel started to cry. He was older than the others in the class. His skin was very pale. He looked like he was made of bread dough. His head was full of lice. I watched as a louse crawled down the back of his neck and disappeared under the collar of his shirt.

The girl Sophie stared out the window without blinking. She was taller than anyone else in the class and she walked like she was shoving the wind out of her way.

I kept remembering Sister Thérèse's face as we walked out of her class. She was crying. And I didn't know the reason for her tears. I didn't know that a saint could cry.

# four

Me and Marcel and the girl Sophie went back to Sister Thérèse's class in September of 1954. The other kids called us the failers. "There go the failers," they shouted when we lined up. Sophie didn't say a word. Me and the dough boy Marcel cried. Tears fell down his cheeks and he caught them in his dirty sleeve.

Sister Thérèse gave us hugs. She gave me my little desk next to hers and put Marcel and Sophie behind me. She told us that God did not fail anyone.

My brothers told me that I had failed because I wouldn't take my slingshot to school. "She can tell the kids that are scared, Mari-Jen," said Alfred. "And that Sophie has no tongue and that boy Marcel is too fat to ever fit into a confession box, so he'll never be saved and you are too scared to do things to help you to grade."

Albert said that I would have to get tough and fight my way at school.

"Fighting is a sin," I said, "Sister Thérèse said it was."

"Kids can't sin," Alfred said.

"Why not?" I asked.

"'Cause your soul doesn't start working until you grow up," said Alfred.

"Yeah, that's right, Mari-Jen," Albert cut in. "Me and

Alfred can do everything until we start shaving. And girls can do anything until they grow tits."

I didn't start to fight because I thought my brothers were trying to trick me. Mama told me that girls didn't have to grade to know how to peel potatoes and wash clothes. And I believed her.

Sophie's mother was dead, and I believed that was why she didn't fight or talk to anyone. Somebody said a lump grew on the mother's brain. It was so big that her head exploded. And then Sophie's father gathered up all his six kids and made them kneel by her bed and pray and then kiss their dead mother goodbye. Mama said the story was true but that her head didn't explode. She said that the poor woman's eyeballs turned inside out and that she died with the whites of her eyes facing the heavens.

I overheard her and Mrs. Landry talking about it one night, so I stayed on the stairs and listened.

"The poor soul must have been looking towards heaven," said Mrs. Landry. "Christ knows she deserved it after all she went through."

"You're not kidding, Tori. It's awful what a woman has to put up with in this world."

Alfred and Albert crept down the stairs and sat beside me.

"What are you doing?" Alfred inquired.

"Just listening to how Sophie's mother got dead."

"They had to put her head in a bag," said Alfred.

"No, they didn't," I said. "Her eyeballs just turned inside out."

Mrs. Landry started to talk about her dead husband,

Zeppie. "I'm some glad Zeppie's equipment wasn't working in full gear, Adele. I don't know what I'd do with six kids."

"I'll say. I got my hands full with three."

"What wasn't working right for Zeppie?" said Alfred to Albert.

"I'm not sure," said Albert. "I think it was his axe handles—he could never split wood too straight."

We went upstairs to bed. Albert said that dead people's hair keeps growing and their toenails and fingernails too, until they fall apart and turn to dust in their graves. They said that Zeppie's hair must have grown down past his suit-coat by now. I told them to stop scaring me.

Alfred said, "That's true, Mari-Jen. Your nails keep growing in case you're not really dead and you might have to claw all the dirt off you to escape."

"And your hair keeps growing," Albert added, "to keep you warm down there, until you can escape."

Mama hollered to us to go to sleep before she came up with the belt and pounded us to sleep. They laughed off the threat under their quilt. I hugged Lizzie and fell asleep thinking about Aunt Clara's white dress.

Sophie and Marcel didn't take the bus to school. They walked. Their houses were very close to the school. You could see their houses when you looked out the school window. Marcel's house had broken windows in it. The kids said his father broke them when he was drunk, and his mother didn't want new ones 'cause her husband would break them again, so she had her sons board up the broken windows.

Marcel had seven or eight brothers and sisters. One of his sisters, Yvonne, had a baby when she was fourteen. Mother Superior took Yvonne to a home for girls when her sweater couldn't cover her swollen belly any more.

Yvonne's baby died. They said her baby was alive when it came out. When she returned home, she didn't come back to school. Her dead baby was buried far away. Some of the kids said Yvonne didn't come out of the house until Father Benoit went there and blessed her and made her come back to church. She used to sit at the back of the church, near the door, with her brothers and sisters. Their mother and father didn't go to church too often.

I asked my brothers how did Yvonne get a baby at school.

"She didn't," Alfred said. "It has to be dark so nobody can see what you're doing to scare the baby, and ruin the whole thing." Albert said you had to be quiet while kissing or you'd have to start the whole thing over again.

Sophie lived with her grandmother after her mother died. Their house was whitewashed every spring. Her grandfather planted carrots and potatoes near the house. Sophie did the housework because her grandmother was blind. Some of the kids said her eyes were almost white and that she walked with her hands in front of her as if there were eyes in her fingertips to guide her. Mama said that Sophie's grandmother didn't have to go to church. "God doesn't want people like that to fall in the pews and break their face in church to prove their faith."

On Fridays, Mother Superior took me and Sophie and Marcel to her office and made us do sums. She had a big chart with the alphabet on it. She pinned it on the wall next to a picture of Jesus. She pointed to different letters with her ruler. She used words like "lower casings" and "higher casings."

Marcel said the letter B was a P. Mother Superior got very cross.

"Are you as blind as you are stupid?" she said to him.

Marcel started to cry again. Sophie would not look at the chart. She acted like she couldn't see it for fog when Mother Superior asked her a question. Mother Superior hit the chart with her ruler. It fell off the wall and landed at her feet. I looked up at the picture of Jesus. I was very scared but Jesus was smiling. She told us to get going back to our class.

Sister Thérèse gave us paper to print letters on. There were no lines on the paper. I made lines with my ruler. Marcel's letters were all crooked. Sophie just stared at her paper. Sister Thérèse put one of her bright stars on my paper. She gave Marcel a ruler to make his lines. He made crooked lines to go with his crooked letters. Sister Thérèse smiled and put a red star on his paper. She let Sophie keep the blank paper on her desk. She patted her on the head and then went to sit down at her big desk.

When we went down to Mother Superior's office on Friday, she read us a story about a leper. She didn't ask us to name the alphabet. She told me to stay in her office when Marcel and Sophie went back to class. She made me sit very close to her desk.

"You are very pale, Mari-Jen. Did you have breakfast before you came to school?"

"Yes, Mother Superior."

"What, Mari-Jen?"

"Porridge and tea."

"Did your mother make it?"

"Yes, Mother Superior."

"Did the twins eat?"

"Yes, Mother Superior."

"How is your Aunt Clara?"

"She doesn't like tea, Mother Superior."

"She doesn't? Why not?"

"It's the bugs that she sees," I said.

"The bugs."

"Yes, the bugs, they float in her tea, she says."

"And who, pray tell, puts bugs in her tea?"

"I don't know."

"Was it your brothers, Mari-Jen?"

"I don't think so."

"Does your mother watch them at all?"

"They were taking in the wood."

"They're apt to try anything, those two."

"They didn't put those marks on Aunt Clara."

Mother Superior stared at me. "What marks are you talking about?"

"The marks that were on Aunt Clara's tits."

Mother Superior removed her glasses. "What in the name of God are you saying, Mari-Jen?" Her voice was angry.

"I mean the bluish marks," I said. "The ones that the hungry babies made through the night when they sucked out all Aunt Clara's milk."

Mother Superior's face got very red, and I watched her open her desk and take out the strap. Her words were shaking from her mouth. "Don't you ever repeat such a filthy story like that again at school!" She made me stand by her desk and hold out my hands. "Don't you ever repeat such filth again!" she screamed. My hands were burning with pain. Pain was running through my body and searching for a way out.

She told me to go kneel in the corner and say ten Hail Mary's out loud. I tried to lift my right hand to make the sign of the cross. It seemed too heavy, so I started to pray without the crossing. I knew God didn't hear all my prayers because I was sobbing too much and I thought you had to bless yourself first to make them real.

Mother Superior told me to get up and go back to my class. She asked me what I had prayed for. I looked at her face. She was smiling. I told her I prayed for forgiveness. But I lied. I prayed for her to die.

When I got back to class, the bell rang for recess. Sister Thérèse looked at my hands. She took out a starched white handkerchief and held it to her mouth. I asked her what the word "filth" meant. She didn't answer.

Outside I told Albert and Alfred what had happened. "Why did she strap you?" Alfred asked.

"'Cause I said filth."

"What kind of filth?" asked Albert.

"She's an old crow," Alfred said, "and we'll get her back."

Mama looked at my hands when I got home. I told her I was punished for mumbling my prayers.

"It's good enough for you, Mari-Jen. Those poor nuns can't have you mumble your way into heaven."

I went upstairs and pulled Lizzie from the cubbyhole. My hands were thawed out from pain then, so I made the sign of the cross on Lizzie before I rocked her to sleep in my arms. That night I asked Jesus if kids could quit school. But I fell asleep before He answered me.

Me and Marcel and Sophie didn't make our first communion until we were older. Mother Superior said we were not ready to commit ourselves to Christ. "How can you take on such a commitment, you three, when you don't even know the alphabet? God would never forgive me for making such a blunder," she hissed.

I knew my alphabet in my head and loved the crooked words that floated like clouds across the blackboard from Sister Thérèse's chalk. "Peter had a little _ _ _ _," she said. She asked the class to fill in the blanks. They shouted out words. "Lump, lamp, limp." Sister Thérèse laughed. I knew the answer. "Lamb, lamb, lamb," I whispered to myself, so I wouldn't forget it.

Mother Superior came into our class to teach catechism to the first communion kids. "Who created us?" she asked.

"God," answered the kids.

"Why did God create us?"

"To know, love and serve Him in this world, Mother Superior," was the reply.

Her next question: "Who are the principal creatures of God?" There was silence, and then Marcel's voice, "The principal creatures of God are angels and men."

Mother Superior stared at Marcel. "Who told you that?" she quizzed. There was a sharp look on her face.

"Nobody," Marcel said in a low voice.

"Then how do you know if nobody told you?"

"I just know," Marcel said. "I just know."

Sister Thérèse smiled. Mother Superior shouted, "Unless you can explain your answers, you will keep your mouth shut!" Marcel turned his head and looked out the window. You could see the church steeple from our class window. It looked like it was built around the white clouds. Marcel watched them as if he were waiting for someone to appear and come to help him.

When Alfred and Albert had made their first communion, the boys had to wear white ribbons around their left arms. I loved watching the girls walking up the aisle of the church in their white dresses and veils. Some of them had a circle of roses on their heads and their veils trailed behind like puffs of white smoke. I couldn't wait to make my first communion. I practised upstairs with a pillowcase on my head. I asked my brothers what the body of Christ tasted like. Albert said it tasted like the flesh of a real person. Alfred said that he was right, and that's why you weren't allowed to touch it or bite it with your teeth or the host would bleed. I asked Aunt Clara if she wore a white dress and veil when she made her first communion.

"No damn way, Mari-Jen."

"What did you wear?"

"Something special." She smiled.

"Did Grandmère make you a dress?"

"Hell, no, she had no thread."

"Did she order you a dress from the catalogue?"

Aunt Clara laughed. She rocked back and forth, back and forth. "Are you crazy?"

"Why?" I asked.

"Because there are no catalogues in heaven, you fool. The angels made me a dress. It was all white, except for the wings—they were blue. But I had to wear my gumboots because they don't have shoes in heaven."

Mama told me to stop asking her questions. Aunt Clara told me that all her dresses had wings, except for the white one.

"Jule broke the wings on my white dress, Mari-Jen. He was just too rough with my wings."

When our class made their first communion, I stood up in my seat to watch them parade up the aisle. A blur of white dresses and veils passed by me to taste the flesh of Christ. Father Benoit asked the class a lot of questions. Marcel was sitting in the back seat with his sister Yvonne and two of his brothers. Sophie sat next to her grand-mother. When mass was over, she took her by the hand and led her towards the door before the other people left. Before they went out, Sophie took her grandmother's hand and put it in the font of Holy Water. Her grandmother blessed herself quickly, then closed her white eyes and walked out the door.

On Monday morning Siser Thérèse had a present for all the kids that made their first communion. The presents were wrapped in blue paper and tied with white ribbons. Mother Superior came in and passed out the presents. Sophie and Marcel and me didn't get one. I watched some of the girls as they opened their gifts. Lucy got a cross on a chain. Another girl, Bertha, got a statue of the Blessed Mary. A boy named Martin got blue prayer beads. Some of the girls got pink prayer beads. Sister Thérèse didn't look over at us.

When the bell rang for us to go home, Sister Thérèse made me and Marcel and Sophie stay behind. She opened her desk and took out three presents wrapped in the same blue paper.

"These are presents for you kids for being so quiet," Sister Thérèse said. "I want you to keep them a secret. Do not tell anyone about them!" We put the presents under our sweaters and walked out.

I ran from the bus to my house. I went upstairs and sat on my bed to open my present. Under the blue paper and white ribbon was a little book. "Butterflies Dance in the Dark" was printed in big white letters on the cover. A yellow and black butterfly with its wings spread open danced on a pink seashell. I opened the book and roamed through its pages. The butterfly followed me from page to page.

I knew the story because Sister Thérèse had read it in class. Its big words read:

> The butterfly has music in its wings,
> It dances to the airs of spring—
> An Irish jig, a Highland fling,
> Why, it can dance most anything—
> Butterflies dance in the dark—
> To the songs of the meadow lark—
> The butterfly hears music everywhere,
> Even in the silence of a prayer.

I took Lizzie out of the cubbyhole and showed her my book. A little leprechaun was playing a fiddle. On another page, a boy wearing a kilt was playing the bagpipes. A butterfly floated around the head of a little girl; she was kneeling by her bed saying her prayers. A butterfly was landing on a big buttercup. On the next page it was flying onto the branch of a tree. There were pages and pages of butterflies in my book. They all looked like they were dancing. On rooftops, on clouds, on window ledges —on the waves. They danced everywhere with open wings, even in the dark. I stood up and stretched Lizzie's arms as far as they could go. I whirled her in the air. Her button eyes were shining. I hummed to her a lullaby. And then her head dropped like she was taking a bow. I held her close before hiding her and the dancing butterflies in the darkness.

I didn't tell anybody about my book—not my mother, or my brothers. I kept the butterflies as silent as they were on the pages, so just me and Lizzie could hear their music.

I was going to tell Aunt Clara when Mama and me went back to the house. My brothers had run off in the woods somewhere so they wouldn't have to come with us. When we got to the house, Aunt Clara was sitting by a window in the kitchen She didn't speak to us. She kept looking out the window. When my mother was in the pantry making biscuits, I went over by her. Uncle Jule was not in the house.

"How are you, Aunt Clara?"

She turned and looked at me. "Did you take my wings, Mari-Jen?"

"No, I don't have wings."

"I can't find them. Somebody was in here and stole them all."

"How can you steal wings?"

"It's easy, you just use scissors and cut them away."

"I didn't take them."

"Then your brothers did."

"They don't have wings."

"They have no father. Maybe your mother stole them. She likes to steal."

I said, "Maybe Uncle Jule stole them."

She started to laugh, an angry laugh that scared me. "He doesn't steal wings, Mari-Jen, he just breaks them when he pulls your dress off."

"I don't have wings, Aunt Clara, but my butterflies do."

Aunt Clara stopped laughing and looked at me. "You don't have butterflies, Mari-Jen."

"Why not?"

"'Cause I own all the butterflies," she said. "The saints know I'm one of them. Saint Butterfly, they call me. Now you keep your friggin' hands off of them."

I didn't tell her about my butterflies in case Uncle Jule would want to break their wings.

When I went back to school on Monday, Sister Thérèse patted my head. "How is my little *papillon*?" she whispered.

I did not know what she had given Sophie for a present. But I heard Marcel tell her, "I already knew the answers, Sister Thérèse, I already knew them."

I waited until Alfred and Albert were snoring that night to whisper to Jesus: "I know my alphabet, Jesus, every letter from A to Z and I know the difference between a vowel and a consonant, but I can't taste you just yet. You'd have to follow Mother Superior, Jesus, from the yard at recess, right into the school to know what I am whispering to you about. Alfred and Albert told me that she is not real. But I know she is because not-real people could not hurt me so much. She doesn't like my friend Marcel either. I heard her telling someone that he was too much like a girl. She called him a freak. If it is okay with you, Jesus, I will stick my tongue out at mass when nobody is looking, and that means I am just licking you until I can swallow you whole. Good night—Mari-Jen. Oh, another wish, dear Jesus. Is it possible for you to straighten out the letters on the pages for me? Sister Thérèse said I can draw real good. Thank you. Amen."

# five

Daniel Peter lived down the road from our house. That's the name my brothers gave the man with the dark eyes, as warm as a baby's heart, who had arrived in Canada after the war from a foreign country and never returned to his home. He was a small man, with a thick black moustache that hung like an upside down V over a full mouth. He moved to Ste. Noire in 1955.

Everyone referred to him as the D.P. "His real name is Mischa, if you can imagine that," I heard Mama say. "He could have started the war and left his country for all we know of that man."

Daniel Peter kept a bull and some sheep and hens and a horse, and a rooster named Tolstoy. Once he had a goat named Babel, but it died during the winter.

Daniel Peter didn't go to church. "The D.P. got no religion," said Mrs. Landry. "He thinks Christ is a flame in your head, as far as I can tell."

Sometimes my brothers would take me with them to visit Daniel Peter.

"Were you in the war?" they wanted to know.

"Why you ask that question?" he asked in his strange accent.

"'Cause we want to know," said Albert.

"Sadness not for children," answered Daniel Peter.

"Did you get shot?" persisted Alfred.

"Much worse," he answered softly, staring into space.

"How's that?" Albert asked.

"My family go to camp, a camp that trade you for death."

We didn't understand what he meant. Daniel Peter stared at us for a long time. I was scared that my brothers had asked him too many questions and he was running out of English. Finally he looked towards the floor and answered slowly. "The enemy, the Nazi, like you more dead than live."

"Uncle Jule got shot one time," Albert told Daniel Peter.

"That's too bad."

"Did you escape?" Albert asked.

"I was rescue," he said, "but my family all get dead."

"Who shot them?" my brothers asked together.

"No more questions, children," he whispered. He looked as if he was going to cry out loud like Marcel.

Daniel Peter let us go out to the barn with him. He showed us his bull, Sol.

"Sol weigh one thousand pound. You must not play with Sol, he not so nice every day."

I was scared of Sol. He was the colour of a thundercloud. His eyes looked like a wild storm was brewing in them. Daniel Peter put a ring in Sol's nose and led him in and out of the barn by the ring. The bull snorted. Daniel Peter made us stand outside the fence when he took Sol out.

One day a man was waiting in the field with his cow. The cow's name was Rinso. Sol ran over to Rinso and started to sniff at her tail. Rinso didn't move.

Albert and Alfred started to laugh. "He got her now," they shouted. We were standing behind the fence. "Look at the size of his pecker," said Alfred.

"Yes," said Albert, "it's even longer than the one he used on Bubbles the cow."

"It's longer than an axe handle!" shouted Alfred.

I didn't know what they were talking about. They climbed on the fence to get a better look at Rinso and Sol. Through the fence poles I could see Sol jumping on Rinso's back. Rinso's front legs wobbled. I was really scared. I didn't know why Daniel Peter couldn't grab Sol's ring and put him back in the barn.

"There he goes," Alfred shouted.

"Let's start the countdown," Albert said.

"One, two, three," they screamed.

"What is Sol doing to Rinso?" I asked.

"He's having fun," said Albert.

"He is going to kill Rinso."

"No," said Alfred, "they're making calfs together."

"You're trying to trick me," I cried.

"Shut up," Alfred screamed at me, "or go home!"

I ran all the way home and took out my book, but I could not forget the storm that I saw brewing in Sol's eyes.

Daniel Peter was very gentle to kids and animals. He said every living creature had a spirit of its own. Sometimes it came in the form of a smile or a pat on the head.

In June of 1956, a nun came to visit our school. Mother Superior took her into our class. She said her name was Sister Madeline and that she was from Montreal. I never saw her smile.

"Sister Madeline is a nursing sister," said Mother Superior. "Do any of you know what nursing sisters do?" Nobody answered.

"Well, she checks children for illness and things tha could stop them from learning or hearing." Sister Madeline was looking at the kids. She stared at us the same way Sol stared at Rinso. She walked over to my desk.

"Are you Mari-Jen?" she asked.

I stood up by my desk and answered, "Yes."

Mother Superior walked over to her. They spoke together. When she left our class, Marcel had to go down to the office with them. He was gone until recess.

After lunch, Mother Superior came to my class and took me to her office. Sister Madeline was sitting behind Mother Superior's desk. "Well, well, Mari-Jen," she said. She didn't smile. I didn't like this nursing sister.

"What age are you?"

She made me sit very close to her. "I am the age of eight," I answered. Mother Superior was standing near the window watching us.

"When is your birthday?"

"In October."

"Do you know what time of the year October comes in?"

"Sometimes in a storm," I answered.

She looked up at Mother Superior. "Do you like school, Mari-Jen?"

"No."

"Do your brothers like school?"

"No."

"Do you know why?"

"No."

"Do you think your brothers are smart?"

"Yes."

"Why is that?"

"They can do take-aways."

"Do you think doing take-aways makes you a smart person?"

"Yes."

"Can you do take-aways, Mari-Jen?"

"Sometimes, when my brothers help me."

"Does your mother help you?" asked Sister Madeline.

"My mother said I don't have to grade to know how to peel potatoes." Again the sisters looked at each other.

"Can your mother read, Mari-Jen?" Sister Madeline asked.

"Yes."

"Does she help you with your alphabet?"

"No."

"Why not?"

"I don't know."

"Why do you think it's important to know the alphabet?"

"To taste the body of Christ."

"That's right," said Sister Madeline. "God gave everyone a brain; they just have to use it."

"Daniel Peter thinks Christ is a flame in your head," I offered.

Sister Madeline's and Mother Superior's mouths opened wide.

"Who is this Daniel Peter?" Mother Superior asked.

"The D.P."

"What in God's name is a D.P.?" Mother Superior asked.

"He is the man from a far country. He lives by my house with his bull Sol."

"Do you go to visit this D.P.?" Sister Madeline asked.

"Sometimes with my brothers. They told me his name was Daniel Peter and that his mother couldn't spell, so she called him D.P. His bull, Sol, jumped on Rinso the cow."

Sister Madeline's face reddened.

"Do you have any friends, Mari-Jen?" she stammered.

"Yes, I have Lizzie; she even sleeps with me."

"Who is Lizzie?"

"My doll."

"Where did you get her?"

"From Santa Claus."

"Do you believe she's real?"

"Yes."

"Do you talk to her?"

"Yes, lots of times."

"Do you think you are Lizzie's mother?" Sister asked.

"Yes."

"Do you ever hit your doll?"

"No, never. Lizzie is very good."

"Are you always good?" Sister Madeline asked.

"I don't know."

"Are your brothers always good?"

"I'm not sure, because Aunt Clara said they stole her wings."

Sister Madeline and Mother Superior looked at each other again.

"Why does your Aunt Clara think they stole her wings?" Sister Madeline asked.

"'Cause they're gone. Aunt Clara told me."

"And what does your Aunt Clara do with these wings?"

"She wears them on her dresses."

"Does your Aunt Clara ever hit you?"

"No, but she gets mad if she thinks I steal her prayers."

"Her prayers," Sister Madeline said.

"Yes, her prayers, through the keyhole, because I won't go in her bedroom any more."

"Why is that?" Sister Madeline asked.

"Because my brothers said I would catch her fits."

"What do your brothers know about fits?"

"They know I can catch them in her bedroom."

Sister Madeline shook her head. She stood up and asked me to read the letters that were pinned on the wall on a black and white chart. She made me stand by the door and cover one of my eyes with my hand. I pretended that I couldn't see the letters. I didn't want to leave Sister Thérèse's class with the world in front of me. Sister Madeline told me to go back to my class and that I would have to come back down the next day. I was glad because I felt like I was talking to a bull.

After school, Marcel told me that Sister Madeline said he needed glasses to read. She was going to take him to a doctor who could make bad eyes good again. The girl Sophie had to go to the office the next morning.

That night, after we went upstairs to bed, I asked my brothers if they saw the nursing sister. Alfred said she came in their class and asked a few nosy questions.

My brothers were in grade four. Sister Thérèse had three grades in her class. Some primary kids and grade ones and twos. She put us in different rows. The primary row was called Buttercup Row and the grade ones were in the Daisy Row. When Sister was writing on the board she just had to say, "Copy this, Daisy Row," and the kids knew which grade she meant.

That year, she told the Sunflower Row about nouns and verbs. I listened in. She wrote a sentence on the board: *The sun sprinkled Jane's nose with freckles.* "Remember, Sunflowers," Sister Thérèse said, "a noun is the name of a person, place, or thing. A verb is an action word." *Sun–thing (noun); sprinkled–action (verb); Jane's–person (noun); face–thing (noun); freckles–thing (noun).*

I liked the new words. Nouns and verbs. I didn't pay any attention to the Sunflower Row when they did their sums and take-aways. I just wanted to find new nouns and verbs.

Sister Thérèse gave me a sheet with words on it and walked away. She passed out the same papers down Sunflower Row. She didn't ask me to turn in my sheet.

After school, Mama told me and my brothers that we had to go down to Aunt Clara's and Uncle Jule's to bring them some fresh bread. She said she was too sick to go. "Make sure you all stay together, and I want you to leave right away." She gave Alfred the bread to carry in a brown shopping bag.

When we were walking along the shore, my brothers decided that they would wait for me by the old turned-up boat. "You go over with the bread, Mari-Jen," Alfred said. "Me and Albert want to scrape the barnacles off the boat."

"We are supposed to be together," I begged.

"We'll give you our fudge on Sunday," Alfred said.

He passed me the bag of bread. "It's only over the hill. Now go. We'll be right here when you get back!"

I ran up the hill to the house. I could hear Aunt Clara's voice. She was screaming at Uncle Jule. Their voices were coming from the pantry. I sneaked in through the door but it slammed behind me. Uncle Jule came out of the pantry.

"Who's with you?"

"Nobody."

"Where's your mother?"

"Mama is sick."

"Where are the twins?"

"By the turned-up boat."

Aunt Clara came out of the pantry. Her sweater was on inside out. "Go upstairs," Uncle Jule said to her as she ran through the kitchen.

"Don't pay any attention to Clara," he said. "I was trying to make her take her pink pills. She always screams when I give her a pill."

Uncle Jule asked me what was in the bag. "It's fresh bread." He told me to put it in the breadbox in the pantry. I obeyed.

He came into the pantry behind me and lifted me up so I could reach the breadbox. He started to sniff my hair the same way Sol sniffed at Rinso. His breath smelled very bad. And then he wrapped one of his arms around me. He was breathing very hard, as if he had a bad cold.

I screamed to Jesus to help me, I screamed to my brothers—I screamed to Mama—I screamed to my Lizzie. I didn't want him to touch me the way he did Aunt Clara but he didn't do anything. He dropped me to the floor like I was broken down and couldn't work any more, just as Aunt Clara appeared in the doorway.

I looked at Uncle Jule's face. There was a storm brewing in his eyes like in Daniel Peter's bull. I got up and staggered out the back door. Uncle Jule came to the door shouting, "If you tell anyone about your aunt, you'll be sorry, Mari-Jen. I'll tell the priest that you came here just to steal Clara's pills—all of them. And you will be punished." He spoke in French to me.

The storm was still brewing in his eyes as he turned and swore at Aunt Clara.

I tried to run to where my brothers were waiting at the shore. But my body was too scared to go fast. I was even too scared to cry. I could hear the waves breaking. I walked along the shore road. The sea sounded like a loud cry. I could hear my brothers' voices. They were laughing and chasing each other around the turned-up boat.

"Hurry up, Mari-Jen," Alfred shouted to me. "Come and play this game. Me and Albert are bulls."

I started to cry and kept on walking home. My brothers followed behind me.

"Did you give them the bread?" Alfred asked.

"Yes."

"Was Aunt Clara in one of her fits?"

"No," I said. "Uncle Jule gave Aunt Clara a pink pill." *Uncle Jule—person (noun); gave—action (verb); Aunt Clara—person (noun); pill—thing (noun).*

I went upstairs when we got home. I pulled Lizzie from the cubbyhole. I told her what Uncle Jule might do to me. I thought I could hear her crying so I rocked her to sleep.

Mama was sleeping on her bed. She had a rag on her head to hold in the pain.

My brothers went down to visit Daniel Peter. He was kind to us. He read stories and taught my brothers how to read maps. He told us about his country. It was called

Poland. Albert said Daniel Peter knew more things than all the nuns put together and he didn't even have to pray.

The next morning at school, Sophie went down to see the nursing sister. She was not there very long. Sophie didn't speak. The kids said the nursing sister just looked at her tongue.

After lunch Mother Superior came for me. The nursing sister had different kinds of games for me to play. I didn't feel like playing. She gave me a blank piece of paper and a bunch of crayons. Mother Superior didn't stay in the office. "You can draw whatever you like," Sister Madeline said. I drew a picture of the sea with a dead fish floating on a wave. I drew a monster for the sun, and then I placed it between two clouds. I coloured my picture black.

Sister Madeline looked at my picture for a long time and then she put it in a folder. She told me to draw another picture of my family. I drew my mother and coloured her dress blue with a white rag tied around her head. I drew Alfred and Albert. They were smiling, with slingshots in their hands. I made a picture of Lizzie dancing in a field. The flowers looked like butterflies. I drew a small picture of me in the corner, watching Lizzie. I coloured my dress black.

Sister Madeline looked at my picture and put it in the folder with the black sea. "Why don't you draw a picture of your relatives?" she said.

I made Aunt Clara wearing her jewellery from the Queen. I drew a picture of Uncle Jule. His picture had no eyes. I gave Sister Madeline the paper. "I'm finished," I said.

She looked at the paper. "No, you're not. You forgot his eyes."

"I can't remember them."

She shook her head. "Dear Lord," she mumbled, "my job doesn't get easier." I didn't tell this nun that Sister Thérèse said I could draw real good.

I wanted to go back to my class but I didn't say anything. Sister Madeline asked me more questions.

"Why did you put a rag around your mother's head, Mari-Jen?"

"Because of the pain."

"Does your mother have headaches often?"

"Sometimes."

"How does the rag help the pain?"

"I think it keeps it in one place, so it won't go all over her body."

"Does your mother ever go to a doctor for these headaches?" Sister asked.

"I don't think so."

"Do you ever get headaches, Mari-Jen?"

"No," I lied.

"Do your brothers get headaches?"

"No ... I'm not sure. They only get mumps."

"Did your mother take them to the doctor?"

"No. The medals cured them."

"What medals?"

"The holy medals."

"Do you go to church every Sunday?"

"Yes, but not when it snows or the thunder comes. Then we can't go."

"Does your mother realize it's a sin to miss mass?"

"I don't know."

"Does she know why you won't be making your first communion for some time?"

"I don't know."

"Do you know why you can't receive your first communion just yet?" Sister Madeline asked. Her voice seemed angry.

"I don't know all my letters."

"That's right, Mari-Jen," Sister Madeline said. "Do you think Christ wants you to stay in primary forever? Do you think Christ likes stupid children?"

"I'm not sure," I answered. "Maybe he doesn't even like stupid big people." She looked annoyed.

"Your mother is going to have to help you if she's worried at all about the needs of your soul," she said.

Mother Superior came back into the office. Sister Madeline told me to go back to my class. I heard them talking together. Sister Madeline's voice was louder. "Mari-Jen is functioning at the level of a dull four-year-old. The poor child does not get any help from her mother. She will never amount to anything in school."

I went back to my class. The Sunflower Row was standing at the blackboard with Sister Thérèse. They were printing sentences on the board. *The sky is blue,* Lucy printed with yellow chalk and read her sentence out loud. I sat in my seat and looked at the globe. The world was in front of me but I wondered about the country called Poland. *Poland,* I whispered to myself. *Poland–place (noun).*

Daniel Peter was standing by his fence when me and my brothers walked home from school. He told Alfred and Albert about a book they should read. "*Gulliver's Travels,*"

Daniel Peter said, "will teach you much about world. Come along too, Mari-Jen. You will like story. I read for you." I loved Daniel Peter's kind eyes. I wished Mama could see the kindness in them.

I stayed home to help Mama when my brothers went down to Daniel Peter's house that night. They came home with a roll of sausage. "Daniel Peter made the sausage," they said. "He puts cornmeal and ground-up beef in it." Mama looked at the sausage.

"God knows what that D.P. put in that. He could have ground up a tomcat for all I know. Throw that in the woods," she ordered Alfred. He went outside and came back in after a few minutes. He and Albert went upstairs together.

When I went up, they were jumping up and down on their bed. Their cheeks were puffed out like they were when they put snowballs in them.

"What are you doing?" I asked.

They started to laugh and bits of food flew from their mouths. "We are eating a tomcat," Albert said.

"Yeah, and he's damn good," Alfred said. "Do you want some tomcat, Mari-Jen?" and then they reached under their mattress and pulled out half a roll of the sausage.

That night before I went to sleep I made up sentences in my head. *Alfred and Albert ate a tomcat*, I whispered. *Alfred–Albert–persons (nouns); ate–action (verb); tomcat–thing (noun).* I had a whole collection of nouns and verbs before I even tasted the body of Christ. Once again I asked Jesus for a father. A strong father who could beat up nuns and eat sausages. I asked Jesus if he had a Saint Urban in heaven. If he did, I wanted him to warn the saint that Mother Superior keeps talking to him. "Urbain, why did you leave me?" I had heard her say one day as I walked to her office. I listened to her strange conversation before I knocked on her office door. She always spoke to the same person. Sometimes her eyes were very red when I went into her office. Once she stared at me with her red eyes before she spoke a word. "Get out," she said, "you will end up just like her." I ran along the hall when I left the office. I didn't want to see her staring at me the way she did. I didn't know who she talked to. I hadn't heard of a saint with a name like Urbain. But I knew he understood French because she never called to him in English. We didn't pray to him in school.

Alfred and Albert said she was probably lost in the woods when she was a kid and was left there by a man named Urbain for the wolves to eat up.

# six

I t was 1959. Mother Superior put me in Mr. Babineau's class. There were grades four, five, and six together, stealing each other's knowledge without even knowing it. An assembly of misfits and abstracts, she referred to this class. I wanted to go back to Sister Thérèse's class. She had put my desk at the back of the room. I was removed from Buttercup Row. Sister Thérèse gave me errands to do. I cleaned the blackboards. I collected pieces of broken chalk and took them home.

The bigger boys were seated at the back of the Misfit Class. A girl named Rosie was fourteen. The bigger boys laughed when she stood up to read. "I'd like to lean on them knockers," someone whispered. Rosie stuttered. She couldn't get all the words out. Mr. Babineau told her to sit down. Mother Superior made me sit in Mr. Babineau's class for a week. The kids didn't like Mr. Babineau. He was tall and skinny and his clothes hung on him. Alfred and Albert said he was made of bones and clothes. They referred to him only as "Bones and Clothes".

"Bones and Clothes has a girlfriend," they told me one night.

"Yeah," Albert said. "She's a widow named Alma."

"You're making that up," I said.

"Like hell," said Alfred.

"Alma got a lump growing over one of her eyes," Albert said. "Some people call it a mouse."

"You're lying," I said to Albert.

"We'll prove it to you, Mari-Jen," Alfred said. "We can sneak up to her window when we see Bones and Clothes' truck at her house Friday night."

We waited until it got dark. Mr. Babineau rode up in his truck. The widow opened the kitchen door and he slid in like a cat. We crept under the kitchen window. Mr. Babineau sat at the table. The widow made a pot of tea. She put a plate of tea biscuits and curds on the table. We couldn't make out what they were saying. Mr. Babineau ate two tea biscuits. The widow was wearing a plain cotton dress and black pumps.

"Something should happen soon," Alfred whispered.

"What's supposed to happen?" I asked.

"Just keep watching," Albert said. "They can't eat all night."

When they were finished, the widow cleared the table. Mr. Babineau walked over to the stove and put in more wood. The widow's yellow cat jumped up on the kitchen table. Mr. Babineau tried to shoo the cat off the table. Its tail shot in the air, but it wouldn't budge. Alfred and Albert began to laugh.

Mr. Babineau made another swipe at the cat. The cat swung at him with its paw. It snarled. It hissed. It then jumped on Mr. Babineau. "You wooden whore!" he yelled.

He grabbed the cat by the tail and swung it around the kitchen. The widow ran out of the pantry. "What are you trying to do to my cat?" she screamed.

"The bitch is trying to kill me!" Mr. Babineau screamed back. The cat had landed in the woodbox.

The widow picked it up and stroked its fur. "Moonbeam, Moonbeam," the widow cried. "My poor little Moonbeam."

My brothers were laughing harder. Mr. Babineau held up a limp, white hand. "Look what she did, Alma." There were red claw marks on his hand.

"Oh, Wilfred, for Christ sake, it's only a cat," the widow cried. Mr. Babineau looked very angry.

It was Alfred who got an idea to knock at the kitchen window. "Make a run for it," he said, "if they come outside."

Alfred pounded on the window with his fist. The widow screamed and the cat flew out of her arms. Mr. Babineau swore. We saw the two of them running in the same direction. They disappeared behind a door near the stove. The cat followed at their heels and made it through the door before it slammed with a bang. We left. On the way home, Alfred and Albert planned ways of blackmailing Bones and Clothes.

On Monday morning, Mr. Babineau came to school with his hand wrapped in a white rag. He said he had cut it on the lid of a can. He wrote a list of words on the board. He called them pronouns. "*I, we, he, she.*" He said they were like cousins of the noun. One of the bigger boys named Cletis poked a pencil in my back. "Hey, you, Mari-Jen, do you know what a penis is?"

I turned around and answered him. "It's a noun."

He whispered to some of the other boys. They started to laugh. Mr. Babineau got very angry. He asked the boys what was so funny. Cletis said, "We are laughing at something Mari-Jen said, sir."

Mr. Babineau looked over at me. "Stand up, Mari-Jen," he ordered. "I want you to repeat whatever it is that's so funny."

I stood up. "It's a penis, sir," I blurted. "I said it was a noun."

His face turned red. He walked over to me and grabbed me by the arm with his good hand. "Down to Mother Superior's office!" he demanded, and led me from the class.

Mother Superior was seated at her desk. Mr. Babineau knocked at her door and she answered, "Come in." He pushed me in front of him. He explained what had taken place in the class. Mother Superior's face grew thick with anger. "Go back to your class, Mr. Babineau," she ordered. My body was trembling.

She grabbed the strap from her desk and walked over to me and pulled me by the hair and dragged me out of the office. She didn't let go of my hair until we reached Mr. Babineau's class. She opened the door and pushed me inside. The class grew silent. She marched me to the front of the class, raised the strap in the air, and shouted, "Take a look at the consequence of filth!" Nobody moved. Some of the kids looked frightened. She continued to shout. "I will not tolerate filth in my school from boys or girls!" She was holding the strap in the air like a sword. And then she ordered me to hold out my hands.

Some of the kids kept their heads down. Mr. Babineau turned towards the blackboard. My hands felt like they were breaking away from my wrists. She then ordered me to turn them over.

I screamed when I saw the blood. It was my own, warm and thick, soft and lingering from my veins, trickling slowly, exposing the consequences of filth. "Sit down, trash!" she screamed. I walked slowly to my desk, my hands held out in front of me. When she left, Mr. Babineau, white-faced, turned towards the class and told them to read silently.

Alfred and Albert ran up to me when we were lined up waiting for the school bus. They had heard. They carried my lunch can onto the bus for me. Albert said, "Spit on your hands, Mari-Jen, and rub them together."

Some of the kids asked to see my hands. "Jesus," one boy said, and went and sat down.

My hands puffed out like bread dough rising. Alfred and Albert made excuses for my wounds. Mama believed them. "Mari-Jen knocked over a statue of St. Jude," they said, "while running down the hall. Knocked the head clean off of him."

That night they planned revenge on Cletis. For Saturday. They knew he'd be going to the store for his mother.

I didn't want to go back to school. Mama made me go the next day. I went back to Sister Thérèse's class. Mother Superior came into our class at ten a.m. sharp. I stood up with the rest of the kids but I didn't look up. She walked down to my seat. Sister Thérèse looked limp.

Mother Superior stared at me and then at my hands. "You should feel shame," she whispered, and walked away. I wanted her to die. I wanted to see her dead and stiff on two wooden boards and I wouldn't touch her hands, not even the way she had touched mine. I would just look at her and say no prayers because I didn't want her to go to heaven. I hoped she'd have to wait somewhere in hell until my swelling went down.

Alfred and Albert made me go down to Daniel Peter's with them after school that day. They bragged about my hands and made me stretch them out so Daniel Peter could get a good look at them. They told him what had happened. His bottom lip trembled. "Bloody Nazi," he whispered. "Bloody, bloody Nazi." He took us into his house and put some kind of white cream on my hands. "It help swelling," Daniel Peter said.

When we got home I asked my brothers what Daniel Peter was talking about. "I'm not sure," Alfred said. "He was talking Polish."

It rained on Saturday. Albert and Alfred put on their rubber boots and went out early. I followed them. I saw Cletis and two other boys walking up to the store. They were taller and bigger than my brothers. Alfred and Albert were hiding behind the building. They waited until Cletis was close to the store and then they sprang at him. Cletis didn't even see them coming. His face looked startled. The other two boys stopped. Alfred grabbed Cletis by the hair and slammed his fist into his face.

"Tell us what a penis is," Albert screamed at Cletis. Cletis tried to get free but Albert kicked him in the legs. He fell backwards on the ground. Alfred kicked him in the stomach. The other two boys ran off. Cletis was moaning on the ground. Blood bubbled from his mouth, as if he were blowing it out with short, uneven breaths.

"You tell Mother Superior and we'll cut your nuts open," Albert shouted at Cletis. They left him on the ground and walked off down the shore road to throw rocks into the sea. Cletis scrambled to his feet and limped into the store after wiping his mouth.

❖  ❖  ❖

I didn't follow them on Saturday evening when they went out. It stormed. I held Lizzie. Mama put blankets on the couch for Mrs. Landry. She expected the storm to last for hours. It didn't. The northern wind slipped through the eaves.

"Thank God it didn't last long," Mama said to Mrs. Landry. "I don't know where them two are at. They'd go out in an earthquake. My nerves are shot."

"They're probably at the D.P.'s," Mrs. Landry said. "That fella is scared of nothing."

Alfred and Albert came in then. They looked like drowned rats. "Where were youse two?" Mama asked. "Out looking for pneumonia?"

"We were watching the lightning over the ocean," Albert said.

"Dear Jesus, youse are trying your best to kill me dead. Get upstairs and stay there." I could hear them laughing as they climbed the stairs.

Mama stood on the doorstep until Mrs. Landry got home. I went upstairs to bed. My brothers were under their quilt, talking.

"Did ya see the way he jumped?" Alfred said. Albert laughed out loud.

"I saw you hitting Cletis," I said.

"Cletis won't bother ya any more," they said.

"He thought he was going to blow up," Alfred said to Albert.

I knew they were not talking about Cletis now.

"Who thought he was going to blow up?"

"Nobody, Mari-Jen," Albert said. "Just someone we met in the storm."

I was afraid to go to school on Monday. But Cletis and the other two boys didn't say anything to me when I passed them in the hall. They were talking about Mr. Babineau. "He damn near got it," some of the kids were saying. "He almost jumped out of his skin when his window blew out. The lightning must have hit something near his house."

On Wednesday afternoon, Mother Superior wanted to see all the girls who were making their confirmation. I had made my first communion the year before with Marcel and Sophie. She gathered us in a spare classroom. She closed the door after we were seated.

"I called you all here for a talk," she said. "Some of you may know something about what I'm about to say, but most of you are ignorant." She walked up and down the aisles. I sat at the back, near the door.

"What I'm about to tell you will not leave this room," she snapped. "When a girl reaches a certain age, she gets what we call monthlies. We call it monthlies because it happens every month. That's providing you're not"—she stopped and looked around the room—"in the family way."

She asked the girls if they knew what she meant. I did, but I wouldn't tell her. "It means you're gonna get a baby," a girl named Agnes said.

"The word is *have*," Mother Superior snarled to Agnes. "These monthlies are our bodies' way of telling us that we must restrain from the sins of the flesh. Or else," she warned, "you know what happens to girls who disobey. Every month your body will bleed. It is the womb crying tears of blood because it is empty. And it had better stay

84

that way until you marry." Her voice rose. The girls were staring at her.

"I hope you understand," Mother Superior continued, "that no girl can join the convent unless her mother was properly married." She stopped and looked around the class. And then she was standing by my desk.

"Mari-Jen, for example, can never join the convent, since her mother is not married." The kids turned and looked at me. I put my head down. *Blood...blood...blood. The womb cried tears of blood. Womb—thing (noun); blood—thing (noun); cried...cried...cried—action (verb); flowing—action (verb...verb).*

Her sermon continued. "Girls who have babies before they marry must be warned. If your baby dies before it is baptized, it will go to a place called limbo. Remember that word, limbo."

My brothers explained monthlies another way. They were almost fourteen then. They had shaved. Each other. Daniel Peter gave them an old straight razor. They wanted to be men. To leave Ste. Noire. They wore their scars and nicks to school. Proudly.

"Youse look like a map!" Mama scolded when she saw their faces. "I'm telling ya that D.P. gave you that razor so youse could cut your throats!" They felt honoured to be so close to danger. They noticed the changes in my body. "Look at Mari-Jen. She's growing tits," Alfred said to Albert.

"You'll be on the rag soon," Albert said. I told them they had the wrong word.

"It's not the way Mother Superior told us."

"What the hell does she know?" Albert said. "Nuns aren't allowed to bleed."

I knew what nuns like Mother Superior could do. She could make my mother send me to school so Mama wouldn't lose her cheque.

I went along to Aunt Clara's and Uncle Jule's with my mother that summer. I could feel my mother's fear. It was my own.

Aunt Clara met us at the door. "I found my wings after all this time, Mari-Jen," she said. "They were in the cellar." She sat at the kitchen table while Mama worked in the pantry.

"Where is Uncle Jule?" I asked. She started to laugh.

"The saints ganged up on him. They locked him in the barn for being bad to me." Aunt Clara looked drawn and pale.

"Do you want to come to the shore for a walk?" I asked.

My mother heard me asking her. "Just take her in the field," she warned. "Don't go away from the house."

Aunt Clara followed me outside. She put her hands in the air as if she were feeling the wind. She was smiling.

Uncle Jule came out of the barn. "Get to hell in the house!" he screamed to us. His eyes were bloodshot. We went inside and I told Mama what Uncle Jule had said.

"The bastard, the miserable bastard," she mumbled to herself.

I followed Aunt Clara up to her room. Her jewellery was broken in small pieces on the floor, as if someone had crushed it with their feet.

"What happened to your jewellery?" I asked her.

"Shhh, Mari-Jen," she whispered and put her hands on her stomach. "Shhh, or you'll wake the baby."

# seven

Alfred and Albert have brewing blue eyes like me, Mama said. "Yours are a soft blue, Mari-Jen," she noted, making the comparison. "It's no wonder I'm in a blue mood, with fall coming and the firewood still to be cut and piled away. It's hard to get them two to do anything any more." She was speaking to Mrs. Landry. "They'd let you burn the drawers off your arse before they'd think of taking in a stick of wood."

"It's the D.P. that got them lazy," Mrs. Landry commented. "Who needs them books of his with snowbanks crawling up your back?"

Daniel Peter never came to our house. He offered once to cut our firewood and store it in the shed. Mama refused. He never offered again.

"What will people think?" she said. "Me here alone with three kids and a D.P. at the end of my axe."

Mother Superior asked me about Daniel Peter. "Does he come to your house?"

"No."

"Does your mother go to his house?"

"No," I said again.

"Are you sure?"

"Yes."

"How can you be certain?"

"I don't know."

"Then it's possible she goes over when you children are sleeping."

"No."

"You just said that you didn't know, Mari-Jen," she shouted.

"My mother won't let him cut our firewood," I offered. "She doesn't want Daniel Peter at the end of our axe."

"Why should she? Your brothers are big enough."

I didn't answer.

Mother Superior shook her head.

"Does she ever mention your fathers?"

"No."

"You and your brothers are illegitimate, you know, you don't have the same fathers."

I remained silent.

"She should explain these things to you. She can't hide these sins forever."

I wanted to leave. I was starting to choke with fear. I kept staring at her mouth.

Albert told me that he and Alfred watched a bullfrog being swallowed up by a snake. "You should have seen it, Mari-Jen. He got him by the head, then sucked him in slowly. The frog's legs were wiggling like crazy as the snake kept nibbling."

"What are you staring at, Mari-Jen?" Mother Superior interrupted my thoughts.

I felt my hands gripping the sides of the chair. I looked past her shoulder and up at the picture of the smiling Jesus. There was no pain in his face. Just that smile.

"Suffer unto me little children." *Suffer—action (verb).*

I heard the ruler slam down hard on her desk. "Mari-Jen Delene! When I speak to you I demand your full attention!"

I looked at her face. There were traces of spit in the corners of her mouth. She swallowed hard. "Get back to class," she commanded, "and take up more space." Once again I heard her call out the name Urbain from behind the closed door. She was mumbling something that I could not make out, but I knew she was very angry.

I walked slowly and went into the washroom. I soaked my face with cold water as I looked into the mirror. The softness had left my eyes. I knew illegitimate meant that our mother was not married.

Two girls came into the washroom. They were in Alfred and Albert's class. Margaret and her friend. I didn't like Margaret. I knew she was Mother Superior's pet and very cruel, like her.

Margaret saw me looking in the mirror. "What are you looking for, Mari-Jen? You won't find it in that ugly face of yours." She walked over to me and turned on the cold water tap and splashed water in my face. "There you go now, Mari-Jen. I washed some of the ugly away, now get going out of here!"

The other girl was laughing. I wanted to tell Margaret that she could soak in the sea for a weekend and she would still be ugly like a piece of seaweed, but I knew she would tell Mother Superior. I heard her telling the other girl that she would be right back, as she left the washroom. I was drying my face when Mother Superior walked in, followed by Margaret.

"Is this where I told you to go?" she shouted as she grabbed me by the arm and dragged me out of the washroom. Margaret and her friend stood looking at me as Mother Superior escorted me out. She took me to her office and made me kneel in the corner. I looked up at the smiling Jesus. I spoke with him in silence.

"Jesus, I hate Mother Superior. I am afraid of her. I think she is going to swallow me up. I am not as ugly as Margaret, Jesus. Margaret is really ugly, but she has a father. I heard her talking to the mirror, Jesus. She was trying to comb her bushy hair and getting very mad. Alfred and Albert said she has to comb her hair with a fork because it is so bushy. But Margaret has a pink comb with big teeth in it.

"'My mother thinks the retard is so pretty,' Margaret said to the mirror. I think she is mad at me for being pretty because she spit on the mirror and called me a bastard. Me and my brothers don't have a father we can name, like Margaret. But we have Daniel Peter and his bull, Sol, but I don't like the bull, Jesus, I hate the bull's eyes, 'cause they remind me of Uncle Jule's eyes and Mother Superior's eyes when she is mad at me, so please, Jesus, when people hurt me, can you close their eyes so they can't look at me? Jesus, I am not really stupid like people think. My head is filling up with new nouns and verbs every day, but I have to keep them a secret between me and you or else they will be taken from me and replaced with nothing but empty pages. Amen."

I told my brothers what Margaret did to me. They told me that they would take care of her. I didn't know what they had planned until I saw them pulling Margaret by the arm behind the school just as the bell rang to go in.

I ran over to the corner.

"Listen here, frog-face," said Alfred. "If I hear any more about you pushing Mari-Jen around, I'll introduce your paper tits to the whole school." Margaret was shaking.

"That's right," said Albert. "First your left paper tit and then your right. Got it?"

Margaret's voice sobbed. "I won't bother her any more, honest, I won't."

I looked at Margaret as she ran past me. Her eyes were soggy from crying and her chest was flat. I wondered if Alfred and Albert had made Margaret tear up her paper tits before she ran into the school.

After school my brothers told me about the Hallowe'en party their class was planning. "Margaret is the witch," said Alfred. "I told her she would just need to bring a broom."

I begged them to take me out with them on Hallowe'en night. "You're so slow, Mari-Jen, you move like a sheep," said Alfred.

"I'll wear my boots," I pleaded. They always came home on Hallowe'en with lots of treats. Mama made them take me to three or four houses and then back home, but I wanted to go farther this year. I wanted to be like them.

Mother Superior explained to the school kids that around Hallowe'en, a night called All Souls Night was reserved for the dead to roam the earth.

We set out where the dead would travel, my brothers and me, just as it got dark. Alfred and Albert were dressed as ghosts, with sheets hanging to the ground. I carried Lizzie for extra protection from the night.

We went to Daniel Peter's house first. He had special treats made up for us with our names on them. Each a bag of molasses kisses and licorice pipes and a bag of chips. We sat on the bank of the road and ate Daniel Peter's treats.

We moved on to Mrs. Bona's house. Alfred said that Mrs. Bona made fudge with Sunlight soap. "Last year," they said, "Enos Petrie ate the fudge and had to go straight home because he couldn't stop shitting on the road after he ate the fudge."

We tasted it carefully.

"It's loaded with Sunlight," Alfred said, and we threw our fudge in the field for the crows.

It was Albert's idea to go visit Aunt Clara and Uncle Jule. I warned them that we were told not to go near their house.

"Mama won't know we were there," said Albert, "unless you squeal, Mari-Jen."

"I won't squeal, but I'm scared of Uncle Jule. He hates kids."

"Then this is a good time to get him back," said Alfred. "He'll never know it was us, Mari-Jen. We're not stupid, so keep your mouth shut or stay here by yourself and wait for us to come back."

I followed behind them. I held Lizzie close to me. A cold breeze whistled off the sea and lifted Alfred and Albert's sheets in the air. A full moon spotted us.

We could see a light in the kitchen of the house from the top of the hill. "We'll sneak in from the back," said Alfred, "and go along the veranda."

We were climbing over the back fence when we saw Uncle Jule walking to the outhouse. He was carrying a bucket. "He must be going to empty the pisspot," said Albert. We watched him walk into the toilet.

"Let's lock him in," Alfred whispered to Albert. "He'll break out after we leave."

"Stay here, Mari-Jen," they ordered. They crept along to the outhouse. Uncle Jule was still inside. I heard the bolt slide into place on the door. My brothers had him trapped. They ran back to where I was standing. We waited for him to start kicking at the door but he didn't make a sound.

"He could be planning one of his old war tricks," Alfred whispered. "He could be armed with a grenade."

"Where is he going to throw it? In the pisspot?" Albert whispered back. "He can't break that bolt in a hurry."

We waited for him to try and kick his way out but he didn't make a sound. "He got a heart attack," I whispered in fear. "He must be dead."

"Na, shut up," said Alfred. "He has to be as old as Zeppie before he wears out."

We heard a moaning scream but it was not Uncle Jule's voice. It came from within the house. "Jesus Christ," said Alfred. "That's Aunt Clara's voice." We crept along the veranda and looked in the kitchen window.

She was lying on the cot in the corner. Her knees were tucked up close to her chin. She looked disfigured. She was holding a sheet between her legs.

"Maybe she's on the rag," said Alfred, but he and Albert did not laugh this time. They were too frightened.

"Let's go in and see her," said Alfred. I was too frightened to move. Albert grabbed my hand and pulled me behind him.

"She'll tell on us," I mumbled.

Alfred and Albert pulled the sheets over their faces and pulled the bag down over my head. We walked quietly along the side of the house. There were no sounds coming from the outhouse. We went in the back door. Aunt Clara did not hear us come in. She was still moaning. I went closer to her. She noticed us standing in the kitchen. Two ghosts and a paper-faced kid. She noticed Lizzie in my arms. She reached out her hands. There was some blood on her hand. "I want to hold my baby," she sobbed. "Let me hold my baby."

I put Lizzie in her bloody hands. She stopped crying then and closed her eyes. I thought she had fallen asleep so I pulled Lizzie from her arms and put a cushion in them. Aunt Clara's eyes were still closed when we left.

"Go wait on the road," Alfred said to me. "We will let him out and make a run for it."

I ran towards the road and looked back. Alfred and Albert were running behind me. Their sheets were flying in the air. We waited for a minute and then Uncle Jule opened the outhouse door slowly and stepped out into the moonlight. We could hear him cursing and swearing as he looked around.

Alfred and Albert removed their sheets and crept back to the kitchen window. I followed behind. He walked over to Aunt Clara and looked at her. She opened her eyes then.

"Was anyone in here?" he asked in a loud voice. "Was anyone in this house?"

Aunt Clara's voice was weak.

"The baby came to visit. My baby came to visit me."

Uncle Jule covered her with a blanket, then put more wood in the stove.

I had a nightmare that night. Lizzie was drowning in blood. In Aunt Clara's blood. She was sinking before my eyes and I could not reach her. When I caught her, she fell apart in my hands.

*The womb cries tears of blood when it is empty. Limbo babies, limbo–limbo.*

Marcel let me try on his glasses. They were round and thick like the bottom of a jam bottle.

"Can you see anything, Mari-Jen?"

"No. Everything is blurry."

Marcel told me he was going to be a priest. He had read the bible from cover to cover with his good eyes.

"What's in it?" I asked.

"Everything, Mari-Jen. Everything is in it."

"Is limbo in the bible, Marcel?"

"There are all kinds of limbo."

"I want to know about the limbo that keeps little babies, unbaptized babies."

Marcel removed his glasses and stared at a cloud. "The angels collect them, Mari-Jen," he said, still staring at the cloud. "The angels collect them and turn them into cherubs." I liked Marcel's story more than Mother Superior's.

"Are you going to live with Father Benoit?"

"No, I'm going to a place in Quebec to study at a seminary."

"Alfred and Albert are going to Africa."

"What for?" Marcel asked.

"To see the lions," I said. "They want to hear them roar."

Sophie's grandmother died on a Wednesday in November. It was snowing. The church bell rang when Sister Thérèse was counting up her stars. We stood by our desks and began to pray. She would go to heaven and she would no longer be blind. Albert said heaven was full of specialists just waiting for something to do.

"Who died?" asked someone at the back of the class. Everyone knew that the slow ringing of the bell meant a death in the parish.

"The church bell has lungs," Alfred told me one day when it rang on a summer afternoon. We were digging creatures out of the sand at the shore. The church bell rang just as Alfred caught one and mashed it between his fingers.

"Do you hear the bell, Mari-Jen? It's whispering death. If you listen hard enough you will hear it. D-e-a-t-h—d-e-a-t-h —d-e-a-t-h."

Sophie's grandmother was buried in a storm. Nobody went up to the new graveyard beyond the hill past the school. I heard the horse and sleigh go by as I looked out the window.

Two men were sitting at the front of the sleigh. One of them was Father Benoit. Another man rode on the back, behind the coffin. It was tied to the sleigh with a rope so the coffin wouldn't fall off on its last journey. The horse stopped and lowered its head. The man up front whirled a whip in the air like a lasso. The horse reared its head and moved on.

Sophie didn't lose her voice when her grandmother died. She came to school the following week and told us she had dressed her grandmother for heaven in a black dress.

Mother Superior took me to her office with her on Friday. Sister Thérèse looked annoyed when I followed Mother Superior out at the hem of her robe. Her office was down the hall from my class.

"Sit down," she ordered when we went in. She sat behind her desk staring at me.

"You're looking rather pale, Mari-Jen. Do you go to bed early?"

"Yes."

She paused, still looking at me, as she took out her notebook and began checking it from back to front. "You've been in school for almost seven years, have you not?"

I didn't answer.

"What have you learned in seven years, girl?"

"I can print," I blurted.

"So what? A monkey can print, Mari-Jen."

"I can pray. Can a monkey pray?"

Her face turned red and her bottom lip trembled. "Are you trying to be smart?" she asked in a shaky voice.

"No, Mother Superior."

"I should say not. Morons don't have much luck with intelligence."

She read through her notebook again. "Have you started your monthlies, Mari-Jen?"

"No."

"Don't lie to me. I know about these things."

"No," I said again.

She stood up behind her desk and told me to stand.

She walked over to the door and locked it. Fear was punching at my insides. I held onto the back of the chair.

"Remove your sweater," she commanded. I undid the buttons one by one. It took a long time. My fingers felt knotted. I was wearing a slip underneath my sweater. She looked at my breasts as she walked towards me. I saw her pull a measuring tape out of a side pocket. And then she wrapped it around my breasts and mumbled something under her breath.

My face was burning. I didn't believe people should be measured to see how stupid they were.

*I am not stupid. Am not—action (verb).*

"I want you in my office on Monday morning following prayers," she ordered, as I buttoned my sweater. She unlocked the office door and let me out.

I went into the washroom and washed my face and hands. I felt really dirty. I stared at myself in the mirror. My red hair looked like a flame. It was tied back at the nape of my neck. My face was pale, almost white. My summer freckles had faded. I wondered where freckles went during the winter. Where did they hide? I wish I could have hidden other parts of me.

*Mari-Jen hides nouns and verbs and freckles. Hides—action (verb).*

We went down to see Aunt Clara on the weekend. Mama and me. Aunt Clara was upstairs in her room when we arrived. Uncle Jule was in the barn.

I noticed a few drops of blood on her floor when I went in to see her. She was in bed. Her face looked bleached. Her jewellery was crushed in small pieces beside her bed.

"Are you sick?"

"No. Frig off, Mari-Jen."

"You don't look good, Aunt Clara."

"I am better now. They cured me."

"Who cured you?"

"None of your friggin' business. Besides, they cured me."

"Who cured you?"

"The saints cured me, Mari-Jen."

"How many were there, Aunt Clara?"

"Three of them," she said, "and a baby."

"How did they cure you?"

"They made me better. They took the pain away after Jule beat me." She paused and looked straight into my eyes. "He kicked me, Mari-Jen. He kicked me when I told him not to touch me or he would wake up my baby."

"What did he do?"

"He put his foot on my guts and kept hurting me. He didn't like my baby." She began to laugh hysterically when she saw me crying.

"You can cry all you want, Mari-Jen, 'cause the saints are bringing me another baby," she screamed, "and if you're real good you can hold my baby for a whole day."

She covered her face with her pillow then and stopped laughing.

Mother Superior was waiting for me on Monday, following prayers. I knocked on the office door. She opened it and locked it behind her. "Take off your sweater," she ordered, "and do not sit down."

I fumbled with the buttons and removed my sweater.

"Pull your slip down to your waist."

Terror scorched my chest. She was standing beside me with a white piece of cloth in her hands. "Christ, Jesus, strike her dead," I pleaded silently. I could hear the sound of Aunt Clara's voice laughing hysterically. I could see the blood. I could hear the laughing again, but it was my own voice this time, growing calmer now as she reached out and slapped me hard across the face. Numbness followed, then silence, then her voice again.

"Stretch out your arms." She wrapped the cloth tightly around my breasts and pinned it in front with four safety pins. "You are not to remove this binding," she warned. "You are to wear it to school throughout the week. I will remove it on Fridays and put it back in place on Monday mornings. Is that clear?" Her voice lowered. "Mari-Jen, you are to tell not a soul except your mother, if she should bother to ask."

She locked the door and let me out. I went into the washroom and threw up. I felt like I was tied to her by a rope.

"Some people have to be tied," I remembered Mrs. Landry saying. An old man down by the shore used to tie his wife to the clothesline. "She'd wander off," she said, "down to the sea, out in the woods, down to the swamp. He had to tie her to keep her safe from herself."

Mother Superior removed the binding on Friday and put it in a brown paper bag. "Did you tell anyone?" she inquired.

"No," I answered quietly. I did not tell anyone that I was being bound to keep me safe from myself.

I watched as she walked to the convent on Friday afternoon. We were sitting in the school bus. She was carrying a black leather case with the brown paper bag in it.

"There goes the beaver," I heard Alfred say to Albert. "I wonder what she has in that case."

I knew. *Mother Superior carries Mari-Jen in a brown paper bag. Carries—action word (verb); Mother Superior—person (noun). I want myself back. Want—action (verb). I hate you. Hate—action, so much action, so much hate (verb).*

Margaret got her monthlies before Christmas. A group of girls surrounded her one morning. They did not know I was in one of the toilets.

"Oh. my God," a girl named Florence squealed. "I'll die. I think I'll die with all that pain." I could see them through the crack in the door, Margaret acting as if blood would pour from her body for a demonstration.

"I was so scared," Margaret gasped, "to see the blood on my sheet. I nearly fainted."

"What did you do?" someone shuddered.

"I crawled out of bed," Margaret explained, "and stood up. I was too scared to walk but then I did."

"Then what happened?" they inquired.

"I nearly fell!" cried Margaret.

The girls let out a moan. "Ohhh...ohhh...ohhh."

"Why didn't you call your mother?" they giggled.

"I did," said Margaret, "but my voice was so weak...but finally she heard me and rushed in to rescue me."

I could see Margaret's face. It was covered in pimples. A

big pimple on the side of her nose looked as if it was trying to tip it over. She was smiling at all the attention she was getting, but it didn't help. She was still ugly.

"Oh, no," the girls screamed. "No, stop—we're gonna cry!"

Margaret continued with her agony. "My mother rushed me to bed and served me weak tea and toast on her best crystal tray. She propped me up on my pillows. Daddy came in and kissed me. He was so worried. He hugged me and wished that I didn't have to suffer so much."

I came out of the toilet. The girls stopped talking and looked at me. I walked slowly to the door.

"Do you think she'll ever have a period?" I heard someone ask.

"I don't think so," said ugly Margaret. "Retarded people aren't like us."

Mama and me took some fudge down to Aunt Clara on Sunday. She was up in her room. Uncle Jule was in the pantry.

"Was Clara sick?" Mama asked him.

"What business is it of yours?" he snarled. "It's me that's looking after her."

Mama didn't answer. He turned to me. "Were you and your brothers here on Hallowe'en night?"

My heart was jumping again. I thought he could hear it.

"They were not allowed to come down this far," Mama cut in.

"We went to Daniel Peter's," I mumbled.

"That's the D.P.," Mama explained.

"I don't give a fuck who he is; I don't want anyone nosing around in here when I'm out."

He left then and went out to the barn. I found a small tray in the pantry and put two pieces of fudge on it for Aunt Clara.

She was sitting on her bed. "I have some fudge for you," I said as I put the tray on her bed.

"I hate fudge, Mari-Jen."

"No, you don't," I protested.

"Yes, I do, Mari-Jen. Fudge makes your hair turn grey."

"Your hair is black, Aunt Clara."

"That's shoe polish. I keep it for my hair."

"Some people put soap in their fudge," I said. "Mrs. Bona gave us soapy fudge on Hallowe'en. We had to throw it away."

I didn't think she heard me. She was staring at the ceiling. "This house is haunted," she whispered. "It's full of ghosts."

"How do you know?"

"They come to visit me all the time."

"You can't see ghosts, Aunt Clara. They're invisible."

"Frig off, Mari-Jen. You're telling lies."

"You can't see a ghost, Aunt Clara."

"My arse. I see them all the time. They wake me up and pull my hair."

"Do they speak?"

"No, they don't talk, Mari-Jen. They got no tongues, only lips. They smile at me with their lips. And besides, I am one of them. Remember that I am Saint Butterfly."

I got up to leave just as she put the two pieces of fudge in her mouth and threw the tray on the floor.


Mother Superior was not at school on Monday. I was very happy. She is ill, said Sister Thérèse, as she asked the class to stand and say a prayer for her recovery. I didn't pray.

She returned to school on Tuesday. I went to her office. She bound me in the white cloth. It was ironed in creases—straight starched creases. I held out my arms like a scarecrow as she pinned the cloth in place. "You must think of this silent bondage as a time of penance, Mari-Jen," she whispered. "Everyone must do penance—every woman. Lord knows it is only penance that has pinned me here. Penance is not a love, girl, it is a curse on the cursed. You will thank me someday for keeping you pure."

I went back to class. Sister Thérèse had put three new books on my desk. I didn't feel like looking at them. The cloth was so tight it was cutting into my flesh.

*Mari-Jen is in silent bondage. Is (verb); bondage (noun); cutting (noun), hurting (noun).*

The following week Mother Superior told me to sit in her grade twelve class. I hated when she did this. Sometimes she made me sharpen pencils. Another time I had to polish the school bell. Other times she just made me wait and clean the blackboards. There were a dozen or more students in the class. They were reading Shakespeare's *Macbeth*. Mother Superior read the part of Lady Macbeth.

A boy named Claude was asked to read the part of Macbeth. He looked embarrassed.

I smiled secretly to myself. How often Daniel Peter had read these words to me and my brothers. I knew some of them by heart.

She began to read in a loud voice. "How now, what news? He has almost supped—why have you left the chamber?"

Claude's voice cut in, shaking weakly. "Hath he asked for me . . . ?"

Mother Superior's voice speaks. "Know you not, he has!"
Claude's painful voice breaks in. "We will proceed no
further in this business!"

"Indeed, we won't," Mother Superior shouted, as she
threw the book on her desk. She was not reading now.

She looked at Claude. "Where did you learn to read?
Under water?"

He did not look up. The others sat without motion.
Locked to their seats.

"Why do I even try?" she screamed. "I walk through this
school as if it were a garden and what do I see?" She paused
and looked around. "Morons! Morons planted everywhere!"

Tears were streaming down her face. She slammed a
closed fist on her desk. "What penance must I endure to
receive a rose?" she screamed. "What penance must I
endure ... again."

At that moment I did not know if Lady Macbeth had
returned or had gone away forever.

# eight

Daniel Peter read from a book he called the Five Books of Moses. He kept his book of prophets on the kitchen shelf next to the stove.

"Are they the same gang that hang around our church?" Alfred had asked. Daniel Peter smiled.

"You have much words, now you need much knowledge."

"Mother Superior said only Catholics are going to heaven," Albert said.

"Then heaven be not full. Maybe God squeeze in some Jew like me to make full house."

"I don't think she's going to heaven," said Alfred.

"Don't think so much, heaven find you before she."

"Are you ever going back home?" asked Albert.

"This is my home."

"But your real home," quizzed Alfred.

"This I make real."

"Don't you miss Poland?" asked Albert.

"Very much. Europe take my vision everyday to my youth, like you," Daniel Peter said sadly.

"Did you have any brothers and sisters?" my brothers questioned.

"Two brother, one sister—very beautiful—like your Mari-Jen—ever so gentle—too much pain for one mind to carry."

"Why did you come to Canada?" This was my question.

"I have pass on ship—ship to freedom—no country left after war."

"Where did the ship land?" asked Alfred.

"In Halifax," Daniel Peter answered.

"Did anyone speak your language?" Albert asked.

"After war I work in Halifax—I cook—I sweep—I wash dishes—I break dishes. I not need much language."

"Were you a maid?" I blurted out.

Daniel Peter laughed and tapped my head. "Little one so clever. I like to teach the mind—so much knowledge unrehearsed in mind."

"Me and Alfred are going to travel one of these days," Albert said.

"You pick right day and you travel far."

"We're going to Africa and maybe some day we'll visit Poland," smiled Alfred.

Daniel Peter did not answer.

"Why didn't you get married?" asked Albert.

Daniel Peter laughed. "My heart more ready but no English."

"We can find a widow for you to marry," Albert announced.

"Please, please, my friend—you *must not* trade emotion for convenience too fast."

"She won't mind. She has a tomcat and a lump growing over one of her eyes," said Alfred.

Daniel Peter laughed heartily. "You make this one up."

"No, we aren't. She's for real," laughed Alfred. "Her name is Alma." Daniel Peter laughed harder.

"Tomcat and lump—maybe she already spoken for—and gone."

"No way. She used to be Mr. Babineau's girlfriend but I think she's mad at him," Albert offered.

Daniel Peter put his hands over his face. "For what reason?" he asked between his fingers.

"He swung her cat around the kitchen and he landed in the woodbox," said Alfred.

Daniel Peter collapsed with laughter. "No more—no more!" he pleaded.

"That's true. He grabbed Moonbeam by the tail and let him drift," they continued.

Daniel Peter laughed until we left for home. I caught a glimpse of him through the window. He had taken his prophets off the shelf and opened the book and smiled down at them.

Alfred and Albert won a writing contest at school when they were in grade eight. Their subject was war. They wrote the story together. They talked about war and suffering. They said that in war all sides were equal because people just wanted to survive. They said how happy they were to have a friend who had survived all the pain. They said Daniel Peter suffered like Jesus. A man from the school board said that they deserved the prize for their kindness. They lost the first prize—a globe. Mother Superior gave the prize to a boy named Fulbert, because she said no mortal can be compared to Christ.

Fulbert wrote about his trip to the doctor in Halifax to have warts removed from his foot. He displayed his scars at recess. He showed the crowd that had gathered around his foot just where the doctor drove in the needles to freeze the warts before he burned them off with something that looked like a hot poker. Some of the kids jumped back. Alfred and Albert joined the crowd. They looked at Fulbert's foot. They whispered to each other. "Hey, Fulbert," shouted Alfred, "me and Albert had warts cut off too—but the doctor didn't freeze them first."

"Oh, yeah," said Fulbert, as he put his shoe back on his foot. "How did he get them off?"

"He bit them off," said Alfred.

The crowd grew larger. "Youse are lying," Fulbert said.

"Is that right?" said Alfred. "Then we'll show you."

The girl Margaret laughed and rolled her eyes. "Why don't you show us then?"

Alfred and Albert pulled down their pants. The girls screamed and scattered like hens in a fox raid. Mr. Babineau came running. He grabbed my brothers by the hair. "What do you two think you are trying to do?" he shouted. "To the office right now!"

Alfred was the first to speak. "Well, Bones and Clothes, have you seen any Moonbeams lately?"

He let go of their hair and began to stutter.

"Moonbeams," said Albert.

"What do you think you're trying to do, Moonbeam?" they asked together.

He walked away, his shoulders slumped, and disappeared behind the school.

The open field beside our house grew thick with tall grass and weeds and garden snakes that slithered across the path. We had planted the path with our feet, to take us down to the sea and to the General Store that could be seen from the top of a hill halfway through the field. Daniel Peter's property was to our right. We took this path to Aunt Clara's house.

Albert and Alfred set fire to the field one spring. They wanted to make the grass grow thicker, so they could hide from their enemies and guard their fort. Their fort was made of old boards Daniel Peter had given them and drift-wood they had carried home from the shore.

The fire went out of control. A sickening swarm of orange tongues licked the corner of the porch. Mama came out of the house screaming, with two water buckets in her hands. She kept filling the buckets from the well, and my brothers splashed the water onto the flames. Their faces were black from the smoke when she hauled them over the steps into the house.

"Finish me off, why don't youse!" she screamed. "My nerves are fried now! Finish me off with fire! What were youse trying to do? Burn me alive?"

Alfred started to say something, but Mama hit him in the face with her hand. He fell back onto the floor. She grabbed Albert, but he blocked her fist with his arms. She grabbed him by the hair and shook him back and forth. He howled when she picked up a piece of kindling and beat the visible flesh on his body. He crawled to a corner of the kitchen with Alfred, and they huddled together with their arms around each other.

I looked at their eyes, set in their black faces. There was something in them I had not seen before. Something I didn't really want to see. I knew Mama had seen it too.

She dropped the stick and went into the bedroom without saying another word. My brothers got up off the floor and went out. I followed behind them. Albert turned around. "Stay home, Mari-Jen. We'll take you some other time." They crossed the black field that they had hoped would grow and guard them from their enemies.

I sat on the step for a long time, until it started to rain. A mud puddle swelled at my feet. I tossed some rocks into the puddle and watched as the water spread out like a big hand trying to catch something.

I heard something flapping. The flour bags on the clothesline had swallowed enough wind to bloat them out like the hanging tits on Rinso, before she was milked.

They didn't come back until later in the night. I watched for them from the upstairs window. Mrs. Landry and Mama were talking in the kitchen. I could hear their voices. "They'd burn the shoes off your feet, them two," Mrs. Landry said. "It's a good job you were home, Adele."

Mama's voice was tired. "I don't think they'll start any fires for a while."

Mrs. Landry sighed. "It's okay for foolish people to start fires. They love to watch the flames. It's the flames that get them excited."

"They're not really foolish, Tori, not like poor Clara."

"No, but they're close, Adele."

"They're not anything like my brother either."

"Well, you'd know more than me. I never had kids, but I saw enough of Zeppie's cousin, Buzzie."

"I thought he was dead, Tori."

"Christ Almighty. He wasn't dead, Adele, when he set his father's head on fire!"

"What happened to him?"

"They put him away, thank God. How could you sleep with a match in the house and that fellow around?"

After Mrs. Landry went home, I could hear Mama walking around the kitchen. She put more wood in the stove. I sat at the top of the stairs for a while. I heard her go to the back door two or three times. I went to bed as the smell of fudge drifted up the stairs and sweetened the dark air.

Marcel practised being a priest on all the sinners he could line up on the weekends. He invited them to his father's barn. Confessions were held at four o'clock. He warned the sinners beforehand that his absolutions weren't the real thing, and that he couldn't absolve Alfred and Albert for starting the fire because he hadn't taken his vows yet.

Amos Dejeune was the first one in confession. Amos was forty years old. He lived with his parents in a crooked house beside the old graveyard. My brothers said that Amos could talk to the dead. Every day Amos walked through the graveyard. He'd stop at the headstones and then bless himself. Then he'd begin his conversations with the dead. Most kids were afraid of him. They would not follow him in the graveyard to listen to him.

We could see him from the schoolyard making his rounds. "There goes Amos," someone said. "He's getting ready to visit the dead."

My brothers followed him one afternoon. Fog draped the tombstones like a damp cloak. Alfred and Albert hid at the edge of the fence until they could make out Amos's form. He made his first visit to one of the oldest stones in the graveyard. "*Bonjour, mon frere*," said Amos to the stone beneath his feet. "The fog is as thick as cream today as I pray for your soul. It is Tuesday, the last day of April, in the year of our Lord 1959. The fishermen sailed early today from the harbour. The sea was as smooth as cat's fur." They said he was talking to an old fisherman, Patrick Pottier, who had died in the eighteen hundreds.

Alfred and Albert ran back to school. A crowd waited for them. They were not disappointed. They said that not only did Amos talk to the dead, but that the dead answered him. They said some of the dead spoke in French and others in broken English. They said some of them were in heaven and the rest were in hell. An old woman, named Mae Renette, was in hell, they believed, because her voice was hoarse when she spoke and it had to be from all the smoke inhaled from the flames.

Amos went to Marcel to ask for forgiveness for going in the Protesant graveyard. Marcel didn't hear any more confessions after this; instead he offered up mass for the souls in purgatory. Amos came to these masses, even though, my brothers said, his friends were either in heaven or hell.

Sol died in the spring of 1959. Daniel Peter dug a hole in his field and buried him. Albert and Alfred helped to dig the grave. Daniel Peter said Sol was too old to be useful. "Are you going to get another bull?" Alfred asked.

"Maybe, but Sol very good bull—hard to find bull like Sol."

"What makes a good bull?" Albert wanted to know.

Daniel Peter scratched his head. "Same thing that make good man—hard work—strong back."

"Why can't you eat a bull?" asked Alfred.

"For same reason you not eat man," Daniel Peter answered, as he continued to dig in the ground. Sol was stretched out ten feet from where they were digging. His eyes were opened wide, as if he were watching his grave being dug. When they were finished digging, Daniel Peter tied a rope to Sol's feet, attached it to his horse, and pulled Sol close to his grave. Daniel Peter pulled the rope over the open grave. He pulled on the rope until Sol fell into the grave on his back. Alfred and Albert helped Daniel Peter fill in the grave.

I looked in at Sol before the grave was filled in. He was staring up at the sky. "Where do animals go when they die?" I asked Alfred.

"They get recharged, Mari-Jen, and then they come back as something else—a lion or a wolf—or even a snake—they roam the world in another form."

"No, they don't, Alfred."

"Yes, they do."

"You're making that up again."

"I am not. If you don't believe me, ask Albert."

"He'll make that up too."

"He doesn't have to, it's true."

"How do you know?"

"Because we know everything."

"No you don't. Then who makes them into something else?"

"An animal spirit," he said.

"Who told you that?"

"I read about it. Some old Indian chief in British Columbia can talk to the animal spirits. Just like Amos can talk to the dead in French or English."

I went home. Mama and Mrs. Landry were out by our fence talking about the weather. I told them that Sol was dead.

"Who cares," said Mrs. Landry. "There's too many bulls on the go here anyway."

"Alfred said animals can come back in another form," I told my mother. She shook her head. "He said an old Indian in British Columbia can talk to the animal spirits, just like Amos can talk to the dead."

Mrs. Landry sighed. "Don't be listening to them, Mari-Jen. Them two will be doing all their talking in an asylum if they don't smarten up."

Daniel Peter took Alfred and Albert with him to Antigonish to get a new bull. They piled the bull in the back of his old Fargo truck. They arrived home with Isaac just as the fog rolled in off the Atlantic.

A group of neighbours gathered to check out the bull. They patted his back and then his neck. "Seems pretty hefty," they said. "I hope he's as good on the hop as Sol was." They laughed, and Daniel Peter agreed.

I went to the store for my mother that evening. I carried a stick along the path. I kept watching for snakes to crawl out of the grass. I was not sure what the spirits did with Sol. I saw someone standing in the field as I walked along the path. It was Uncle Jule. He did not move as I continued to walk along. I kept watching him as I ran and crawled under the pole fence, near the path. The hem of my skirt got caught in the fence. I heard it rip as I pulled on it. Uncle Jule had disappeared when I turned around.

A light rain fell. I don't remember getting to the store. "You look like you were wrestling with a bear," the woman at the store said.

"It was a snake," I said. "It must have been a snake."

She shook her head as she passed me the brown sugar.

In the fall, before I was twelve, a doctor came to our school. She was from the Health Department in Halifax. Mother Superior said she was a psychiatrist. Dr. Mitchel wore steel-rimmed glasses. Her dark hair was pulled back sharply into a bun. Her skin was very pale, almost like Marcel's, but her face was lean and cold, like frost had set into it and never melted. Mother Superior made me go to the office. I sat opposite the doctor. Mother Superior left us alone. "I am Dr. Claire Mitchel," she said. "Do you know why Mother Superior asked you here?"

"No."

"How old are you, Mari-Jen?"

"Almost twelve."

"How old are your brothers?"

"Fifteen."

"Do you get along well with your brothers?"

"Yes."

"Do they ever hit you, Mari-Jen?"

"No, not now."

"Did they ever hit you?"

"Just sometimes, but not hard."

"Why did they hit you?"

"I don't know."

"Does your mother ever beat you?"

"No, not me."

"Does she hit your brothers?" Dr. Mitchel asked.

"Sometimes, but not now."

She kept writing down my answers on a sheet of paper.

"Do you like school, Mari-Jen?"

"I like Sister Thérèse. She gives me books."

"Do you like books?"

"Yes."

"Do you know your alphabet?"

I did not answer.

"Your name, Mari-Jen, can you spell it?"

"Sometimes."

"Can you spell it today?"

"No."

"Why not?"

"I forgot."

Dr. Mitchel stared at me. "I think you know how to spell it, Mari-Jen."

"Sometimes," I said.

"Have you started your monthlies?"

"No."

"Are you sure?"

"Yes."

"Do you have any friends?"

"Yes."

"Who are they?"

"Daniel Peter is my friend."

"Who is Daniel Peter?"

"He is my friend and Alfred and Albert's friend."

"Where does he live?"

"By our house. He's our neighbour."

"Do you visit his house?"

"Yes."

"Alone?"

"No, with my brothers."

"Does Daniel Peter have a wife?"

"No, but he has a bull, a new bull named Isaac," I answered.

Dr. Mitchel took off her glasses. "Is he your friend?"

"He tells us stories about Poland and he reads us stories from old books."

"Do you know how old your friend is, Mari-Jen?"

"Old like you," I replied.

The doctor put her glasses back on and wrote something on the sheet. "Does Daniel Peter ever hug you?"

"No, he just taps me on the head."

"Are you afraid of him?"

"No."

"Would you let Daniel Peter hug you?"

I did not answer.

"Would you let him hug you, Mari-Jen?" Dr. Mitchel asked again.

"He doesn't hug people, just bulls."

"Do your brothers hug you?"

"No."

"Does your mother?"

"She lets me sleep with her when I am sick. I can feel her hugging me in the night. I hear her whispering that she would love for me to get better."

She stared at her notebook.

"I hug Lizzie," I said.

"Who's Lizzie?"

"My doll. I hug Lizzie every night."

"Would you like to play some games with me, Mari-Jen?" Dr. Mitchel asked.

"I don't know," I said.

"I have some puzzles here. Do you think you could put them together for me?"

"Maybe."

Dr. Mitchel took out a board with circles and squares and triangles cut out.

"Now, Mari-Jen, do you think you can put the shapes in the correct openings?"

I put the square peg in the round hole on purpose.

"Too bad, Mari-Jen." She put the board away and asked me more questions.

I was careful not to mention my collection of nouns and verbs. I knew she would tell Mother Superior about them and they would be taken from me. Sometimes at school, you had to be very smart to appear very stupid.

"What kind of stories does Daniel Peter read to you?"

"Good ones."

"How do you know they are good?"

"I like them."

"Do you remember them?"

"Sometimes."

"Are they about children?"

"Sometimes."

"What else are they about?"

"Countries. Different countries."

"Poland?" she asked.

"Yes."

"Do you know where Poland is?"

"In Europe."

"Very good. Did Daniel Peter tell you that?"

"No, my brothers did. They're going to visit Europe."

"Oh, they are?" she said with a queer smile on her face.

"Yes, Alfred and Albert are going to travel all over the world."

"Would you like to go with them?"

"Yes."

Dr. Mitchel handed me a blank piece of paper and asked me to print my name.

I printed it out.

"Can you read the letters?"

"No."

"Why not?" she asked.

"I just can't."

"Can you print your brothers' names?"

"No."

"Lizzie's name?"

"No."

"Can your Aunt Clara read, Mari-Jen?"

"I don't know."

"Did you ask her?"

"No, but she knows about the Queen."

"Who told her about the Queen?"

"I don't know, she just knows. And my mother can read if she wants to."

"Does she ever read to you?"

"No, just Daniel Peter."

"You like Daniel Peter, don't you?"

"Yes."

"Does he ever tell you he likes you?"

"Yes. He likes me and my brothers."

"Does he have a girlfriend?"

"No, but my brothers said they could get him one."

Dr. Mitchel rubbed her forehead. She looked tired. "Mari-Jen, I think this will be all for today. I will see you again on Monday."

I left the office. Mother Superior met me in the hallway. "Come with me," she said. I followed her into the empty classroom. She removed my binding for the weekend. She slapped me hard across the face when I showed her the red marks under my arms. "It's a small price you have to pay, girl, to protect your body from sin," she thundered. "I'll not listen to petty complaints like this. I am trying to save you from a life of misery." She walked out and left me in the room.

I went to the washroom and soaked some toilet paper in cold water and put it under my arms. My skin tingled. Small shivers exploded inside of me. *Fuck Mother Superior. Fuck—fuck—fuck (verb) (action) (action) (verb); Mother Superior (noun) (noun) person (noun).*

Alfred and Albert went out after school. I went upstairs and stood in front of the old mirror and removed my clothes. My breasts were round like balloons. They started to change after I turned ten. I was afraid of the changes in me. I heard mama telling Mrs. Landry that I was filling out at an early age, just like she did.

On Monday morning I went back to the office to see Dr. Mitchel. She asked me if I had told my mother about seeing her.

"No," I said.

"You don't talk with your mother very often, do you?"

"Sometimes."

"Sometimes is not enough." Her voice sounded like Mother Superior's.

I did not answer.

"Who do you talk to when you're feeling sad?"

"Lizzie."

"Lizzie is not a real person, Mari-Jen. She is a mere object of affection."

"I talk to my brothers."

"Your brothers are not responsible for you. You must talk with your mother more often and tell her what makes you sad," said Dr. Mitchel.

I wanted to leave. I did not want to answer any more of her questions. "You can leave now, and tell your mother I will be sending her a report on my visit with you," she said flatly.

I went out into the schoolyard. It was empty. I watched Amos as he jumped over the fence and went into the grave-yard. The sun was shining down on his friends. He leaned against one of the tombstones. Amos Dejeune was a lucky man. He had many friends to talk to when he was sad.

# nine

My mother made us go to evening mass during Lent. The Co-op truck was loaded with church-goers. Alfred and Albert walked to church when they got older. "The truck is for old people and kids," they said. "It smells of blue veins and rheumatism and mortal sins."

When I was thirteen, a missionary priest from Quebec came to our parish during Lent. His name was Father François Poulaine. He was much younger than Father Benoit, and thinner, with dark eyes piercing out over high cheekbones. His voice was deep, like he had a bad cold.

I confessed my sins to Father Poulaine. "Bless me, Father for I have sinned. It has been six weeks since my last confession."

"Your sins?" the deep voice said.

"Father, I used a verb on Mother Superior."

"What—what are you saying?"

"A verb, Father." My throat was drying up.

"You put a verb on a nun."

"Yes, Father."

"How you do that?" the priest asked.

"I swore, Father."

"You put a swear on Mère Superior."

"Yes, Father. But to myself."

"Mon Dieu, how that one work?"

"I said, Fuck Mother Superior, Father."

The priest cleared his deep throat.

"You put precious mortal sin on your soul. For this you will suffer and make long penance of ten bead."

He began his absolution on my verb. I left the confession box and went to kneel at the foot of the altar. The sanctuary light flickered slowly, its permanent flame open like the wounds of sorrow on the crucified Christ.

Alfred gave Albert his sins to take to confession. He waited for him in the main church. And there they divided their penance, a full rosary, in two.

On Good Friday, my mother took Aunt Clara to church. She wore her white dress. We sat at the back of the church. Mama warned Clara not to talk out loud. Aunt Clara smiled, "Your mother is crazy. She doesn't even know the names of the saints."

Mother Superior sang in the choir with the other nuns. Sister Thérèse played the organ. They were joined by twenty or more school kids.

"Who in Christ is screeching like that?" Aunt Clara asked out loud.

Mama told her to be quiet.

"They are scaring me."

"Be quiet, Clara."

"They can't sing."

"Yes, they can."

"My arse can sing better than that."

"I'll take you home," Mama warned.

"They sound like tomcats."

"Take her outside!" Mama ordered.

I took Aunt Clara by the hand and we went out the side door. She was very angry. "Your mother don't own the church." She spit on the ground. Her face was flushed. "Your mother can't throw people out of church."

"She didn't throw you out."

"Yes, she did."

"You were making too much noise."

"So what?"

"The priest will be mad."

"To hell with him. I didn't like the singing; it's too loud."

"It's Latin—they were singing in Latin."

"Then they should stop."

"Do you want to go for a walk, Aunt Clara?"

"Where to?"

"Down to the shore."

"No, I'm scared of the waves. They'll rush up and swallow me."

"The tide is low."

"So what? The waves are still there."

"The waves can't get you if you just look at them."

"Jule is going to drown me, you know. He said he was."

"No, he won't."

"Yes, he will, Mari-Jen. He drowned my baby."

"You don't have a baby, Aunt Clara."

"That's because Jule drowned him in a bag."

"How do you know he drowned him?"

She started to scream. "He showed him to me, Mari-Jen; my baby was in the bag with a rock. And then he drowned him somewhere."

"I'll tell my mother to make you some fudge after mass."

Aunt Clara stared at the sea. She could hear me but she didn't bother to answer.

"Can you hear him, Mari-Jen?" She was speaking in whispers.

"Hear who?"

"My baby—he's crying."

"I can't hear him."

"You got shit in your ears, Mari-Jen."

"No, I haven't."

"My baby is crying for me to come closer."

"I still can't hear anything, Aunt Clara."

"He wants me to go down on the breakwater."

"We can't, Aunt Clara, mass is nearly over."

"I want to go now," she insisted.

I heard the people coming out of church. "We have to go now, it's time to go home." I took her by the hand and we went to meet Mama.

When we got to the truck, Aunt Clara didn't want to get in.

"I don't like this truck," she argued. "It's full of spiders."

"Get in, Clara," Mama's tired voice begged. "Nothing will hurt you in the back of a truck."

She finally climbed in. Two women took her by the arms as she climbed the step. She sat on a bench near the cab of the truck.

Mama's face looked tired and drawn. Dark circles cut an edge in her skin under her eyes. I didn't know what a woman should look like at thirty-five.

She kept a picture of herself, taken when she was

seventeen. Her hair was black and thick. She had a straw hat on her head. Mama was smiling; she wore white gloves and white high-heeled shoes and nylons.

"I was going to church in Halifax," she'd said, "when that picture was taken."

"Who took the picture?" I wanted to know.

"Nobody you'd know, Mari-Jen," she half-whispered. She took the picture from me and put it away. Every now and then I'd catch her looking at it. And then it would be put away for long periods.

She and Aunt Clara did not look alike. They had the same colour hair and blue eyes, but Mama's were softer.

I heard Aunt Clara screaming. "When is this damn truck ever going to stop!"

"You'll be home soon," Mama assured her.

"I don't want to go home, Adele. I want to go to the shore."

"Not today, Clara. I'm too tired."

"Then Mari-Jen can take me."

"Maybe on the weekend, Clara."

"To hell with the weekend, I wanna go now."

Mama told me to take her home when the truck stopped at the crossing.

"Take her in, Mari-Jen, and make sure she doesn't follow you home."

I walked along the shore road with her. Aunt Clara didn't ask to stop. We walked over the hill. I kept looking for Uncle Jule. He wasn't out in the field. I took Aunt Clara through the main gate and we went along the veranda to the back door and into the kitchen. I told her to go upstairs and to stay there. When I left, she was still standing in the kitchen. I ran along the veranda and out through the gate.

I looked back to see if she was following me. I was walking along the road over the hill when I heard someone behind me. It was Uncle Jule. His steps were gaining on mine. I started running, and I could hear him calling my name. But I didn't stop running. I ran towards the fish shed. I was hoping to see someone there. A fisherman. Anyone. There was nobody in sight. Uncle Jule was getting closer to me and swearing.

"You little bastard, what has she been telling you about me?" He was drinking again.

I ran towards the road. I knew I could out-run him when he was drinking but my heart was beating so fast I thought I would spit it out. I saw a truck coming over the hill. The driver stopped and spoke with Jule. I saw him get in the truck and watched as the truck turned around and drove away.

I walked down to the water and took off my shoes and started to walk along the shore. I walked a while before looking back. In the distance I could see my grandfather's house. I knew Aunt Clara was there all alone. I knew that she could never out-run him. I knew that I could not get away from Mother Superior either, so on Tuesday morning I asked Mother Superior to leave the cloth on forever.

"You're more stupid than I thought, Mari-Jen. How will you clean your body?"

"I have other ways, Mother Superior. I have other ways," I mumbled to myself.

"Go to Sister Thérèse's class and stop babbling," she ordered.

I went outside and sat on the step. I looked down towards the sea. I could hear the faint murmur of the voices it held. I wished that Uncle Jule and Mother Superior were dead. I wondered if their eyes would stay open if nobody closed them.

Mother Superior caught me out on the step. She lifted me up by the hair and sent me flying through the door. I didn't feel the pain until I was sitting in my desk. I sat at the back of the class. The younger kids turned and looked at me. I was crying out loud. Sister Thérèse gave me a package of tissues and a notebook.

"Here, Mari-Jen, you can write in this."

The notebook had different coloured pages in it. They were green and blue and red and orange and yellow and pink. I took out a pencil and began to write in the air like a mime.

"The sea cried." *Sea (noun) cried (verb) (a very sad verb).* Mari-Jen wants to be dead. *Mari-Jen (noun).* I wasn't sure which one was the verb, so I just wrote—*wants to be (all verbs).*

Sister Thérèse smiled when I looked up at her. She knew I was smart. She knew it, and had to keep quiet to keep my nouns and verbs safe.

Alfred and Albert started going to dances before they were sixteen. They slicked back their hair and put shiny studs on the back of their jackets and boots.

"Youse look like you were drowned," Mama gasped, when they left for the dances.

"It's the style," Albert said. "Everybody looks like this."

"Some looks—what happened to your curls?" she snarled.

"They make us look like girls," said Alfred.

"How come I don't have curls?" I asked Mama.

"What for, do ya want to go through life looking like Curly Kate?" she quipped.

"I like curls. I want to let my hair grow so I can curl it," I said.

"Suit yourself, but you take care of it."

I wanted to go to the dances with my brothers. I heard them talking about them afterwards. They danced to the music of Little Richard and Chubby Checker. They changed the words of "Blueberry Hill" to "Graveyard Hill." They sang to each other—"I found my thrill on the Graveyard Hill, and we did it together on Graveyard Hill."

Father Benoit put a sign on the Co-op Hall. "No Twisting Allowed."

He warned the young people in Sunday sermons that he would not stand for such lurid, sinful moves. The girls were afraid to dance the Twist and the boys went along with them. "They dance like sticks," said Alfred. "Like they have lead up their arse."

Alfred and Albert did the Twist together. Father Benoit gave their names on the altar. Mama cried in church. She forbade them to go to the dances. They sneaked out the upstairs window and jumped off the porch. They crawled back in through the window after midnight. They said they would take me with them some night if I didn't squeal.

Daniel Peter's birthday was in March. Albert said we would have a party for him and dance all night. Daniel Peter would not tell us his age.

"You are young or old like your wisdom," he said, smiling.

"He means you're as old as your wisdom," Alfred said to Albert.

"Then he's pretty old," Albert said, "close to seventy maybe."

Daniel Peter laughed loudly.

"You make old age for me very quick."

He made us a cup of cocoa. We were sitting at his kitchen table. Alfred and Albert had tied a ribbon on their winning story and they gave it to Daniel Peter as a present. He read it slowly to himself. He got up from the table and went into his bedroom. He stayed there for a while.

"Maybe he is mad at us," I said to my brothers.

"No he's not," Albert said, "but maybe we should have given him the story before."

"Why?" asked Alfred "We were going to keep it until we went away and then give it to him before we left."

Daniel Peter came back into the kitchen. He was smiling.

"This is best present somebody give to me since my family . . ." He didn't finish. He looked like he had been crying.

My brothers looked at him but didn't say a word. Daniel Peter took out the chess set and challenged my brothers and me to a game. I always lost because I wasn't sure where to move my pawns. Alfred defeated Daniel Peter. And then he and Albert challenged each other. They played for over an hour before Albert called out checkmate. Daniel Peter sat at the table.

"Remember, my friend, the best force come from the mind, not the fist." He put up his hands in a mock fighting gesture. Alfred and Albert laughed. They raised their fists in the air and awkwardly wished him a happy birthday before we left. On the way home they said we couldn't dance at his party because Daniel Peter looked too sad.

Mother Superior made me sit in her grade twelve class to clean the blackboards before school finished. I listened to her read to her students. She held their attention with her sharp, screeching voice. She spoke really loud.

"Pay attention," she demanded, "and listen for the subtle hints of the author." The author was Shakespeare. His subtle hint, she explained, was death. Death to the hero and heroine. Romeo and Juliet. Suicide to mend a broken heart. The students rolled their eyes when her back was turned. I tried to read some of the words when Mother Superior went out of the class, from the reader I found on the desk. She could never read from Shakespeare like Daniel Peter could.

Once, after a reading of *King Lear*, Alfred and Albert said they had seen Lear standing in the field looking down towards the sea.

Suicide was the word that made Alfred the champion of the spelling bee when he was in grade six. Sister Thérèse had taken her class to watch the competition between the grade six classes. There were five grade sixes that year. Albert made the finals but lost out to Margaret. He was asked to spell "magazine". He smiled. He let out a half whistle and began to spell. "M-a-g-i-z-i-n-e." Margaret smiled. The judge called out, "Incorrect." Albert ran his fingers through his hair. Margaret stood up straight. It looked like she was going to bow. Mother Superior smiled at her. She took a deep breath and began to spell. "M-a-g-a-z-i-n-e." There was a loud clap. It came from Mother Superior's white hands announcing Margaret's victory. The competition was between her and Alfred next.

They were tied after a dozen words. And then came the word "suicide." It was Margaret's turn first. She looked nervous. She took a deep breath and opened her mouth. "S-u-i-c-e-d-e." There was no clapping. The judge called out, "Incorrect." Alfred stood at the front of the class. He straightened his shoulders. He looked towards Albert and began to spell. "S-u-i-c-i-d-e." Albert stood up and clapped. Mother Superior ordered him to sit down. The judge gave Alfred his prize. A *Webster's Dictionary*. Margaret's lower lip trembled. She was not used to losing. She was a champion of words—in English and in French. She had never lost.

Alfred and Albert stood up together, smiling. A group of mourners had gathered around Margaret. They patted her on the back for her attempt at "suicide." She wiped her tears with a starched, white hankie. I noticed the initial M embroidered on the edge of it.

She dipped her big nose into the hankie; the letter M was wrinkled and crushed.

Alfred and Albert walked slowly past Margaret and her mourners. They challenged each other to spell the word "loser" before walking out of the class with Webster by their side.

They ran to Daniel Peter's house when we got off the school bus. I followed behind. They wanted to be congratulated. Daniel Peter beamed. He looked through the pages of the dictionary and then looked over at me.

"You, Mari-Jen, learn many word." He paused. "I will teach." He told us to sit down and he began the lesson.

Alfred and Albert welcomed the challenge. They never missed a word. It was my turn. Daniel Peter asked me to spell the word "books." I swallowed hard. He repeated the word slowly. My voice cracked. "B-o-o-k-s." He cheered loudly. My brothers grinned.

Albert held out the dictionary when we got home.

"I won it," he beamed, "in a spelling bee." Mama shook her head.

"That's good, now spell the word 'woodpile' and get busy."

He threw the dictionary on the table. They changed their clothes and went out to the woodpile. I heard the axe coming down hard on the block. There was a little break and then the axe splitting again, hard, swift, deep, and angry.

I knew why they were angry, but Mama didn't. She had her own pain, and went into her bedroom and tied the rag tightly around her head, before the axe had even hit the block.

I knew what the word "suicide" meant. So did Romeo and Juliet. I knew Margaret would learn to spell it correctly from now on. I knew you didn't have to die to understand some things. Words could die if they were never read. Daniel Peter's eyes died when my brothers read to him about the war. And my feet died when I tried to dance without music.

# ten

There were unbending rules in my mother's house. Particularly the kitchen. No running when a cake was in the oven. No walking on the wet floors. No fires during thunderstorms. No hanging around when there were visitors. These were the rules of her kitchen.

Albert and Alfred flattened their birthday cake in the oven. They were twelve or thirteen at the time.

"It's as flat as St. Joseph's feet," Mama wailed when she looked in the oven.

They had chased each other over the squares on the new oilcloth. I loved the smell of newness in the kitchen. Its bright pattern of red and black blocks looked daring. I played hopscotch by myself on it when Mama was hanging out clothes.

We ate the flat birthday cake. We didn't mind—it was spring, and Daniel Peter had promised to take us for a long ride and ice cream.

He piled us into his truck. Alfred and Albert sat in the back of the truck. They wanted the danger of speed and wind. Daniel Peter drove thirty miles an hour. They told the kids at school that the truck hit ninety miles at one turn. They were called liars. They laughed in the faces of their accusers and showed their wounds.

"Take a look at these," said Alfred. "A rock got me when the truck spun on two wheels." His two elbows were scraped and bruised.

"That's right," Albert piped up, "look at my knee."

It was red and swollen. They were bruised from falling off the porch roof.

"It was hard to keep standing in the back of that truck," they beamed. "We're lucky we've only got a few bruises."

Daniel Peter drove for miles until we came to a store near a lake. An eagle hovered over its borders and spread its elegant wings against a purple sunset. Daniel Peter watched the bird for some time.

"My, my," he said slowly. "Freedom very beautiful, very beautiful indeed."

Alfred and Albert ordered double-scoop chocolate cones and I ordered vanilla. Some of my ice cream dripped down and smeared Lizzie's wool hair. The man behind the counter smiled.

"You have handsome children," he said to Daniel Peter.

Daniel Peter bowed his head. The gesture was in thanks, I knew that. I knew what he was telling the man without even speaking. My brothers knew it. They swirled their tongues over the ice cream and produced two chocolate smiles. They climbed in the back of the truck and tapped the hood with their fists.

"We're ready, Father," they shouted, then sank their teeth into one of their sweet, frozen moments of spring.

Daniel Peter did not speak to many people.

"It's his accent," Alfred said. "Some people think he's talking D.P. when it's really English."

I didn't know what D.P. was or how you could speak it.

"It's like French, Mari-Jen," Albert explained, "only slower."

Daniel Peter stayed home most nights and kept company with the prophets in his book. Alfred and Albert helped him with the work in his barn.

Daniel Peter was very grateful. He told us stories. He said Poland was very much like Ste. Noire.

"Me and brothers play game same like children in every country. We give funny name to bird in sky. We swim for river. Pretend drown. We put line under country we like to see after peace. We put name of girl we like in tree." He read to us. He taught us how to spell. He told us about shipwrecks and natural disasters. He told us about the darkness of war and the light of survival.

He told us when we were older, and really listening, about the woman he had loved and lost to that darkness.

"She very, very pretty in nature, pretty in spirit," he said in a choked voice. He never mentioned her again. We walked home that evening without saying a word. We had no name for the man whose arms were as empty as his heart.

Mama said a man like him would not find a wife in Ste. Noire.

"Why?" Alfred wanted to know.

"'Cause of the difference."

"What difference?" said Alfred.

"The religion," she explained.

"So what," said Alfred.

"So what," she sighed. "Youse should know by now Catholics can only marry their own kind."

"What kind is that?" said Alfred. He and Albert started to laugh.

Mama got very cross at them. "Youse two will know the difference if ya start sniffing your noses in another religion."

"Everybody got the same God," said Alfred.

"You're crazy," she screamed. "Some people have no use for the man on the cross."

Mama was crying. "There are rules in Father Benoit's church and youse know them. No confetti, no scarlet lips, no bare shoulders or mixed marriages," she shouted, before throwing my brothers out of the house.

Mrs. Landry had walked in the house then and caught the tail end of the anger.

"You're right, Adele," Mrs. Landry said, pounding her fist on the kitchen table. "Remember when Ada's daughter married that Presbyterian, she dropped dead three months later."

They sat at the kitchen table and drank their tea. There they gave thanks to the only God they knew. The man whose son died under the storm of Calvary. We did not mention any of this to Daniel Peter. And I did not mention to my mother about Daniel Peter's visit to our school.

I saw his truck parked by the side of the road when I went to sharpen my pencil.

"You're looking very green, Mari-Jen." It was Sister Thérèse's voice speaking to me. "Go to the washroom and wash your face in cold water."

I went out and walked down the hall. He was talking to Mother Superior. I heard their voices. Daniel Peter's quiet and gentle voice—cutting in on hers—warning her, his argument like prose against her verbal banter.

"She very much intelligent," he said. There was a delay. Silence.

And then Mother Superior's voice, loud and splitting. "She doesn't share her brothers' intelligence. She is retarded. She cannot read or write. She doesn't know black from white."

"You make very big mistake, ma'am," he said.

"What would you know?" she thundered. "You're not even one of us."

Daniel Peter's voice grew louder. "I know when human spirit broke—the same happen to intelligent."

Mother Superior's voice trembled. "I've tested her and so have others, and there's nothing there."

"You and others make very much mistake, the child very smart." Daniel Peter shot back. "Mari Jen not have intelligent problem—have only problem with showing intelligent."

"How would you know?" she screamed. "You cannot teach."

Daniel Peter seemed to chuckle. "And what you teach child?"

I heard Mother Superior's ruler slam down on her desk.

"I am a nun, a Superior, and a teacher of academics and religion. Our own Catholic religion and you are a . . ."

Daniel Peter cut off her words. His voice was even. "What you are saying, that I am foreigner. Excuse, ma'am—your God is same like me."

I ran down the hall and back to my class. Later, Mother Superior gave me a letter to give to my mother. I threw it in the stove after school. I watched her words burn and crumble in the flames. Albert and Alfred had opened the letter.

Mother Superior felt that Daniel Peter was a bad influence on us. My brothers laughed.

"Burn the damn thing, Mari-Jen," they urged. "We'll say you lost it."

I went to her office the following day.

"Sit down," she insisted.

"Did you give your mother my letter?" she inquired irritably.

My whole body shook.

"I lost it, the letter, I can't find it."

I saw her hand move towards me, like some black beast of prey. The slap stung. My head rolled against the back of the chair.

"And he calls you intelligent; he comes here and introduces me to insult."

She slapped me harder the second time. "It's no use trying to teach you people any principles or manners. What does your mother know anyway?"

She sent me back to my class. But she did not write another letter.

I told my brothers what had happened in her office.

"The bastard," they hissed. There was frustration in their eyes. I had seen it before. It was there when Mama hit them. Hard. More than once. She kept a leather belt to keep them in line. But she also used kindling, whatever was in reach when her anger was stoked. She measured their punishment. Twelve lashes for Alfred. Twelve lashes for Albert.

I threw up after she beat them. They didn't. They swore. They made plans. They'd get away early and never return. I cried. I was not one of them. They were identical. Their fears and pain and plans were identical. I was the odd one out. But they never beat me. They used threats on me.

"You tell, Mari-Jen, and Lizzie goes on the block," they'd warn.

That evening we went to visit Daniel Peter. He had the same look of frustration in his eyes. He knew he was on the outside looking in. He made us a cup of cocoa and afterwards he read from the book *Gulliver's Travels*.

Alfred and Albert smiled. Their journeys had begun in Daniel Peter's kitchen.

I don't know where my brothers were the day the taxman came to our house. I saw the car parked by the house when I was coming from the store.

It was a black car with silver spokes on its wheels. I walked over by the car and saw my reflection in its shiny door. It looked new and important to me. Inside, the seats were a deep red. I imagined me and Lizzie sitting in the back with the windows down. The wind would dance in and out of the open windows while Lizzie slept, and later I would tell her about the colours that passed by. The colours of spring, and how later in the evening the fog snuffed them out. I had to roll up the windows to keep her warm. The car was a Chevrolet Impala.

I walked into the porch but didn't go any further. I heard their voices.

"She is slow, they say." Mama was speaking, almost embarrassed, as if she were describing a bad batch of bread. "The yeast must have been too slow to rise," she'd say, if the bread was a bit flat. "It's just a bad batch and that's that." This was her tone talking to the man. My mother's voice again, urgent with anger.

"Your brother didn't have the decency to even write. Here I was swelling up with shame—and waiting for him to come back to marry me—he said he would. I'm willing to bet he doesn't even know her name, or give a damn. He should burn in hell, for marrying someone else, and putting his handle on somebody else's kids, the bastard, after what he did to me..."

Mama was crying now, like she cried when someone had died. The man's voice was kind.

"Patrick was never any good, Adele, never reliable. They didn't have any kids, she left him after a year—nobody knows where he is. How is Mari-Jen?"

There was a pause. I didn't know if I should walk in and answer for myself. But I didn't. I stood by the kitchen door.

"She's all right, she don't look slow. People think she's real pretty." I thought to myself, Margaret's mother said I was pretty. Mama says I'm pretty. I didn't hear another word between them. I went outside and stood in the shade of the house by the porch. It was cool and quiet. Spring had broken the earth. I twisted the toe of my boot into the ground. Mud covered my boot, thick brown mud, like chocolate icing on a muffin. I could see the shiny bumper on the man's car from where I stood.

I knew there would never be mud on his car. It would be washed away. The shine would be brought back to life to collect the people's taxes.

Mrs. Landry had said that they would tax a fart if they could smell it soon enough. She hid her electric radio and clock from them. They were gifts that her sisters had sent her from New Brunswick for Christmas the year Zeppie died.

"I don't trust them," she told my mother. "They're like hounds sniffing things out."

She hid the radio and clock under the bed. Word was passed out at church that they were coming to Ste. Noire—and people were prepared.

We didn't have anything new to hide from the taxman. Our furniture was old. Our radio was full of static.

"That damn thing sounds like it has bad nerves," Mama said. She was trying to listen to the weather forecast but the noise kept coming and going.

Alfred and Albert hit the top of the radio with their fists to steady the voice. It worked for a while and then went out again.

People got their tax bills in the mail. Our post office was at the Crossroads, next to the barber shop and general store. People waited for the mail truck to come. In spring and summer they sat on wooden benches, across from the post office. They were mostly old men who waited there, telling time with watches that hung on a chain. They had nothing left to fit into time—their work was done.

They watched everyone go by. They kept their backs to the sea. The sea had been good to them. They praised it. Praised its danger and wealth in the same breath. It had claimed their neighbours and friends, and had never let some of them go.

I was still playing in the mud when the man walked by. He stopped and put out his hand.

"You're Mari-Jen, aren't you?" He spoke softly and touched my face.

He had fiery red hair and blue eyes. He held my hand. I kept looking down at the mud. I didn't know why I wanted to show the taxman my collection of nouns and verbs in the cubbyhole. Nobody knew they were there. Just me and God and nearly the taxman.

He let go of my hand and walked away. He turned once and looked back at me. I thought he was going to ask me if I would like a drive in the shiny car. But he didn't.

I went into the house. I asked Mama about the man who had just driven away. She didn't look at me.

"Did he tax us?"

"No, there was nothing of value here for him."

"I like the taxman," I said.

"Why?" she asked sharply, and then went into her room and stayed there for a long time.

He never returned. The next taxman who came was older with grey hair. He drove a truck when he came to our house to look for something of value.

My brothers made their confirmation that year. Mother Superior said confirmation was a renewal of baptism. They were old enough to renounce Satan on their own.

The bishop came from Antigonish and blessed the devil out of my brothers. They said he slapped them harder than he did the other kids. This was part of the ritual of confirmation.

"Do you renounce Satan?" he asked, as he went through the row of children.

And then he came to my brothers. "Do you renounce Satan, James Alfred?"

"I do renounce Satan."

"Do you renounce Satan, John Albert?"

"I do renounce Satan."

They renounced the devil together. I believed them. Mama said she'd have to wait and see. "They're geared for anything, them two."

She said little babies couldn't renounce Satan when they were baptised because they couldn't speak for themselves.

"That's why youse need godparents," she said, "so they could ward off the devil for you until you're old enough to get rid of him yourself." My brothers' godparents lived in Halifax. My godparents moved to Quebec when I was a baby. We never really knew much about them.

My brothers told me that the devil could speak a dozen or more languages.

"He's good in French and English and Greek and even Russian," said Alfred.

"He knows almost as many languages as God," said Albert, "except Latin. That's the one language that God hid from the devil so he will never know what goes on in confession."

I was glad to know that. I was scared of the confession box, the darkness it held against you when you unravelled your sins.

There were two confessionals, one on either side. The priest sat in the middle. Left and right sinners gathered together. He opened a square slide and you could see the shadow of his face. His left ear. I always confessed into his left ear. I don't know why. It just seemed like the correct thing to do.

Someone else waited on the right side. I knew they were there. I wondered what they had to confess. I knew they'd be listening. My brothers did it all the time. They knelt quietly in the dark and eavesdropped on your soul.

They timed people's penance. They threatened some of them.

"We're telling your mother," they'd say. "We overheard you in confession."

They had a collection of pocket knives and whistles and marbles that kids gave them, so they wouldn't tell their mothers their sins.

The girl Margaret made her confirmation with my brothers. She wore a beautiful white dress that her aunt sent to her from the United States. Margaret's face was as white as her dress. There were dark shadows under her eyes. She had not been to school for a few weeks. Mother Superior said Margaret had a bug. After confirmation, Margaret did not return to school. Mother Superior gathered the bigger kids in the auditorium and made us pray, in French, for a miracle.

"A miracle," she said, "that would cleanse Margaret's blood, and let flow into her sunken veins a vibrant river of red energy." At recess the kids talked about Margaret's bug. The bug's real name was leukemia.

Somebody said that her white cells were eating up all her red cells and that Margaret would die. Her parents took her to the Children's Hospital in Halifax and stayed by her side. Margaret was fifteen when she died the following spring, the same age as my brothers.

Mother Superior made all the school kids go to the funeral. We marched in triple file to the church. Margaret's coffin was opened at the foot of the altar. We had to walk by and say goodbye to her. She was wearing her white confirmation dress. Her body looked like it had shrunk and was ready to fly away if someone blew on it.

Her mother and father were seated in the front pew. They were dressed in black, like two slumped shadows that were hidden from sunlight. I heard her mother's low, muffled scream as I walked down the aisle. A group of housewives, standing at the back, mumbled to each other.

"They are finished, them two people." And then they shook their heads and sank into the back seat.

Alfred and Albert did not go into the church. They stayed in the porch with Emile, the bell ringer, before the mass of the angels for Margaret began.

Mama said that Margaret would be restored to good health and be as plump as she ever was, once she reached Paradise. And it would be in this condition that she would greet her mother and father at the Pearly Gates after their deaths.

Marcel told me at school the next day that death itself could be a miracle.

"How's that?" I asked.

"It's part of the mystery, Mari-Jen."

"Who told you that?"

"Nobody. You don't have to be told—you just have to feel it."

"They why do you cry, Marcel?

"Maybe for people who don't understand it."

"I don't, Marcel."

"You understand more than a lot of people, Mari-Jen. You always have. That's why I like talking to you. That is why you're my best friend." I wasn't really sure where Margaret was going to go. All I could think of was the way her mouth was curled.

Alfred took a deep interest in diseases after Margaret's death. He looked for books in the school library that would explain collapsed lungs and braided bones and hidden tumours.

He and Albert examined pictures of skeletons and joints and muscles. Daniel Peter opened a battered trunk and gave Alfred an old medical book he had bought in Halifax. In it, Alfred found chapters on fits and diseased livers and babies born with two heads. He said he believed that Aunt Clara had epilepsy, and the fear and uncertainty of it caused her delusions. Mama shook her head.

"Look for what's wrong with youse two," she said, "while you got your nose in that book."

He laughed as he read from a chapter on the effects of "The Minds of Genius."

# eleven

rs. Landry was not really sick when she left Ste. Noire—just old. My mother said her younger sisters in New Brunswick were worried about her here alone. One of her sisters and a niece came to get her when I was thirteen.

Mama helped her pack her clothes and personal belongings. She gave us her radio and some dishes and bits of furniture.

They arrived in an old black panel truck that had a pair of dice hanging from the mirror inside the cab. "Dear Jesus," said Mrs. Landry when she saw the truck driving into her yard. "They're liable to drive me straight to the nut house in that rig."

Before she left she had signed over the house we were living in—it was Mrs. Landry's house willed to her by an old aunt—to my mother. "You were good to me," I heard her tell Mama in the kitchen. "There was many a storm that passed over our heads in this house."

Alfred and Albert loaded her furniture on the back of the truck—old beds and bureaus, a china cabinet, trunks, a spinning wheel.

Mrs. Landry insisted on taking her tomcat, Lasnip, with her to New Brunswick. Her sister asked, "What in the hell are you going to do with a tomcat in New Brunswick, Tori?"

Mrs. Landry shook her head defiantly. "The same damn thing I did with a tomcat in Cape Breton."

My brothers laughed. They made a crate out of an old wooden box and lined it with straw, then put Lasnip in the crate. The cat hissed and snarled and tore at the straw.

They left before dark. The fog was just starting to roll in off the sea. We stood on the hill and watched them drive away. Mrs. Landry cried. I saw her turn and look back at her house. I knew we would never see her again. Mama knew it too. There was something about the way people promised to visit. To catch up on things.

The morning after Mrs. Landry left, Mama heard something scratching at our door. Lasnip stood on the step, hungry and worn, with bits of hay stuck to his grey fur.

Mama was depressed for months after Mrs. Landry left. She said she had nobody to talk to when the thunderclouds gathered in the sky like an approaching army and threatened her world.

Lasnip stayed in the old house and only ventured out to look for meals. He sat in the empty window like a dusty ornament. "That cat is half-human," Mama said. "He's like a spirit guarding that house."

Mother Superior set up a memorial in honour of Margaret. She gathered the students in the auditorium. It was the fall of 1961. A picture of Margaret was hung in the front hall. An inscription under it read: "Rest in the sweet valley of Jesus, dear Margaret." Margaret was smiling. She was standing in an open field wearing a flared orange dress. An orange ribbon swirled above her head like a lasso. She was holding a book in her hands. The memorial would be given to the student with the highest average in grade twelve.

Alfred and Albert were in grade eleven. It was their first year to write provincials. The exams were prepared and marked by the province. Every student in the province wrote the same exams. The marks and results arrived through the mail. Mother Superior boasted about the results of her students' marks. There were very few failures under her thumb, she said.

Alfred and Albert had had to buy their high school books starting in grade nine. Daniel Peter saw to it that they had the money to get their books. He paid them for their chores around his farm. He saved their salaries and smiled proudly when they showed off their books. They said they were subtracting the weeks before they would leave Ste. Noire, but I didn't believe them.

He saved their old books and taught me from their ink-blotted pages. He tested me by asking me questions and kept a record of my progress. I didn't have to write anything down.

"This very much shame," he'd say, because I was never tested like this at school. I got hundreds in English and spelling and history and geography. I had great difficulty in math. It was my hardest subject. My world was held together by nouns and verbs in the cubbyhole. "*Daniel Peter is a great teacher.*" *Daniel Peter (proper noun) is (verb) teacher (noun).* I was not interested in adjectives and adverbs. I wanted the names of people, places, and things, and the action of a verb. *I liked the taxman. Liked (verb) taxman (noun).*

*Mari-Jen wants to be dead. Mari-Jen (proper noun) wants to be dead (all verbs).* I went over my new and old sentences. They jolted my memory, like the names on tombstones.

Margaret was buried in the new graveyard. Amos climbed over its fence and made his acquaintance with the newly dead. We saw him in the graveyard when we drove home from school on the bus. He looked like a dark smudge against the white crosses and marble stones, leaving his fresh prayers wherever he stopped.

Aunt Clara had not been feeling well for a few months. Mama had to wash her when we went down to the house. Her knees and ankles would swell up and turn red. She could not come down the stairs on her own. Mama rubbed a liniment on Clara's sore joints.

"Poor Clara would be better off dead." That's how Mama reacted to Aunt Clara's illness. Mama said Grandmère had the same condition. I knew that my mother was very tired. She looked old sometimes. Her pretty face was pale and sad. That is why she said that Aunt Clara would be better off dead. She needed somebody to look after her all the time. I tried to help.

"Mari-Jen," Clara said meekly. "Take me to the shore with you."

Uncle Jule came up to the room one morning. I didn't speak to him.

"Call someone to take her to a hospital," he said to Mama in a cold voice.

We called from the store. An ambulance arrived the next day from Antigonish. A nurse and the driver helped Mama put Aunt Clara on a stretcher. She screamed when they picked her up, like a child being held over deep water. She was very frightened and confused. I didn't watch as the ambulance drove away.

The nurse said it was probably arthritis that was causing her a lot of pain. Mama said she knew that it was. It was something that got in the family bones. I wished that my mother would not get it.

I looked over at Uncle Jule. His beard had grown longer. It covered most of his face. There was nothing in his eyes. He stared out the kitchen window, past the fields, to where the high tide was breaking on the shore. He turned to Mama and told her to clear out Aunt Clara's things. "She won't be back here," he said. We piled her clothes into a cardboard box. Wool stockings, frayed underwear, cotton dresses, dark buttonless sweaters —these were the things he spoke of. I put her white dress and the seashell that I found under her bed in a paper bag. I claimed them as my own.

That afternoon I burned the white dress. I watched the flames lick up the cotton and turn it to ash. I didn't want to be reminded of that dress piled on the floor. I kept the shell and put it in the cubbyhole. My mother was relieved when they took Clara away. She didn't have to go back to the house and deal with Uncle Jule any more.

She was taken to the hospital in Antigonish and later put in a nursing home there. She lived for years in the company of her saints.

Mother Superior called me to her office that week. "What is wrong with your Aunt Clara?" she inquired.

"I don't know."

"Aren't you people concerned?"

"Yes."

"Then you should act concerned."

"I am."

"I suppose she was nothing but a burden to your mother and uncle," she added.

I didn't bother to answer. She was annoyed with my silence but I didn't care. She stared at me. Her lips were pale, as if someone or something had sucked all the blood out of them.

"You know, Mari-Jen, I've asked the good Lord many times why he has to take children with great potential and leave the broken behind. Do you know what I am saying?"

"No," I lied.

"Children like Margaret"—she was almost whispering—"with such potential for life, so much to give."

I stared at the floor. I knew what she was saying.

"Look at me when I'm speaking to you!" she shouted.

I had seen anger in her eyes before but this anger was different. This anger was directed at God and neither one of us would bother to answer her.

Later that night, I repeated her words to my brothers. Alfred curled his fists into a ball. "She's cracked, that woman is cracked."

Albert spoke out. "She should never have been put in the same room with kids."

Mama heard us talking and came up the stairs. "Youse keep your mouth shut about nuns. There's enough bad luck around here." She was in a rage, her body trembling.

Alfred spoke up. "She has no right to judge anyone's intelligence."

Mama shot back. "What do you know?"

"I know more than she'll ever know!" screamed Alfred. "Mari-Jen is not the retarded one at school. You ask Daniel Peter."

"What are youse trying to do now? Have me lose the cheque when ya take off from here?"

There was a long silence. Mama pointed her finger at me. "You stay away from the D.P., Mari-Jen . . . or I'll report ya myself." She left and went down the stairs and out the back door.

My brothers swore again. "It's no use trying to get through to her, she'll never understand. It's too late for her."

I never went back to Daniel Peter's house. Alfred and Albert told him what had taken place. He was very sad, they said, as if they had told him someone had died.

I waved to him in the mornings and after school when he was out in his field.

There were changes in me that I could not explain. Fears. They crawled inside my head at night and back over again in the morning. I wet my bed. I hid the wet sheets from Mama and washed them on the weekends.

Alfred and Albert came up the stairs one day when I was sitting on my bed. I didn't hear them. I was sitting there without a top on. Just the binding.

"What in the hell have you got on, Mari-Jen?" Alfred asked.

"My binding."

Albert laughed. "Is that the new style, Mari-Jen?"

"It's not mine; Mother Superior makes me wear it." I had just removed the wet sheet off my bed.

"Jesus Christ," I heard Albert say. "That woman really is crazy."

"Take that off and leave it off, Mari-Jen."

When Mother Superior called me to her office on Friday, I was not wearing the binding. "Where is it, Mari-Jen?" she demanded.

"It's gone."

"Where did it go, you fool?"

"I gave it away."

Her face went pale. "What do you mean, you gave it away?"

"I just gave it away."

She walked over to me and hit me hard across the face. "Leave this office!" I heard her scream. I walked slowly back to Sister Thérèse's class. My head was pounding. I could see the younger kids looking at me and feel Sister Thérèse take my hand and lead me to the back of the class. I felt a cloth on my face and Sister Thérèse's hand lowering my head between my knees. I saw the blood then, in little pools, round like coins, at my feet.

Sister Thérèse shouted to someone to wet some paper towels in cold water. They ran to her with them, two of the kids. She held the damp paper across my face. I swallowed hard and deep the taste of my own blood.

Alfred and Albert wrote their provincial exams in June. They sat with Daniel Peter in the evenings and discussed the questions.

I longed to go down. I stood on the hill and looked towards his property. A few sheep grazed in the eastern pasture. A mother and her lambs. The lambs chased each other at the ends of their tails. Their mother looked up and called them to her.

I could see Tolstoy, the rooster, strutting towards the chicken coop. He stopped and flapped his wings as if he was shaking the day's dust from his feathers before retiring for the night.

I heard Mama's voice calling to me as I walked back to the house. "What are ya doing on the hill?"

"Just looking down at the sheep."

She eyed me curiously. "You're getting too big, Mari-Jen, to be hanging around grown men. Grown men get funny ideas around pretty girls."

"Daniel Peter would not hurt anyone."

"He's a man. You're too pretty to be around men at your age. There's no telling what he's thinking."

"He's thinking good things, because he's a good person."

"That man is a foreigner, Mari-Jen, a D.P. God knows what side he was on in the war. He could be a German spy."

"He has been in Cape Breton for years. Why would he hurt us now?"

"Don't argue with me," she cried. "He could be waiting for the right minute to spring."

I tried to explain to her how good he had been to me and Alfred and Albert.

"They are full of tricks, them people, I know," she shouted. "I seen a good many of them in my day."

My brothers came home then. I heard them laughing as they came in the kitchen. They had heard part of the conversation.

"Daniel Peter is not really Polish," said Alfred. "He's really a German spy."

"You needn't make jokes," Mama threatened. "You could wake up some morning with a bomb in your face."

"That's right," Albert said. "The man has a satellite in his bedroom. And don't forget that picture he has of Hitler on his wall."

"Why do you think he chose to live so close to the Atlantic?" asked Alfred. "I've seen them. Haven't you, Albert?" he said. "Those Germans coming ashore by the breakwater. That submarine was quite a sight. Like a whale coming up for air in the moonlight."

"Yes," said Albert, "and Daniel Peter waiting there with his truck parked arse end to the sea—in no time he had a truckload of Germans headed for here."

Mama threw a piece of wood at the door, but they were already outside. I watched their silhouettes in the closing of the evening from the upstairs window. They were walking back to Daniel Peter's house. I curled up on my cot and cried for the man I really knew.

I wet my bed again that night. Mama caught me washing the sheet. "Is that sheet wet?" she asked, pulling it from my hands. "You pissed the bed. Why didn't ya get up and use the pot?"

I tried to stay awake at night. I opened the window and let the breeze blow the sleep from my eyes. I outlined Aunt Clara's face in the dark. Her black curly hair, tangled like sheep's wool. I heard Uncle Jule's voice, ordering Mama to cut it. Short. I remembered the blood on her hand—it was a Hallowe'en night. I fell asleep then and dreamt about

Uncle Jule. There was a wild storm. The waves were pounding at the door of his fish shed, the froth of their fury oozing in between the cracks. The water was hot, very hot, and the fish heads swam around in the barrel without bodies, their heads moving from side to side as they struggled for air. Their eyes were wild as they tried to dive down deep to the bottom of the barrel and then his hands lifted up the barrel and he emptied them out. The sea was calm again, but now babies' heads were everywhere, floating on waves, scattered in the sand, on top of the breakwater. They were all crying. Uncle Jule gathered them all up and put them in the empty barrel and the crying stopped.

"Mari-Jen, why are you crying?" It was Alfred's voice. He was leaning over my cot and holding my arms. The sun was shining. Albert came up the stairs.

"He did cruel things to Aunt Clara," I sobbed.

"Who did cruel things?" Albert asked.

"Uncle Jule. He jumped on Aunt Clara. He did to her what Sol did to Rinso. I saw him."

I saw the muscles in their necks strain.

"Was that in your dream, Mari-Jen?" Alfred asked.

"No, it's for real. He did it to her."

Alfred and Albert looked at each other. They turned to me. "Did he ever do that to you, Mari-Jen?"

"No, I got away. I always kept my distance from him." I heard them swearing as they went down the stairs.

Mama was out at the clothesline when I came downstairs. I soaked my wet sheet in the tub of hot water on the stove and poked it down with a stick. She looked at the sheet when she came in. "We're going to have to air out your mattress, Mari-Jen." We went upstairs and pulled it off the springs. It wasn't heavy. It was only a small cot. We carried it down the stairs and leaned it up against the back fence so nobody could see it.

"Put some creolin in a bucket of water and wash out those stains," she ordered. "That's all I need now, more problems, with you and your busted kidneys. I can't deal with another sickness right now." Mama looked at me with a worried look in her eyes. "I'll make you a good batch of fudge after your mattress is aired out," she said, as she walked back to the house. I knew she didn't want me to know that she was crying.

# twelve

My brothers waited eagerly at the post office for the results of their provincials. They chatted with the old men on the benches until the mail truck drove up and emptied its lot at the back door.

They had taken a run down to the shore when the post mistress put the envelopes into my hand. "I guess this is what your brothers have been waiting for this summer," she said, smiling.

I ran with the two envelopes down to the shore. I expected to meet them on the way, but I couldn't see them anywhere. Small coloured dories bounced up and down on the waves. The fishermen were in for the day. Two of them sat facing the sun. In their chapped hands they held some torn nets and they spliced them together again, swiftly, with the wooden hooks the fishermen used. All the while they kept an eye on the dories, as if the dories were children who might wander out of sight.

I walked along the sand-coloured road a little farther. I could not see my brothers. I looked down towards the breakwater. An army of seagulls stood on the pier, as if they were lining up for a rally.

I looked over towards the fish shed. Uncle Jule's shed was the last one in the grey row. The door was open and swinging back and forth in the wind. I watched for him to come out.

Mama hadn't gone back to the house since Clara left. "There's no reason to go there," she said. "He can damn well help himself." I knew she was relieved. I could see it in her eyes. She had changed after Mrs. Landry left. Grown heavier. Her hair was greying and thinning out. She was fading slowly, like a cloth left in the sun too long.

I had gone into her room one afternoon when she was sleeping. Her breathing was heavier. Her folded hands were crossed over her breasts. In her left hand, she clutched a picture someone had taken of her as a teenager. She was forty-two years old now.

I left the room before she woke up. Nothing I could say or do would make her younger. And yet there were so many things about her that I and Alfred and Albert did not know. I knew that she both hated and loved looking after me and my brothers. But something was missing.

My brothers ignored her as much as they could. They had stopped calling her Mama when they were fourteen years old. She never questioned them about it. I knew she was aware of it, but she never said a word.

We were all sitting in the kitchen one rainy afternoon when Alfred asked about their father. "Is he still alive?"

"Is who still alive?" she asked.

"Our father. Is he still alive?"

There was both anger and fear in her face. "What the hell difference does that make now?" she growled.

My brothers were looking at her. Questioning her. She was very uncomfortable, and angry. I wanted them to stop.

I knew that she would have married their father. That she had looked at that wedding dress for a long time. I could see the tears clouding her eyes.

"We'd still like to know," said Albert. "Maybe even visit him someday."

Her face was scarlet. She wrung the sweat from her hands into her apron. "It's too late for that. The man is dead. He died before you were born." The conversation stopped. She went outside. That afternoon they buried both their father and their mother.

"Your father is still alive, Mari-Jen," said Alfred.

"How do you know that?" I asked.

"I heard grown-ups at the store talking one day. They said we had different fathers."

"Yeah," Alfred said. "No stranger can change that."

I didn't tell them what I already knew. I didn't want them to tell Mama.

The slamming of the shed door startled me. The wind had picked up. Sand swirled in the air as if children were throwing handfuls of it at each other. I stopped and looked at the door. I could still see the two fishermen from where I stood. I walked slowly along the breakwater. I thought that Alfred and Albert may have gone down on the left side of it. Some kids had fastened an old plank to the wharf and they used it as a diving board. The water was so clear I could see the coloured stones on the bottom of the sea. A jellyfish lay on the sand. Someone had crushed it with a rock and smeared it about like dark paste. Seaweed and kelp floated onto the shore from grey waves. I called out their names but nobody answered. I turned back and walked down towards the fish sheds. I knew the two fishermen could see me. I felt safe.

I saw the arm first, dangling over the fish table, and then Uncle Jule lifted up his head and steadied himself on his free elbow and he looked long and dazed out towards the sea. I walked closer to the door. I knew he couldn't get up and chase me. His eyes were almost sealed. He was trying to see through the narrow slits of vision he had left, like a newborn kitten brought out into the sunlight. He was alone in the shed. I ran along the side, between the sheds and up on the road. I kept running until I could hear only the seagulls calling each other.

Alfred and Albert were out in Daniel Peter's field when I saw them, repairing a broken fence with Daniel Peter. I called to them and held up the letters in the air.

They came running. "I went down to the shore looking for you," I said to Alfred.

"We didn't stay there very long, Mari-Jen," said Albert. "We came back here."

They ripped open the envelopes. Alfred let out a squeal. "I made it! Look at these marks!" Albert's face beamed as he read his results.

There was a letter of congratulations along with their results. They had achieved the highest ranking in the province for grade eleven.

Albert threw the paper in mid-air. He had scored higher in the sciences and maths than Alfred, but Alfred scored higher in literature and history. They ran towards Daniel Peter with the papers in their hands.

I watched the three of them from the road. Daniel Peter patted them on the back. I could not hear their conversation. I ran up the hill to our house. I wanted to be the first to tell Mama.

She was in the kitchen peeling potatoes. "Alfred and Albert got the highest grades in Nova Scotia," I said excitedly.

"There'll be no need to be cursing that poor nun now," she said without looking up.

"She didn't make up the exams. Everybody wrote the same ones."

"It's her that showed them that work, Mari-Jen. They wouldn't leave her here all them years to teach empty heads."

"Mother Superior doesn't even like my brothers."

"No damn wonder," she protested, "with all the trouble they caused her over the years."

"It's Daniel Peter who taught us what we know," said Albert, as he walked into the kitchen. Alfred agreed.

"That man can't even talk English," Mama snapped. "Youse don't know what you're talking about!"

"That nun is a fruitcake," Alfred said. "She's fully responsible for Mari-Jen not getting anywhere under her roof."

They went back out. They didn't come home that night. I waited for them in the dark. I didn't eat my supper with Mama. I wasn't hungry. The smell of the stew climbed up the stairs. My stomach curled. I made it to the pot just in time. I couldn't identify what was coming out of me. It looked like poison, like the lime mixture we made to pour in the outhouse in the spring. "It eats up the slop, Mari-Jen," Alfred explained to me the first time they threw it in the toilet. "If we didn't have this, then we'd have to build a new outhouse every time this one filled up," he explained, "or else we'd all have to run and shit in the woods, winter and summer."

It started to rain the evening that I waited for them. I held Lizzie close to me. Mama called to me to come downstairs. She had turned on the radio, the one Mrs. Landry had given us. "It means there's a storm brewing, all that static," she cried up the stairs. She began to panic. "Are them windows closed upstairs? Put some rubber boots around the chimney!"

I threw the old rubber boots I found in a box around the chimney. I circled them like children playing a game. The upstairs of our house was never fully finished. There were no walls. We ran around the chimney when we were kids, chasing each other in a game of tag. I believed that people who had walls were rich like Margaret. I had heard her describe her new bedroom to the kids at school.

"The walls are dreamy," she'd said. "A snowy blue with a white ceiling and my curtains hang like lazy summer clouds on the big windows." I longed to visit that bedroom and look out at the world from behind a cloud.

That year I nailed cardboard around the partition near my cot. I drew flowers on the cardboard and coloured them in with my crayons. I imagined that I lived in a castle surrounded by gardens high on a mountain and my mother and father hugged me every morning when I came to the table for breakfast. And later I would roam through the gardens and water the thirsty flowers while Lizzie slept in a wicker carriage by my side.

Mother Superior said daydreams were a sin. She said it just before I made my confirmation. "They drain you of good mental and moral thoughts, and keep you lazy."

I never mentioned my daydreams to her no matter how often she asked me what was roaming through my head. "What do you think about, Mari-Jen?" she asked.

"I don't know."

"What do you mean, you don't know?"

"I think about different things."

"What are they?"

"God sometimes."

"What about God?" she quizzed.

"What He looks like, if He really has a beard, if He really looks like Shakespeare."

"What difference would it make and what do you know about Shakespeare?"

"Not much. I just looked at his picture in a book."

"Do you think about men?" she asked sharply.

"No, just paper men that I look at in books."

"Do you daydream about them, Mari-Jen?"

"No, I just look and close the book."

"It's too bad you can't read what these men have written, Mari-Jen," she said sarcastically. "You wouldn't have to look so much."

Marcel told me at recess that God had to do some mean and powerful things to man to keep him in line. "You have to understand, Mari-Jen, that Sodom and Gomorrah was just one example."

"What did God have to do, Marcel?"

"It's simple, Mari-Jen. He had to let man know that when he starts playing God, God will start playing back."

I always believed Marcel. He found answers for questions that nobody else could answer. He said there was a reason for why he and I had to stay behind in class when the others went down to see a movie.

"It's because we don't have our dime to pay our way," I said. We had to stay in the class and do schoolwork. That was Mother Superior's rule. No money, no movie. It hurt Sister Thérèse deeply to leave us behind but she did not make the rules. We knew that. Marcel said the answer would come to me sooner or later.

A flash of blue lightning filled the upstairs window and then the rain pounded the roof and sent crude gusts of wind along the eaves. Mama sobbed.

I ran down the stairs with Lizzie. Mama was pacing the floor with her hands over her ears. Her hair hung over her face and revealed slivers of her pale skin between the strands.

"Dear Jesus, why don't you take me and get me out of my misery! I cannot take any more of this."

My body was cold, freezing cold. I tried to say something but my throat was pulling my own words back in. It took me a few minutes to hear the rattling of my own teeth. I put the cuff of my sweater in my mouth to ease the trembling. I had not seen her go on like this before. She looked like Aunt Clara.

I tried to take her hands but she wouldn't let me. I found a bottle of holy water on the kitchen table and made the sign of the cross.

She screamed again, but this time to Mrs. Landry. "My God, Tori, why aren't you here! I can't stand it!"

I cried out to my brothers. I was calling their names when I saw Mama at the back door. She was kicking the storm door with her feet. It flew open and slammed against the house with the force of the wind. She ran outside into the force. I ran after her. The wind and rain tore into my flesh. Mama stumbled onto the ground as I pulled at her dress and felt it rip in my hands. Her feet were bare.

"Let me die, Mari-Jen. Just let me die," she begged.

She seemed weightless now as she struggled out of my grip and ran towards the road and fell again. I wrapped my arms around her body and pulled her back up on her feet. Lightning bolted. A spotlight on us. Her eyes looked dead and the voice that cracked in her throat seemed to come from a far distance.

I started to walk with her towards the house when she fell out of my arms. This time I could feel her weight when I pulled her up. I held her arms and steadied her on her feet, the way a mother would with a child just learning to walk.

The rain stopped suddenly and the wind softened and took a new direction. Little bursts of lightning fizzled and went out like wet firecrackers.

I walked backwards towards the house, still holding onto Mama's hands. She had stopped screaming. I sat her on a chair and went to get some water and a towel to clean her up. "Come and sit on your bed, Mama. The storm is over."

She followed behind me. I pulled off her dress and dropped it on the floor. I took off her slip and underclothing. I was fifteen years old and I had never seen my mother naked. She had gone out of her way to hide her body from me, dressing quickly if she thought I was coming into the room.

And now she stood before me, naked, and I saw and felt the blue jagged scars on her belly. The ones my brothers would never see or feel. I covered her in her warm nightgown and she lay on her pillow and pulled up the quilt to her mouth. I felt her hand reach for mine and I let her hold on to it until she fell asleep.

I had not thought of Uncle Jule all evening, but he came to my mind after the storm. I went upstairs and put on the light that was hanging on the rafters from a cord. It swung around when I pulled on it. I lay on my cot and watched the swinging until it stopped. I thought about Margaret's empty bedroom. Was it still blue? Did her mother remove the white cloud of curtains? What purpose did they now serve in their childless house?

I looked at her parents when I saw them in church. They were still dressed in black grief after three or four years.

I missed Aunt Clara. I missed her pranks and her saints. I wished that old Mrs. Landry was still living next door. I now realized that she was like a mother and friend to Mama. I missed her quick steps to our place. In and out of storms she'd appeared without warning. I had not seen Lasnip for a few days.

"He probably went to the woods and dropped off," Mama said. Dropped off was her way of announcing sudden death.

When I woke up, the light was still on. The sun was shining. I looked over at my brothers' beds. Something looked different. Most of their clothes were gone. The map above the bed was taken down.

I got up and ran down the stairs. Mama was still sleeping.

It was almost ten o'clock. A sickening feeling washed over me. They had told me they were leaving Ste. Noire as soon as school was finished, but I didn't believe them. I dressed quickly and ran along the road towards Daniel Peter's house. I saw them coming out of the barn. We met on the road. Alfred kept looking towards the sea when he spoke.

"It's something we have to do Mari-Jen," he said. "We have been planning this for years."

Albert agreed as he leaned over and kissed the top of my head. "We will come back for you someday, Mari-Jen," Alfred said.

"Daniel Peter has been saving money for us. It's enough to get us on the road. Tell Mama that we will be okay." Daniel Peter stood by the barn. His eyes looked tired and strained. They left with him in his truck. He drove them to the bus station. I watched it move slowly along the road. Its front tires dipped into two shiny puddles filled from the previous night's rain. The water splashed up over the road. I saw a brown frog on the edge of the splash. Its limbs moved in violent jerking motions. The frog's insides gushed out of its skin, as if it were trying to turn itself inside out. One of its back legs swam in one of the puddles. It was dying piece by piece. I ran to Daniel Peter's woodpile for the axe and sliced away its misery. I walked back up the hill with my own still intact.

I went and sat on the step. Mama found me there. "They're gone," I said. "They left Ste. Noire." There was no expression on her face. "They had to go sometime, sooner or later, Mari-Jen," she said flatly. "They were getting too big for me to handle."

I went around the house and threw up. I saw Lizzie lying near the back door. Her body was soaking wet. I had forgotten that she was in my arms when Mama ran out. I took her inside and washed her in the little tub. Her hair was tangled and muddy. One of her arms had come off.

"She'll dry on the line," Mama said. "The wind is blowing from the northwest." She heated up the leftover stew while I hung Lizzie on the clothesline.

I sat on the doorstep and looked over at Lizzie. Her body looked disjointed with one arm.

I remembered that Alfred was wearing his green shirt; it was his favourite. Albert would be sitting by the window of the bus while Alfred would be checking the maps, subtracting the miles from Ste. Noire.

"Your dinner is hot." Mama's voice called through my thoughts. "Come in the house, Mari-Jen," her voice demanded. "You been sitting there for hours."

Alfred would fold the map, being careful not to crease the world. I did not know where they were going. Without me. They said they had enough money to get them on the road. I did not know what road they would take. What city they would venture to.

"Take your doll in from the line, Mari-Jen," Mama's voice cried out. " I will sew her arm back on for you."

The sun was sinking when I took Lizzie and her broken limb off the line. I sat on the step with her and watched the sea swallow the sun. The evening sky was spotless of clouds and birds and fog. It looked like a painting, draped blue-black above the clothesline, above the sea, above the trees. The wind didn't stir as darkness fell and the crickets sang louder than I ever heard them before in Ste. Noire.

# thirteen

Mama made new clothes for Lizzie, as if she were a new baby in the house. A bright green dress. Two pink nightgowns. She knit a soft warm blanket and wrapped it around her. She sat by the stove in the evenings and said her rosary. I went upstairs and turned on the light. I sat on Alfred and Albert's bed. I didn't want to sleep. A full-faced moon toasted the window. A warm glow drifted in and lingered at the top of the stairs.

They had been gone two weeks. Their names were in the paper. They were being congratulated in their absence. Daniel Peter saved the clippings.

He told me he had when I met him on the road. "You eat little, Mari-Jen, too much flesh fall from bones," he said. He looked older. His shoulders slumped and the light was gone from his eyes.

"Their names are in the paper," I said to Mama. "People are talking about them." She didn't answer.

I hated the nights. They pulled me into a grave of darkness and dangled the faces of the dead in front of me.

Old Zeppie walked around his house. He was hunchbacked and his hair had grown down over his shoulders. He kept calling to his wife, but she didn't answer, so he kept walking around the house, calling her name. The tomcat,

Lasnip, kept running from window to window as Zeppie circled the house. Finally, Zeppie put his right hand up in the air. It was then that I saw the axe. He started to chop at the house and swung at the door. It fell over. He went to the windows and smashed them with the axe. He grabbed Lasnip by the tail and cut him in two. And then Zeppie disappeared with half of Lasnip into a fog.

I woke up screaming. I could hear the sound of my own pain. It was still dark. I slid off the plastic. The light dangled from the rafter. It was too early to get up. I went to the cubbyhole and took out some books. I read *Butterflies Dance in the Dark* out loud.

*Are they sleeping? What strange town looms before their eyes?* They would laugh at my dream. I knew they would. "Mari-Jen, I told you that hair grows on the dead," Alfred would say. They would joke and tease me.

They had told me one day that they went to a Presbyterian wake just to see how they were sent off. "They had a net over the dead man's face, Mari-Jen." It was August, and the corpse had his hands down by his sides. "Jesus," said Albert, "he looked like he was ready to spring on you if he didn't like what he heard. I was going to nail a few Hail Mary's on the corpse, but I changed my mind."

"The people prayed for him in church and sang a dozen hymns and then they sank him into the sod. No smoke, no chains rattling, no blessings—they just sang a few Gaelic hymns at the grave and let him fend for himself. Nobody cried," said Alfred.

"You can say one thing about the Catholics," added Albert. "They sink you in fine style, with a sprinkle of holy water and a dash of clay, like they were preparing a roast for a grand feast."

I went back to sleep. Mama called me to come downstairs at eight o'clock. "Mari-Jen, come down and eat your porridge." She was at the bottom of the stairs. She didn't come upstairs any more.

I wasn't hungry. I watched the steam rise up over the bowl and disappear. "There might be a letter today," I said.

"They left two weeks ago."

"Go get your wet sheet, Mari-Jen."

"I don't have a wet sheet." I didn't bother to tell her that I didn't put it back on the cot.

I threw the porridge outside for the birds when Mama went in her room. Alfred liked porridge more than Albert. He said it stuck to your ribs and kept you full all day. He told me when I was about six or seven years old that he read about a mountain climber who got lost for a whole week and survived. "He had eaten porridge that morning," said Alfred, "and it kept him alive because it clung to his ribs like a crow on a wire and his body kept dipping into the porridge when it got weak."

I had asked Mama and Mrs. Landry if that could be true. "It's only true," said Mrs. Landry, "if the man prayed. . . . For sure, prayers and porridge would get you through a war if you had enough of both."

I went to the post office. Slowly, I kicked rocks into the ditch along the way. It hadn't rained for over a week. The ditches were dry. Brown wisps of grass ran in and out and along the sides of the drain like uncombed hair.

There was no mail. No letter. I walked home at a faster

pace. Maybe Daniel Peter would be out in his field. He might have heard something. I would call him to come to his gate. She couldn't stop me from asking him questions out in the open. But he wasn't home.

"There's no mail." I knew she heard me so I kept up the conversation. "I wonder how Aunt Clara is and old Mrs. Landry."

"They are all gone, Mari-Jen," she said sadly and walked away. She said it as if they were dead. Physically dead. No voices, no faces, no appearances. They came to me like ghosts. I remembered old Mrs. Landry calling from her step. "Mari-Jen, did you see my tomcats?" The three of them had disappeared one by one after Zeppie died. "They probably got caught in snares," she had said, "chasing that she-cat of Vange's."

"Why would they chase Vange's cat?" I'd asked my brothers.

They laughed and said that Vange, a neighbour who lived farther up our road, had a she-cat named Flortine who used to sit on the fence and wait for all the tomcats to come and visit her and then they'd do it in the moonlight.

"Do what?" I asked.

"Oh for heaven's sake, Mari-Jen," Albert said, "they'd all sit on the fence with Flortine and fart."

Somebody had given Lasnip to Mrs. Landry when he was a kitten. He didn't like to roam.

I never knew if Aunt Clara had had a cat. I never saw one there. Uncle Jule hated cats, and kids, and nuns. "They are all useless," he said. "They serve no purpose with their scratching and nagging and novenas."

He never went to church. "Don't be forcing those kids to go to church," he'd tell Mama. "They'll end up as neurotic and predictable as you are." She never bothered to answer him.

Mama lit vigil candles for him on Sundays. "It's to guide him back home," she'd explain. "To show him the way." She warned me not to say anything to him or Aunt Clara about the flame that burned for his troubled soul. Guide him back from what? He was more damaged than my mother would ever know.

They were gone over a month when the word came with the card. "They Vancouver now, work, enjoy, see new place—say hello and love to you—and two dollars for you—to say hello back." Daniel Peter read from the card. He was driving up the road when he saw me and stopped. He passed me the two-dollar bill. He couldn't hide his excitement. "You keep for you and mother, Mari-Jen, boys be okay. I write back tonight."

I ran to the store with the money. I bought a box of candy for Mama and me and went home. I passed her the change and told her the news that Daniel Peter had given me. "Alfred and Albert are in Vancouver. They sent two dollars. I bought some candy for us. They are working, Mama—they like it in Vancouver."

"You can't trust that D.P., Mari-Jen. You can't trust people from other countries, and that's that!"

She wouldn't take any of the candy. I took it upstairs and sat on their bed.

❖ ❖ ❖

Everything about school was different in September. I was too old for Mother Superior's questions. "Why did your mother let them go?" she demanded to know.

"She didn't."

"They are gone, are they not?"

"Yes."

"Did your mother throw them out?"

"No."

"What do you think this makes my school out to be, a dropout centre?"

"I don't know."

"Of course you don't!" she screamed. "You know very little."

I didn't answer.

"I don't see why you should return. There's nothing we can do for you here. It is beyond my infinite mercy to elevate your brain to any form of intellect. I have tried to spare you the pain of the vulnerable."

I left her office and walked down the hall. I heard her calling my name. "Mari-Jen, return to my office!"

I sat in front of her.

"I will fill out some forms," she began, "and send them on to the department that looks after these things. Is there anything you have to say?"

There were words coming off my tongue, but they were not my own: I remembered Daniel Peter's kind face dip in and out of the misty pages as he read the words that I recited loud and clear to Mother Superior.

"Nought's had, all's spent," I took a deep breath and continued:

"Where our desire is got without content
'Tis safer to be that which we destroy,
Than by destruction dwell in doubtful joy."

I could hear Mother Superior's bones rattling. Her whole body was in motion as she inched off of her chair. A swipe of her hand sent the bell flying to the corner with a dull ring.

"How dare you?" oozed out of the froth in her mouth. "How dare he steal my words. Who is he to teach you? Get out of my office! Get out of my school!"

I met Marcel in the hallway. He had lost a lot of weight.

"Mari-Jen, I will be leaving before Christmas to live in a seminary in Quebec."

"That's nice, Marcel."

"Father Benoit made all the arrangements," he said eagerly. "He'll be taking me to the train station in Port Hawkesbury."

"Then you won't be coming back, will you, Marcel?"

"Not for a long while, Mari-Jen. My sister is getting married to the father of her dead baby before I leave. Father Benoit made the arrangements for the marriage."

I wanted to wish him luck but it wasn't luck he needed. It was peace. I did not say goodbye to my friend. There was no way I could tell Marcel that I loved him. I went into the washroom and cried.

Sister Thérèse knew I would not be coming back to school. Her face was a patchwork of sadness and regret. She came up to me before I got on the bus and put her arms around me and whispered, "I will pray for you, Mari-Jen."

She cried then. I did not look at her face. I went to the back of the bus and lowered my head. A spider squirmed along the floor. It looked so helpless after being walked on. I decided to do the spider a favour and crushed it to death under my foot.

Mama accepted Mother Superior's decision without question. "She can get you a cheque every month, Mari-Jen. I just got to fill in some papers."

My eyes were dry as I climbed the stairs. My voice was somewhere out of reach of my throat because I tried to scream and I tried to cry but I could do neither.

I did not come down for supper. I heard Mama calling to me but I didn't answer. I knew she would not come upstairs to get me.

I opened the window that faced the road before it got dark. I could hear Daniel Peter's voice calling to his sheep. They always obeyed him, the animals. Alfred and Albert obeyed him too. Even when they didn't want to do their homework, he always won out. "Work first—play second," he'd say and then put on a pot of cocoa.

I put my elbows on the window ledge and listened to the sounds of a village under darkness. I wondered if Amos still spoke to the dead when he went home.

Sister Thérèse had told us one day that the nuns did not speak to each other in the convent after a certain hour.

And what were Margaret's parents saying to each other? Did they wait for darkness to curse heaven for their loss?

Amos was alone now. His parents were dead. He visited them day and night, and turned the earth on their graves as if he were trying to air them out, like a quilt in spring.

In the silence of the convent, I imagined Mother Superior removing her white binding and folding it neatly beside her bed. That's what the kids at school had said the nuns wore to conceal their womanly forms. They did not bloom like ordinary women. They don't even bleed, they said, because of the vows they took. The vow of chastity kept them pure and bloodless. Nobody knew how it worked, it just did and that is why they were all so pale. They were drained by chastity and vows.

I didn't tell my mother when I started my monthlies. I thought it would have frightened her, to know that I was just like her. Alone and bleeding.

# fourteen

I gave Daniel Peter the news to send to my brothers. I told them that I was no longer at school and why. I mentioned that Marcel had left for Quebec to become a priest.

I had seen Marcel for the last time at church on Sunday. Father Benoit asked everyone to pray for Marcel and his chosen vocation. "You have listened to God's call," he said to him, "and have answered it wisely." Some people cried. I watched their faces, their public displays that rose to the surface at times of sorrow and salvation and escape.

His family was in church. His mother was very heavy. She looked burdened by all of this and the going away of her good son. His father sat at the end of the pew, unshaven and rum sick. I had never seen him sober. People said it was a miracle, a priest coming out of that house, out of that racket. Marcel knew what the people were saying. He forgave them. He believed in miracles, no matter where they came from. He came over to me to say goodbye before the Co-op truck left, and held my hand.

"You will always be my friend, Mari-Jen," he said. There was a peaceful look on his face. I was glad that he was happy and getting away from that house. The truck started to move. And then he was gone. He left for Quebec that afternoon. When we got home, Mama said Marcel would make a good bishop some day.

"He's not even a priest yet," I said.

"Makes no difference, Mari-Jen, as long as you're a Catholic, they can pick you from a potato patch and make you pope if they have to."

I knew Alfred and Albert would be happy that Marcel was leaving Ste. Noire. They always liked him, even when he was fat and they said he would never fit into a confession box.

Sophie was at mass on Sunday. Someone said she was going to Halifax to live. She had dropped out of grade eight to look after her sickly father, but now he was dead and Sophie was suddenly free, no longer needed at sick beds. I was happy for her. She was a loner. She used to walk to school with Marcel. I wondered if he was thinking the same thing I did. That death had been her companion for so long, she'd be lost without it reaching out to her. Some of the villagers believed that only certain people had a knack for being around the sick and the dying. They believed they had certain powers bestowed on them to give comfort. They were known as the extra hands of Christ here on earth.

I had watched Mother Superior in the choir that day. Her mouth opened like a bird waiting for a worm. Tasted, then swallowed—down her throat and into her stomach where it would coil in the darkness and die under the weight of her hymns. I knew what she and Uncle Jule could do to people, but I didn't like the hate that lived inside my heart.

I lingered in familiar spots in the church. Near the rope in the porch where Alfred and Albert had stood and rung the bell for old Emile. I held the rope when I was sure nobody could see me. I was sure I could feel the warmth of their hands on the rope.

"I miss them," I told Mama one Sunday night. It was in November, and a stiff breeze lingered noisily outside the kitchen window.

She didn't answer but I saw her wipe the tears from her eyes when she thought I wasn't looking. I knew she missed them. Once I heard her call out to them at night. Could she see their faces in the cool and prayer-filled darkness? I could hear her praying, sometimes for hours, after I went upstairs.

They were identical, except for the scar above Alfred's right eyebrow. He said the axe had came loose from the handle and landed in his forehead when he was splitting wood. They were ten years old at the time. I saw the blood when he came around the corner of the house. Albert had him by the sleeve of his sweater leading him towards the door, but Mama had stopped them and washed his face with cold water on the step.

"Get a bag of sugar," she said to me. She lifted a fistful from the bag with her bloody hand and sweetened the wound. The blood stopped. She washed it out later with creolin and water and taped it closed. A straight scar was all that remained. Did she remember the scar? She must have.

There were glimpses of her that I did not recognize. She could have let him die. Bleed to death. The closest doctor was ten miles away. Other county children died. One of Zeppie's sister's sons was scalded to death. He fell in a hot tub of water when his mother went out to the clothesline. She had found him, Mrs. Landry said, "peeling like a banana when she came back in." But this was long before my brothers and I were born. She said the women in the village took turns holding him all night and soaking him in tubs of cold water to ease the pain. And then he died, just as the sun was rising, in his mother's arms. There was no doctor to tend to him, she said, because it was winter and no way of getting the word out.

Mama cried when she heard the story. Just as she had cried when Father Benoit bid farewell to Marcel.

I made up excuses not to go to church. Headaches, sore legs, ringing in my ears. I couldn't fool her. I didn't have what it took to be convincing. "You have to go to mass, Mari-Jen," she warned. "What will people think?"

I didn't care. Their thinking couldn't reach me now. I went along with her. People asked about Alfred and Albert. I always answered, "They're in Vancouver, working." My answers satisfied them.

I watched for Mother Superior to open her mouth. She always directed the choir by opening her mouth first and then lifting up her arms as if to lift the music out of the mouths of her choir. I always knew when they hit a sour note. Her arms spoke for her. Swaying in anger, stopping in mid-air, she lifted them swiftly and wildly above her shoulders and then straight down at her sides, she'd let them rest. And then the meek voices of the choir rose and fell flat like a dead battery because they were scared of her.

I knew it annoyed her to lose control. Sister Thérèse did not look up from the organ. She could feel the pressure of Mother Superior behind her as her white fingers slept on the keys, and she waited for instructions to start again.

Along the side aisles, three or four people shuffled their way, making the stations of the cross. An old woman bowed her head slowly as she came to each station. She closed her eyes as she prayed, the agony on the walls too much for her to bear at such a close range. I had not made the stations of the cross since my brothers left. They had said that our school bus driver, Bertie, looked like Pontius Pilate. Mama warned them of the dangers of mocking dead men from the bible.

"We're not making fun," Alfred said. "They just look alike."

"How in the hell do youse know what Pontius Pilate looked like?" she asked. My brothers ran outside laughing. The next morning they asked Bertie if he thought he looked like Pilate. Bertie smiled and said his wife thought he looked like that famous Jimmy Durante, in Hollywood.

There are strange cravings that come out of loneliness, like a long and laboured birth I heard the women talk about in the back of the Co-op truck. I stuffed some old clothes belonging to Alfred and Albert, and lay the forms on their bed. I propped them up. Their stuffed feet dusted the floor. I ripped a pillowcase in two for their heads and used buttons for their blue eyes, black wool for their hair. I drew their noses with a pencil and then their eyebrows. Red crayon completed their mouths. Smiling, they looked back at me. I talked to them out loud as I carried them over to the window. They looked out. "Daniel Peter should be in his barn," I said. "You'll see him any minute now."

I lay them in their bed at eight o'clock every evening. Then I read to them and told them what was going on in

Ste. Noire. I told them how much I missed listening to Daniel Peter read from his old books. And how I was scared that I would forget my history and geography. I told them how dull life was since they left. And about the pain inside my heart that made me cry. I left them only to go to church and down to the store.

Just before Christmas a parcel arrived from Vancouver. It was addressed to me. I ran home with the parcel wrapped in my arms. Inside were warm red gloves and a scarf. There were little rhinestones on the front of the gloves. There was a blue flannel nightgown for Mama. She took the nightgown and put it in her room. There was a short note in the parcel. "Getting along just fine—hope you are well. We plan to travel next summer. Will write soon."

I put on my gloves and scarf and went out for a walk. I hoped to see Daniel Peter out in his field and show him my gifts. I saw his truck turning onto our road. He stopped when he saw me. I held up my red hands, displaying the rhinestones. He smiled broadly "Very pretty hand," said Daniel Peter, as he rolled down the window of his truck.

"Alfred and Albert sent them to me," I said proudly.

"Look to this," said Daniel Peter, holding up a pair of black gloves. "They not forget my hand. You here wait. I have book for Christmas for you."

Daniel Peter parked his truck and went into the house. He returned with a bag of books. "You must look to book, Mari-Jen."

I took the bag of books and walked back home. I went up the stairs. I had put the stuffed dolls near the chimney when I went out. It was the warmest spot upstairs when you were not in bed. The pipe from the kitchen stove gave off a lot of heat. You had to be careful not to trip over it.

I sat them on the side of their bed. "Look what Daniel Peter gave me," I said out loud, and began to read the nouns and verbs from one of the books. I was so happy, I forgot to thank them for my presents until I put them to bed that night.

"Who are you talking to, Mari-Jen?" Mama shouted up the stairs.

"I'm just looking at the Christmas catalogue," I lied, "and talking out loud." She didn't answer me.

The next Sunday, I put on my new scarf and gloves and walked down to the crossing with my mother to wait for the Co-op truck. Nobody noticed them. They asked Mama about Aunt Clara. "How is Clara doing in the home?" an old woman asked.

"Mon Dieu," said another. "Me, I miss Tori's face in the truck."

They really didn't want answers, just conversation. Nobody seemed to answer each other. They just buzzed like a swarm of flies trapped in a jar.

When we got home, I repeated the conversation to Alfred and Albert. "You should have seen Mother Superior this morning. She was so mad she turned white. The organ broke down during mass."

Sister Thérèse waved to me when Mother Superior's back was turned. I smiled up at her.

That evening I brought Alfred and Albert to the window to watch the snowflakes fall. The night was so still. I could see old Mrs. Landry's house. The flakes fell in front of my eyes like a blurred vision. The wind whistled softly from the south and sent the snowflakes through the empty windows of the house. A white sprinkle from an invisible hand. I reminded myself to look in at the pattern they created on the floor in the morning.

I turned to Alfred and Albert and told them the story of an artist that Marcel had told me. He said the artist went out into the wilds with his canvas and looked for shapes that the forces of nature had created. Snowdrifts, the curvature of the sands when the tide was low, broken tree limbs on the ground after a storm. Once he had painted the remnants of a forest fire. Three black sticks, against a blood-red sunset. The middle stick was higher than the other two and the sun shone on it like a crown of glory. The artist had called the sketch "Energy," because that's what you'd get from looking at it.

I asked Mama if we could send Alfred and Albert a Christmas present. "What with?" she asked. "You're only getting a small pension and I'm getting less."

Some government agency was sending me a cheque. I was embarrassed when it arrived in the mail in its dull brown envelope, sealed tight like a fistful of poison. I didn't want their cheque that crawled out of my hands and crawled into the hands of the general store owner at the end of the month. "You're paying up, Mari-Jen," she'd always say, with her eyes staring at me from under her glasses.

She always put what money was left over in a white envelope. "Here, Mari-Jen, give this to your mother." She put the paid-in-full bill in the envelope with the balance.

When I was going out the door she'd whistle in her inflated voice, "Don't lose the change, your mother will need it."

I didn't turn around. There were too many eyes following me. I got away as fast as I could and took a deep breath before cutting into the fresh air with a "frig you."

I was getting tired of a one-way conversation with my brothers, so I gave them voices. I drew a scar over Alfred's right eyebrow so I'd know who was who when they spoke.

"I want to look out at Daniel Peter's property," Alfred's red mouth pleaded. I carried him to the window and positioned him there. He stayed there for a long time, watching for Daniel Peter to move about the field.

"Is Tolstoy still cross?" spoke Albert, from his perch on the bed.

"He is," I said. "Daniel Peter has to lock him in the barn when people visit."

"I'm tired," Alfred whispered. I carried him to his bed like a cripple and covered them both with their quilt. They settled down and were quiet.

I went downstairs for a glass of water before I went to bed. Mama was banking the stove for the night. She put two pieces of hardwood in the stove and closed the drafts. "Did your nightgown fit?" I asked, without looking at her.

"I don't know," she answered, then went into her room for the night. I heard her crying when I went to bed.

It was three days from Christmas Eve and neither one of us had mentioned a tree. We always had a little Christmas tree when we were younger. Alfred and Albert and I took the axe and headed for the woods. Mama always let us decorate it with the ornaments that Grandmère and Grandpère had used on their trees. Round glass balls and plastic country churches with doors that opened.

Uncle Jule said he hated Christmas—hated Christmas trees and meat pies that slid down the gullets of the spiritual pagans who ate until dawn and kept one eye open for the miracle in red. He would never put a Christmas tree up for Aunt Clara. Mama had pulled a dusty homemade wooden tree from the attic, dusted it off, and set it upon Aunt Clara's dresser. It was under this tree that St. Nick left his miracles of toilet water and wool stockings and tins of hard candy. These were the gifts given to Mama for Clara from some church organization.

Alfred and Albert and I carried our trees out of the woods, shook them out like a dog out of water, and carried them home. My brothers nailed two flat boards together and hammered them to the bottom of the tree for a stand.

On Christmas morning we dashed under the tree to collect the same colouring books and crayons we had seen in the general store window for over a month.

Daniel Peter didn't celebrate Christmas. "He'll have to explain it someday," Mrs. Landry had said, "when Saint Peter gives him a going-over at the gate."

Daniel Peter bought presents for us but we didn't put them under the tree. They had lost their shine by Christmas morning. The puzzles had already been pieced together and the books read and the candy eaten.

On Christmas Eve, Mama and I went to midnight mass. Before I left, I sat Alfred and Albert by the window facing the road. They could watch us as we walked over the hill.

We passed Daniel Peter's house as we walked to the crossing to meet the Co-op truck. His kitchen light was still on. I wondered why he was still up. The Co-op truck was loaded with church goers. We had to stand near the back. Sister Thérèse came over to our seat in church and passed me a box of candy. There was a young girl on the cover, dressed in green velvet, stringing lights on a tree. On the way home, in the back of the truck, some younger kids sang "Jingle Bells."

A light snow began to fall when Mama and I walked home from the crossing. Daniel Peter's house was in darkness. We walked past it, not saying a word, as if it were an open grave.

Mama's voice cracked like frost. "Hurry up, Mari-Jen, you're so slow." She was ten or more steps ahead of me. I knew she was tired. I had watched her head drooping at mass. She was ready for sleep. There would be no Christmas morning rush this year. We had a small chicken for our dinner. My mother made a couple of raisin pies and a batch of date squares. They would sweeten our Christmas.

She went straight to bed when we got home. I went upstairs and tucked Alfred and Albert under their quilt. I knelt beside their bed and sang "Silent Night" to them. I turned out the light and curled up on my cot. And in the silent and coming miracle of the night, I heard my brothers whisper, "Merry Christmas, Mari-Jen."

# fifteen

er ankles were the first thing I noticed. Swollen—over the sides of her shoes like the ragged edges of a pie crust. I thought she was afraid of climbing the stairs, but I knew her feet were too heavy and awkward now to climb the stairs.

"Are your feet sore?" I asked, looking down at the swelling.

"It's part of the change," she said matter-of-factly. "It's to be expected."

"Why don't you go to the doctor, Mama?"

"What for, Mari-Jen? The doctor can't make me younger again."

I had overheard conversations on the "change" between my mother and Mrs. Landry. "I got a few questions for my Maker," Mrs. Landry had said. "If we ever meet face to face, I'll ask how come it's the woman with all the workload and the man with all the strength? First it's the monthlies and then babies and then after all that, women are dried out like a prune with the change. And the God-damned man just stands there and looks on, still full of strength, with a hard-on you could tie a horse to."

I looked at the married couples sitting in church. Some of the husbands and wives didn't sit together. Margaret's parents did, always. They looked dried out from living.

They stared straight ahead at the altar. I imagined they could see Margaret kneeling there on her first communion day and at her confirmation. They believed Margaret was so pure and good. I knew that heaven would have to make some changes in Margaret.

"You are so stupid, Mari-Jen," Margaret had whispered. We were standing in line, waiting to go to the water fountain after taking the cod liver oil capsules we were forced to take at school. "I'll bet you don't even know what you're swallowing," she said. "It could be rabbit shit for all you know."

She had an audience—four or five other girls laughing and coaxing her on. They were all about twelve years old. "Do you know what the capsules are for, Mari-Jen?" she asked.

I didn't answer.

"I'll tell you, dummy. They grow lumps on your chest." The girls squealed with laughter. "Do you know what the lumps are called?" she quizzed.

It was my turn at the fountain. I had swallowed my capsule and stepped up on the wooden step to reach the tap. I felt the step slide out from under me. My head hit the side of the wall before I fell to the floor.

I heard their laughter. Mother Superior came roaring down the hall. She pulled me up by my collar. "Can't you even take a drink of water without making a fool of yourself?" she spit as she talked, and sent me reeling into her office.

I told Alfred and Albert what Margaret did to me. They sneaked into the cloakroom the next day, and filled Margaret's and the other girls' lunch cans with rabbit shit. At lunch time, they sat behind them when the girls opened their lunches. They said Margaret screamed and turned white and started to throw up. And soon there was a chorus of sickly white girls running to the washroom, their stomachs turning from the smell of rabbit shit under their noses, instead of their sandwiches and sweets.

*Poor Margaret. I hope heaven can make you nice.* I didn't know if it was all right to speak to the dead because I felt sorry for her parents. They seemed to be good people and maybe Margaret would have turned into a nice person had she lived. I did not grieve as they did for the dead—I grieved for the living—for my brothers, for my swelling mother, for my friend Daniel Peter, for my aunt Clara, so broken, like the wings on the fallen angel that Albert glued back together for me and placed on top of our Christmas tree when I was seven. I had found the angel with the broken wing in Grandmère's attic and rescued her from Uncle Jule. I hid her under my sweater until we were safely out of his sight.

I did not grieve for Uncle Jule when Father Benoit knocked on our porch door and told my mother that he was dead. Mama called for me to come downstairs. It was spring. The sky was dark. Black clouds burst open, and rain fell heavily on the roof of the priest's car as we drove along the shore road to Uncle Jule's. Someone had found him hanging in the barn. A crowd had gathered when we arrived.

Mama went inside the house. Father Benoit walked into the barn. I stood beside the car. I could hear the sound of their voices coming from the barn, and then a loud thump as someone cut the rope. Father Benoit's voice was louder than the others, calling out in Latin to his God that one of His flock had fallen out of grace from a rafter of despair.

The hand of the wind moved slyly around the barn and thrust open the door.

Six or seven men stood over the lifeless body of Uncle Jule as the dead language of Latin floated among them. There was a deep red gash around his neck. A purplish blush smeared his face. He had shaved off his beard since I'd last seen him. The rope he had used was coiled at his feet like a serpent's snare.

"Hail Mary, full of grace," I cried aloud. My prayers were not for him. "The Lord is with thee, he cannot hurt her any more, blessed art thou amongst women." Women like Aunt Clara, like my mother, like me. "And blessed is the fruit of thy womb."

I heard Mama screaming out my name. "Mari-Jen, get in here and say your prayers!" I did not realize I was praying out loud. A group of women were in the house, sweeping and washing down the living room walls.

"They'll be waking him here," Mama said. "The men will prepare him in the barn." She did not say his name out loud. Father Benoit came into the house and spoke with her.

"I'll have the funeral on Wednesday morning, Adele. You know there'll be no mass."

Mama didn't answer. The women busied themselves after slowing down to listen to the priest. They raised a hand to their brows and released their secret thoughts to each other with their eyes.

Mama took me upstairs with her to get Uncle Jule's suit for his burial. She climbed the stairs slowly. His bedroom door was partly closed. Inside the room, the walls were bare and dark. I had never been in this room. Faded wallpaper peeled like dry bark. A cast iron bed with one broken leg rested against the wall. An old quilt covered it. A bureau, with most of the drawer knobs broken, was pushed up against the door of the closet.

"Grab the end of it," Mama ordered, and we pushed it away from the door.

"What if he doesn't have a suit?" I asked. "What will we do?"

"We'll find something," she said, annoyed. A blue suit coat hung on a nail. Inside it was a faded white shirt and a striped tie. They looked as if they had all been removed from his body as one garment.

"I'll air out this jacket and soak the shirt in Javex," said Mama.

"What about pants? Dead men wear pants, don't they?" I asked.

"Don't ask such stupid questions, Mari-Jen, and keep looking," she screamed. I found a pair of grey dress pants thrown in the corner.

"I'll spruce these up," Mama panted, grabbing them from my hands.

"He didn't believe in God, you know," I whispered, almost to myself.

"Everybody believes in one God or another, Mari-Jen."

"He hated the church."

"That was the war talking, Mari-Jen. People get funny from war. God has ways of taking care of funny people."

"Then why won't Father Benoit give him a mass?"

"How do I know? I'm not God. And that's why Father Benoit will leave everything to Him."

"Father Benoit is burying him outside the fence in unconsecrated grounds, Mama. You wasted your nickels on all those candles."

"So what, Mari-Jen. God will still find all His lost souls. We are all part of the flame." She took his clothes and left the room.

I stayed behind and looked around. I wasn't looking for anything in particular. I wondered if he had walked out of this room and headed straight for the barn. From here to death. When had he pushed the bureau up against the closet door?

His war medals were pinned on a bar, all six of them, with a sharp pin on the back of the bar. An imprint of King George was on the medals. He looked solemn and geared for victory. There was a picture of a much younger Uncle Jule in uniform. Below the picture, on the frame, was inscribed: "For King and Country." I threw the picture against the peeling walls. I had hated the man, hated his cruel ways of handling women, and I was positive that he had not hung himself for King and Country.

In one of the drawers, under some old shirts, is where I found the picture of a young woman. Her hair was blond and styled in deep-set waves. Her lips were puckered up, as if she were throwing a kiss to someone or had just swallowed a worm. She was kind of pretty in a way. On the back of the picture was written: "Love forever, Ruthie."

I went downstairs. More women had arrived and were scrubbing out the pantry and washing the dishes that were on the shelves. "Hang these dishcloths on the line, Mari-Jen," Mama ordered. "And the white shirt." I walked along the veranda. I could hear the voices of the men in the barn.

I hung the shirt out first and then the dishcloths further down the line. Someone had put the suit coat and pants on hangers to air out. I stood on the veranda and looked at the clothes on the line. The rain had stopped and a soft breeze shivered through the clothes.

This attention would have annoyed him, I thought to myself. He would never have allowed strange women in his house to clean up his sins of disorder.

The house was filthy. I could sense Mama's shame around the women. "I haven't been here since Clara left," I heard her say to them.

"Jule wanted things his way. He wanted to be alone." They looked at her and spoke in turn. "You know men, Adele," said one old woman. "They'd live in a barn and eat surrounded by cow shit."

"What will become of the house?" asked another.

"God knows," Mama answered.

I went back out on the veranda. Two men came around the corner of the house carrying a washtub. It was filled with water. "Gadet is on his way down," said one man to the other. "He'll drain the blood from him in jig time before he turns black."

I threw up over the veranda railing. I remembered Alfred and Albert telling me that Gadet stabbed the dead and sliced open their veins to drain their blood.

"He does it mostly in the summer months," they'd said, "'cause the heat would cause the corpse to explode and fly right out of their coffins."

People called Gadet when their animals were sick. He had worked with a veterinarian when he was a young man.

"And knew more than the vet," they'd added. "He knows just the right vein to stab," Albert had said, "so he's useful around animals and corpses."

I went into the house and stayed there. Some of the men went for the coffin. The women had set up the two barrels in the living room. I went up to Aunt Clara's room before they brought in the coffin. The room was musty and full of dust. I opened the windows and aired it out. It had gone so long without sunlight and air, when the wind ran in it seemed to gasp like someone caught stealing.

I heard the truck drive in with the coffin in the back. The coffin was black with six dull silver handles. Two men came out of the barn to help the other two remove it from the truck. They didn't see me looking out the window.

Later, I watched them parade across the yard with the body of Uncle Jule. The sun ducked behind a cloud. It looked like it was going to rain again. They steered the coffin towards the back door. I went to the top of the stairs. They had secured the coffin on the two barrels and opened the lid. I heard a gasp escape from a cracked throat.

"Dear Jesus," it said, and I knew it was Mama's voice.

Someone began the rosary. Their prayers floated up the stairs like whiffs of stale air. I went back into Aunt Clara's room. It had started to rain again and large drops of rain washed down the open windows like tears of sorrow from one of Aunt Clara's saints.

Anxiety hugged me abruptly. I wanted to go home, away from this morgue of despair. I hadn't told Alfred and Albert where I was going. They were alone. Mama called to me to come downstairs but I didn't move.

There was no way I could get out of the house without passing the coffin. My body ached. I heard Mama's voice calling to me from the bottom of the stairs. "Get down here, Mari-Jen." I walked slowly down the stairs.

"Don't put on a show in front of people," she warned. "You have to respect the dead."

I followed her into the wake room. A few people were milling around. Prayers were spilling from their lips. Softly. I wanted to warn them that they would be wasted. He didn't want their prayers. Spiritual energy filled the room. A vigil candle flickered at the head of the coffin. Red—a brilliant red flame of energy danced above the man who had died loaded with whiskey and despair. There were signs of agony on his bloated face—clean-shaven and exposed. For the last time he seemed to take one last look at the world from an open slit in his eyes, and I knew if he could protest, he would scream, "Fuck off!" and scatter the flock.

We stayed at the house until he was buried on Wednesday. We slept in Aunt Clara's bed. A few of the neighbours kept a nightly vigil during the wake. I went upstairs before it got dark and stayed there.

Mama was anxious the day of the funeral. "Don't forget to touch him, Mari-Jen, before we leave for the church."

"I don't really want to," I protested. "He wasn't really related to us."

"He was part of the family, Mari-Jen," she wailed. "Don't talk so foolish."

"But he has no blood left in him. They drained it all."

"Makes no damn difference. Dead people are still

family." This was her logic. She could not stand to be criticized by the people for sending him off without a touch.

The room was full when we stood by the coffin. Mama reached out her hand and let it fall slightly over his brow. I could feel her body trembling. She nudged me with her elbow. My hand reached awkwardly towards his hands, as if they were creeping up on some insect I wished to crush. I could feel the beads that were braided in his knuckles and then his cold hands against my flesh, probing for an opening in me, on me. I imagined them moving, tracing my skin that was now on his, and even in death he had the last move. I could feel something leaving my body, running in hot streams down my legs and running into the seams of the wooden floor.

"It's not her fault," I heard someone whisper. Someone ran for a bucket and the mop and wiped up the floor. I ran upstairs and into Aunt Clara's room. Mama came into the room just as I was removing my wet underwear. Her face was flushed.

"Why in the hell didn't you go earlier? I got enough to deal with. I don't need you pissing yourself in front of people."

"I didn't know it was happening!" I cried.

"Take them bloomers off, Mari-Jen. We got to get going."

"But I don't have dry ones to put on."

"That's not my fault. You'll have to go without them, or pin your slip."

We went downstairs. I had pinned my slip between my legs. People glanced at me with pity in their eyes. The coffin had already been put in the back of the truck. Mama and I sat in the front. The six pallbearers sat in the back of the truck with the coffin. They were all veterans.

I sat with my head down, in the middle. The driver spoke to Mama about the weather. Father Benoit was waiting for us at the front of the church when we arrived. He instructed the men to bring the coffin in as far as the porch. A handful of people gathered. His sermon was brief.

"Suicide leaves you on a road that leads to nowhere. No map to find it. All those who believe in Him do not live in despair. May the good Lord have mercy on his darkened soul. Amen."

The men removed the coffin from the porch and loaded it on the back of the truck. Mama and I didn't go up to his grave. I could see a gathering of men beyond the graveyard fence. They were standing in bright sunlight on unconsecrated grounds that would soon swallow up and decay the whiskey-drinking man who put a rope around his neck, just inches from the wounds near his heart. That night I asked Jesus to forgive me for not liking Uncle Jule. I knew he was not right in his mind, because his mother had left him and never returned. "But he hurt soft women in hard places, Jesus, and laughed when they cried out your name."

# sixteen

I never did go back inside my grandparents' house. I waited for Mama by the door as she cleared out the papers and sold some of the furniture. The house was put in her name since she and Clara were the only living survivors of the estate, and Clara couldn't be named legally, so it went in her name. Uncle Jule's fishing boat and gear became my mother's property. She sold them and put up the house for sale. Part of the money went towards Aunt Clara's keep. "It's only fair," she told the man who came to our house to clear up the legal end of the sale.

She sold the house to an American tourist. He liked the ghostly splendour of the place, he said—the view of the ocean and the fog that hung around the eaves like lace, just before sunset.

She gave most of the money to the parish. "People go queer with too much money," she explained to me. "They lose track of religion and live high on the hog."

"Father Benoit must be rich and queer," I said, "'cause lots of people leave money to the church."

"He don't count, Mari-Jen. The only thing that goes in that man's pockets are his hands. Priests and nuns don't get paid for what they do."

"Alfred and Albert need money," I said. "They would like to travel."

"Then they should have travelled back to school," she said angrily.

"They will. They are being smart," I answered defensively.

"They should be. Their father was . . . " She caught her words and stopped talking abruptly.

I went upstairs and sat beside their still figures and put my arms around them.

That night I dreamt that they came back for me in a shiny new car. It was the same car that the taxman had, except the interior was a royal blue. Alfred was driving, and Albert had rolled down his window and shouted my name. I was walking to the store when I saw the car coming up the road. When I ran over to the car, Daniel Peter was sitting in the back. Alfred told me to get in and we would all go for ice cream at the store near the lake. I asked them if we were going to take Mama with us, and they both turned and looked at me sadly before telling me that she was dead.

I woke up screaming. The sun was streaming in through the window. I could hear Mama walking around in the kitchen. She had heard me scream. I went downstairs.

"You better eat, Mari-Jen. People are noticing how skinny you are getting."

"I'm not hungry."

"They're gonna think I'm not feeding you, for Christ's sake."

I sat at the table and nibbled at the porridge.

"I had a dream last night about a car. Just like the one that taxman was driving." She didn't look at me. "He never did come back, did he, Mama?"

"Did you ever see him again, Mari-Jen?"

"No."

"Then I guess he didn't come back."

"Do you know his name?"

"It's Marcel. Marcel James McGrath," she said slowly.

"How come he didn't come back?"

"How do I know, Mari-Jen? I'm not a mind reader."

"I wonder where he lives."

"How in the name of God would I know? I didn't follow the man home."

"We had the same colour hair, me and the taxman."

"You think of the craziest things. Why don't ya just eat before you disappear altogether under them bones of yours."

Mama's face was very pale. I knew she hated foreign conversations. She got stuck on the answers just like Mother Superior had when Alfred and Albert cornered her in front of an audience. "Your Margaret wasn't as pure as you thought," they said to her.

Her face went pale.

"Do you want to know how we know?" Alfred had asked.

"Explain to us what a bastard is, Mother Superior," said Albert.

She began to stutter and stammer. "You two are . . . "

"Are what?" asked Alfred. "How do you know what we are? Prove it. And prove you're not."

She continued to stammer. "People know who their mothers are . . . "

They had slapped their knees in a mock gesture of laughter then and sent her flying off in a scurry of rage. They were standing in the hallway with the other grade eleven students. They had just finished writing their provincials and had not yet laid claim to victory.

Mama was out at the clothesline when I heard her talking to someone. It was our neighbour Vange, who lived farther up the road. I went by the porch door so I could hear their conversation.

"She was sick for a couple of months," I heard Vange say. Mama was crying. And then she turned and walked back to the house. "Poor Tori's gone," she told me, as soon as she got near the door. "Her sister found her dead in bed," she sobbed. "Vange just got the news at the store. The priest in New Brunswick called Father Benoit to let her parish know."

We went inside and began to say our rosary. Mama was still crying. "Dear Jesus, there's nothing but death flying in my face this spring; my nerves can't take it," she wailed. She went and wrapped a cloth around her head and went to bed. I knew she had one of her headaches again.

"Whenever Mama looks like a pirate," Alfred had said, "she has a headache." I remember laughing when Alfred told me that and Mama threatening to feed our fudge to the crows if we didn't shut up.

I went upstairs and told Alfred and Albert about Mrs. Landry's death. I had already told them about Uncle Jule.

"You should not have looked at him." Albert spoke sharply. He was sitting by the window with Alfred. I had opened the window and a warm breeze slipped past them like a wave of a hand.

"I didn't want to. She made me do it." They were looking at me as if I'd made a grave error. "It wasn't my fault!" I protested. "I had to."

"Stay away from the dead, Mari-Jen. Stay away," warned Albert.

I ran downstairs. Mama was sleeping. I went down over the hill and looked for Daniel Peter. His truck was gone. I kicked the gravel on the road out of frustration. I wanted to hear Daniel Peter's voice. He would know if the dead could hurt me.

I remembered him reading stories to us from Ovid. I believed every word he read about people being turned into flowers and trees and even the wind. He would tell me if it was okay to turn things into people and if Uncle Jule could hurt me.

Daniel Peter was not afraid of the dead. He said the dead were responsible for the spiritual energy the world possessed. I wasn't sure if that included Catholics, but Daniel Peter had never lied to us.

I went back home. I told Alfred and Albert that Daniel Peter was not home and that Mama had a bad headache. They didn't speak to me for a long time. They just sat there, looking out the window.

A sharp pain cut away at my flesh inside my belly. I lay on my cot and curled up my knees. I had felt this pain before, just before my monthlies, but they had stopped suddenly, just after my brothers went away, and had not returned. The pain went away after I rested. I went downstairs and took Lizzie back up with me. She had been sitting in the rocking chair in the kitchen.

I took off my blouse and skirt and walked over to the mirror and removed my underwear and stood naked. I had not been aware of the changes in my body. My breasts were fuller, and yet the fullness of them seemed at odds with my bony shoulders and thin arms. My ribs protruded out from under my breasts, and I ran my hands over them as if I were rubbing a delicate piece of cloth over a washboard.

I felt my belly, its sunken hollow being supported by two hip bones that looked like bookends on an empty shelf, and I stared in the mirror at what little was left of me at seventeen years of age.

The fears in me had voices. Dark, haunting voices. They spoke louder than I ever could. Uncle Jule's voice scared me the most. It spoke after dark. Always after dark. It cried, always cried. "You'll end up just like them." Nobody else could hear him, only me. I told Alfred and Albert to listen hard. "Pay attention," I told them, but still they didn't hear him after dark.

I didn't mind old Zeppie's voice or his wife, Mrs. Landry, calling to me. Their voices were softer and they just wanted to know if I had seen their cats. But I didn't want the dead to keep calling.

I kept my light on after dark. I crawled in bed between my brothers and covered my face with their quilt.

I told Mama that I had heard voices. She looked at me the way the blind would turn towards a frightening sound. She was sitting by the stove. The blue of her eyes dimmed, as if they were ready to go out above the dark circles under her eyes. Looking at her, I was sorry I had said a word.

"What voices, Mari-Jen?" She seemed to whisper, as if she were afraid one of them would answer her.

"They're just in dreams, Mama, I guess," I tried to assure her. "I was always afraid of Uncle Jule."

"Do you hear his voice, Mari-Jen?"

"Sometimes after dark. I think he's upstairs with me."

Her eyes were still on me. "He was tortured, Mari-Jen, driven to despair. That woman just left him behind like a dog."

"I hated him," I said. "He was never very kind to us."

"He can't hurt you now. Just say your prayers when you hear his voice. He'll go away."

Mama prayed for things to go away and for things to stay just as they were. She prayed for storms to be over and for sickness to disappear. She prayed for the souls in purgatory and for those on their way there. Prayer was her pill for fear, and yet for the first time, I realized she felt that God had never bothered to answer someone like herself, a woman who had traded her flesh, her empty womb, in her confusion to stop her tears of blood.

And I could do nothing for her now but watch her head lean against the back of her chair, her face flushed from the heat of the stove, but offer up to her one of my secrets, and I ran upstairs and took down an armful of books, and read to her out loud from *Butterflies Dance in the Dark*, and I watched her lips smile. And the tears rolled down her cheeks as if someone or something might appear and take it all away as suddenly as it had appeared, out of nowhere.

# seventeen

When we went to church on Sunday, Mama let me carry her prayer book. We sat in the back seat of the church as usual. Alfred and Albert had always called it the charity pew because people who sat in it didn't pay their church dues and they didn't have a pew of their own. Mama couldn't afford to pay church dues. My brothers sat upstairs when they could get away from her, before they got older and stayed in the porch with Emile, the bell ringer. They said God could hear their prayers faster than those sitting downstairs, since they were closer to the clouds, and besides, you didn't have to pay rent on your soul if you sat upstairs.

This was another reason why she gave money to the parish. Her dues had been lean over the years. Her spiritual penance for bringing herself and three illegitimate children to church had consumed my mother with guilt and now she was paid up, as they say, and we could sit in the back seat like souls out of debt—paid in full—whatever it was she thought she owed them.

I opened the prayer book and began to read words from it to myself: "I will go in to the altar of God, to God who giveth joy to my youth. *Introibo ad altare Dei, ad Deum qui laetificat juventutem meam.*"

I read words from the Gospel according to Luke: "Now it came to pass, when Jesus drew nigh to Jericho, that a certain blind man sat by the wayside, begging. And when he heard the multitude passing by, he asked what this meant. And they told him that Jesus of Nazareth was passing by. And he cried out, saying: 'Jesus, Son of David, have mercy on me.'"

I was collecting the nouns and verbs of Jericho when I heard Mama whisper to a woman seated in front of us: "Mari-Jen, she can read that whole book from cover to cover." I did not look up. I did not want to see the disbelief in the woman's eyes. I knew it would be there, lingering like the blind man in the Gospel, for some kind of vision. Mama's spirits brightened. She took comfort in knowing that she had not been slapped in the face with a retard.

She offered safe pieces of her past life to me—images of a young girl bleeding rose petals for rouge on a Saturday night. I loved the new spark in her eyes.

"Me and this girl Eva did it to give us colour," she quipped. "We were so pale, you'd think we'd just fell in a flour barrel."

"Eva's aunt sent her mother lipstick from the States," my mother explained, "and Eva would steal it on Saturday and we'd hide behind the store and put it on each other and head for the dance. It was great walking in with our stolen red lips, the envy of every girl there."

"Did you dance?" I asked.

"Sure, all right. Mind you, we'd go out between square sets and cool off and redden our lips some more."

I envied my mother those privileges. I had never danced. Alfred and Albert had promised to take me but I never got to go. I asked her over and over again about the dances, the music, the swirl of their dresses as their partners swung them to the pulse of the music.

"They were so much fun, Mari-Jen. Sometimes there'd be three or four fiddlers playing to their hearts' content, their sweat rolling down their chins and dripping into their shirts—strathspeys and jigs and reels. But on they played with their shirts drenched and clinging like layers of fresh skin to their backs and the prompter called out until his throat closed up and he kept it that way until the following Saturday, to keep it ripe, and he'd sing out again, like a river panting: 'Allemande left, and allemande right.'"

When I went upstairs I wrapped a sheet around my waist and swirled around and around. I took Alfred in my arms for a partner, then sat him down and danced with Albert. I imagined the music was coming from the cubbyhole, the porch roof—every dark corner of my upstairs world. I released Albert from my arms and picked up Alfred again, and we danced until the music stopped and a soft rain fell against the roof.

I spent my summer nights swirling in and out of music that never played for me.

Daniel Peter told me that summer that my brothers were working on a ship that was sailing for Europe. I didn't question him. He was looking at me the way a child would study a corpse, full of wonder and fear. I wanted to get away.

"Mari-Jen," he said, after much hesitation, "you very much pale, no blood find your face for long time."

"I have to go now, Daniel Peter," I said, and walked home slowly.

I had no reason to stay outside in the summer. There were no trees to climb on my own, no frogs to dangle on the end of a stick, no snakes to kill before sunset.

"One crow sorrow, two crows joy, three crows a letter ..." It came from Albert, the letter addressed to me. The letter was brief.

"Dear Mari-Jen and Mama—We are working on a ship going to London. We are on our way, then on to France, to use up our French. Alfred and Albert." My mother read the letter out loud. It was the first time they had called her "Mama" in years.

I imagined them on a boat in the middle of the Atlantic with slingshots in hand. They used to stand on the wharf and fire rocks into the sea. They made a contest out of it. Alfred had a better aim. He usually won. His rocks always landed five or ten feet farther out than Albert's.

There was a yellow square on the roof above the bed where the paper map had hung up for so many years. I took an old rag and nailed it over the square. I did not want to see how far they were getting away from me. I didn't dance with them that night. I could not hear the music, no matter how hard I tried.

He returned in the night—Uncle Jule—his voice as cruel and raw as it had ever been. "They don't need you, Mari-Jen, or want you, or else they would have taken you along."

I woke up in a cold sweat. He had stopped talking but continued to laugh. His voice cracked like static.

"Shut up!" I begged in a low voice. "Leave me alone." I began to pray but his voice dampened my prayers.

"Prayers won't help you, Mari-Jen. Don't be listening to your stupid mother."

"Go to hell!" I cried.

He laughed louder. "I'm already there. Nobody needs you, Mari-Jen. You're a retard."

"I can read," I sobbed. "I can read words. Daniel Peter knows I can read. He taught me how."

"Is that why your mother won't let you go to him?" the voice asked. "You might do too much reading for him."

"Daniel Peter is my friend."

"Nobody needs you," the voice cried. "Your brothers don't need you."

"They'll be back!" I screamed. "They'll be back as soon as they see the lions."

His voice disappeared then and sank into the darkness of the night.

I hadn't covered Alfred and Albert when I went to bed. Their limp bodies lay on the bed in the heat. Alfred's leg hung loosely over the bed as if he had started to get up but decided against it. I was terrified of new dangers that I could not name.

I got up and went over to them and shook them lightly. "Do you hear him?" I pleaded. "Did you hear what Uncle Jule had to say?"

Albert woke up. "Go back to bed. You're caught in a dream."

"I am not, Albert. He was here. I heard him."

"Do you see him, Mari-Jen?"

"No, but I heard him."

"I didn't hear him. Go to bed!"

"He said you and Alfred don't need me. And Daniel Peter doesn't need me."

"You need sleep," Albert scolded. "Now go!"

I sat on my cot and rocked back and forth. I stripped off my nightdress and dropped it on the floor. I didn't know I was bleeding again until I saw the patch of blood on my nightdress. "The womb cries tears of blood when it is empty." I remembered Mother Superior's words. Exactly. Nobody really understood what she meant then.

I didn't ask Mama if she knew what Mother Superior was talking about. It would have embarrassed her to have to explain sex like a recipe for tea biscuits or bread pudding. She and Mrs. Landry had never mentioned the word "sex" in any of their conversations. They referred to sex as "it."

"By the look of her, she must be at it day and night," I remembered Mrs. Landry saying of a young woman who rode in the back of the Co-op truck with her husband. They had been married two weeks earlier. I kept looking at her in church. She looked normal to me. I searched her face, her hair, her hands, trying to figure out what "it" was that Mrs. Landry had seen.

She was kind of pretty in a way, with thin wisps of blond hair strayed loose from her bun. She wore face powder, a light coating of it, and pale pink lipstick. Her husband was tall and thin, and red-faced like a fisherman. They stared at each other when they thought nobody would catch them. And then the man caught a stray wisp of her hair in his rough hands and tucked it gently under her hat. The woman smiled. A few months later, her belly began to swell and she did not come back to church until her womb was empty, and she carried the smiling fisherman's son in her arms.

I never told anyone that I knew what "it" was. I knew Daniel Peter would have understood its meaning. I suspected that Mother Superior might know all about "it."

Sister Thérèse would understand these things, but she was bound to silence. They were the daughters of the vow. Chastity, silence, obedience, poverty. But I knew, like me, that they spotted their own blood when they least expected it.

The blood on Aunt Clara's hand must have been from a cut. I had not known then, nor did she, Saint Butterfly, that she could not bear children. This is how Mama explained it one day: "Clara lost most of her woman parts from an operation when she was younger. They thought she had cancer. That's why she was as sassy as a goat. Grandmère and Grandpère let her get away with everything."

I had an occasion to witness sex. Under the wharf where the plank had been removed by young boys for a smoking hideout. They were naked, the couple, when I spied them between the planks. I lay flat on the breakwater looking down at them. They hollered like banshees in the sand. And then the man rolled over on his back and the woman, still attached to him, sank lower and lower, until he gave one hard push and she hollered again and said, "Fuck, fuck." I thought she was mad at him. But then they lay in each other's arms and shared a Black Cat cigarette and smiled, as a chain of blue smoke rose in circles and disappeared in the salty air.

I got up and ran towards the road. They never knew I had seen them, when I was supposed to be at the store buying flour.

On the way home I thought about Mrs. Landry and Zeppie. Had they done it like this? Probably not. Someone would have noticed the look of her after doing it day and night.

# eighteen

y mother knew the storm would be heavy, as she called it, that summer day before it even started. "My God, look at those storm clouds," she wailed, pointing to a dark buildup of clouds forming in the northern sky.

"Make sure the upstairs windows are shut," she ordered. I closed them tightly and sprinkled the panes with the bottle of holy water she gave me. "Put a boot in each window, Mari-Jen."

I took Alfred and Albert from their bed and set them on the floor near my cot.

"What in the hell is taking you so long up there? Get down here!"

I heard Alfred and Albert laugh as I went down the stairs.

Mama was pacing from the kitchen to the living room and back. She held her rosary in her hands. "I hate summer and its damn storms. I wish God had found quieter ways of warning people."

"Storms are electrical, Mama. They are just part of nature."

"Who in the hell told you that?"

"I know about them. They are not a threat from God. Daniel Peter told me all about storms."

"He doesn't know what in the hell he is talking about. Storms are for God-fearing people."

"You can't believe in a God you fear, Mama."

"Where in the sweet Jesus are you getting them ideas, Mari-Jen? Is that D.P. giving ya them queer books to read?"

"No, Mama, he is not. Daniel Peter is a very smart person."

"Is that so? Then what is he doing here? There are no places here for him to pray."

I didn't answer her. I went up the stairs just as the rain pounded the roof and a clap of thunder screamed from a black cloud. I went to the window facing the road and looked out towards Daniel Peter's house.

He was walking towards his barn with a lamb in his arms. I waited until he was out of sight before I left the window. A flash of white lightning zigzagged in mid-air and disappeared into an open window of Mrs. Landry's house.

I heard Mama call my name but I didn't answer her. She was at the bottom of the stairs. "Get down here, Mari-Jen! Get down here before the house goes up in flames!"

There were other voices screaming. Uncle Jule's was louder than Mama's. He was cursing and swearing. "I'll get you, you little bastard, I'll get you."

Alfred and Albert were warning me. "Go and hide. Hide from them."

And then Mrs. Landry's voice called to her cat. "Get in here, Lasnip, you fool. Get in out of the storm." Then old Zeppie screamed. "To hell with the cat. Let him drown for all I care."

The noises stopped suddenly. I walked down the stairs slowly. Mama was kneeling by the couch with her head in her hands. She was trembling.

"It will be over soon," I whispered. "The rain has stopped."

I went to the porch and opened the back door. A soft westerly breeze fanned my face. I looked down towards the breakwater. I wondered if the lovers had taken shelter under the wharf from the storm. Nobody would spy on them in the rain. They could be at it and smiling with their Black Cat cigarettes without anyone ever knowing. I envied them.

Beyond the hill, in my grandparents' old house, the American hung his flag above the door and captured the fog that rolled in off the sea on an 8-mm camera he had bought in Japan, somebody said.

I told my brothers about the wharf lovers that night. "Are you sure she's not a mermaid and he some sort of sea lion?" asked Alfred.

"I saw them and they didn't have any fins or fish scales on them. Just flesh," I announced out loud.

My brothers laughed. "Imagine," said Alfred, "if Mother Superior knew they were there, she'd sink her teeth into their bare arses to make them stop." That made me laugh. I had not laughed for so long. I felt my bones loosen and my head get lighter.

"Mother Superior has a cane," I heard myself say. "She walks with a cane now."

"She's been in Ste. Noire too long," said Alfred. "Far too long."

"She doesn't go up in the choir any more," I said.

Mama called to me. "Mari-Jen, you better go to the store. We need some eggs."

I got up slowly from my cot and went downstairs. "Get

a box of Dodd's kidney pills too. My kidneys are acting up again."

I took my time walking to the store. I opened my mouth and drank in the fresh breeze. Daniel Peter's truck was in the field but I didn't see him anywhere.

I was nearing the store when I decided to walk down to the sea. *They could be there, the lovers, under the wharf, already naked.* I began to run until I reached the sand road.

The wet sand slowed me down. I looked behind and saw my footprints following me. When I reached the wharf, I crept slowly over the planks until I reached the hideaway. They had probably just left, because their footprints were fresh.

I walked back to the store. There were a few people standing around when I went in. I asked for the eggs and kidney pills. "Your poor mother not feeling well, Mari-Jen?" the store owner asked.

"She said her kidneys were acting up again."

"The poor soul," said the woman. "There's so much sickness going around. It must be in the air. People can't do anything outside any more without getting caught."

"Poor Mother Superior is not too good," a voice behind me said.

"It's no wonder," said another, "with all the work that woman put in over the years. She's due for a rest." I took the eggs and pills and left the store.

That night I had a dream about a group of nuns gathered on the wharf. There were about fifty of them lined up. They each took a turn looking through the planks. I couldn't hear their conversation. Finally I saw Mother Superior take her cane and poke it in a stabbing motion down on the lovers. I ran towards the wharf and grabbed the cane from her hands, and then I threw her into the sea. I then grabbed the other nuns and threw them in on top of her. But they all had the same face—the face of Mother Superior. I woke up before I knew if she had drowned or reached safety.

The next morning was Sunday. I heard Mama rustling around in the kitchen. "Get up, Mari-Jen. It's almost ten o'clock. You'll be late for church."

Mother Superior wobbled into church with her cane. I watched her walk to the front pew. I wanted to go up to her and warn her to leave the lovers alone.

I told Alfred and Albert about my dream. They thought it was funny. "We used to take the girls under the wharf," said Alfred. "There's something about the sea that drives you bare-naked."

"You're lying. You never got bare-naked under the wharf."

"We did so," Albert said, "especially when the tide was low. We had all kinds of bare-naked parties there."

"These lovers are older," I said. "Older than me and you."

"Who are they?" asked Alfred.

"I don't know. I don't know them."

"Then you're guessing their ages by looking at their arses. How can you tell how old an arse is by looking at it, unless the owner is eighty or more?"

I put names on the lovers. She Aqua and he Wave. I knew they were real but I had never seen them in Ste. Noire. *Aqua and Wave are wharf lovers. Aqua (noun) (proper); Wave (noun) (proper); are (verb) (action); improper action.*

That's what they would be told in confession, the wharf lovers—improper action—if they bothered to dress and tell. I wondered how they would begin. "Bless me, Father, for we have sinned, on sand, on sea, on shells."

The winter froze the lovers out of my life. I wondered where they had gone, if they grieved for the sea as I did.

Two young men delivered a load of firewood to our house before the winter. Their mother sat with my mother in the back of the Co-op truck. "You'll need to stock up soon on wood," I had heard her say to Mama. "I'll have my sons look after that wood for youse."

They arrived on a Saturday afternoon. I heard the truck turning into our field. Mama went outside to talk with them. I pulled the curtain over and looked out the front-room window. They were tall and lean, the young men, with their red plaid shirts buttoned halfway up their chests. The older one did most of the talking, while the other one laughed at whatever his brother had to say.

I saw Mama walking towards the house. "Mari-Jen, did you take the axe from the woodpile? You can't chop wood with a knife, you know."

I wanted to scream at her. "I am not a child. I do not go around woodpiles stealing axes and bucksaws. Look in the fuckin' porch where you put it yourself. I am me, Mari-Jen, not handicapped, not slow, not without feelings!"

That's where she found it, the axe, in the porch behind the woodbox. "Take it out to the young fellows, Mari-Jen, so they can split the wood. They haven't got all day."

I threw my coat over my shoulders but didn't button it up. I dragged the axe behind me like a dog with a crippled tail. I recognized them from school as I got closer to the truck. They were part of the group that teased me the day Mother Superior beat me in front of the class.

"Take a look at this," I heard the older one say to his brother.

"Yeah, check out the fuckin' headlights on her for a retard."

"Too skinny," said the older one. "There's more meat on a toothpick."

They laughed out loud. I pulled the axe from behind my back and positioned it in both hands. They stopped laughing and looked at each other and then back at me. I stopped walking and lifted the axe with both hands lightly over my shoulder. I wanted to split them in two.

Neither one of them spoke. I stood my position for a minute or more. I heard the jangle of keys. The older one had removed them from his shirt pocket and was checking them over carefully.

I felt rage boiling in my belly and its fumes expanding in my nostrils. I felt warm and yet cold, and not yet ready to let the idiots in front of me go.

I looked at their faces. They were not smart faces, just dumb, as if they'd stumbled onto something they could not use their muscle on.

"Going somewhere?" I asked. Neither one of them answered. "My brothers are in Europe. Do either one of you know where Europe is located?"

They eyed each other. "Fuck knows," said the younger one.

"We gotta split this fuckin' wood," said the older one, "before we go."

"Ya better hand over the axe," the younger one snapped. "We're not beavers, we can't chew it up with our teeth."

They chuckled between them. I did not hear Mama come up behind me until she hollered, "Give them the axe, Mari-Jen, before the damn snow falls."

I threw the axe on the ground and ran towards the house. I could hear their laughing voices as I ran into the house and up the stairs. I pulled Alfred and Albert from their bed and threw them on the floor. "How dare you leave me here!" I sobbed. "You bastards."

They lay on the floor in the corner. One of Alfred's arms had come loose and lay across Albert's back. I left them there and sat on the floor beside my cot.

I heard the truck leave. It was getting dark outside when Mama came into the house. I could hear her putting wood into the stove.

"Mari-Jen," she called up to me, as the smell of balsam filled the air. "Them two nice fellows did us a big favour, saving us from freezing this winter, let me tell you. Thank God for people like them."

# nineteen

I sewed Alfred's arm back on that night and then sat on his bed and rocked him in my arms. He didn't move, even though he'd have another scar to deal with; he didn't move.

I was proud of my brothers. Proud of their strengths and their journeys. They had taken the world from above their head and run after it. Not like the two brothers doing favours to keep the chill from the arses of people going nowhere.

"I'm so proud of you," I whispered to Albert, "so proud of you and Alfred." I put the two of them in their bed and covered them with their quilt.

I went downstairs, where Mama was stirring a pot of stew. "You better eat, Mari-Jen. We'll have to go to bed soon. You can't burn wood all night just to look at the four walls. I can't afford it."

"I'm going for a little walk," I said. "I want to get some fresh air."

"You can poke your nose out the door and get that, Mari-Jen."

"I need a walk, Mama. It's a nice night. There's a full moon." I buttoned my coat and wrapped a scarf around my head and pulled on my red gloves.

I walked slowly over the hill. I didn't know why it got dark earlier when the fall and winter arrived. There were so many questions I needed answered. *Why was the sun closer to the earth in winter? What is the deepest part of a woman called?*

I could see the glow from the light in Daniel Peter's kitchen. He told me he was going to get a television to keep him company. He said he was going to put an aerial on the roof of his house so he could get a good picture. I wanted desperately to watch the television with him, to learn things, to see the faces of people who didn't know me.

Mama said there was a television in the home where Aunt Clara was. "They got everything in them places," a woman at church told her. "The foolish are luckier and happier than most of us."

The priest was going to have Amos put in the home, but he kept hiding when people went to his door. "He'll never survive without a graveyard to roam through," the woman said. "His only words are for the dead."

I kept walking until I came to Daniel Peter's gate. I could see him standing by the stove. I went as far as the kitchen door and turned back. He would think something was wrong. A young girl under a full moon, wearing red gloves, asking to watch a television—a boxful of strangers. I ran from his door for fear he might catch me looking through the window.

Mama was putting kindling in the oven to dry for the morning fire. "Did you get enough air?" she asked as I came in the porch.

"It's getting too chilly," I lied.

"Well, it's not too chilly in bed. That's where I'm headed after I put the kindling in the oven."

"It's only seven-thirty. I'm going to listen to the radio for a while."

"Don't put it on too loud. That's all I need tonight is them Sirams in my ears with this headache."

"They're the Supremes, Mama, and I'll keep the radio down low."

She went to bed. I turned the dial on the radio until I got an American station. It was from Detroit. The Beatles were singing "She was just seventeen." I turned the volume up a bit and swayed to the rhythm of the music. I imagined they were singing to me, Mari-Jen, nearing eighteen years, in the village of Ste. Noire and too cold, too cold to dance alone.

How easily the taxman, James McGrath, came to me in my dream that night. Older and with a slight limp, he walked towards Mrs. Landry's house. It was raining heavily. He stopped a couple of times and looked around, then continued to walk until he came to the open doorway. Once inside, he leaned in the doorway and looked towards our house. He kept calling out something, but I couldn't hear him over the sound of the rain. I ran outside but Mama pulled me back in by the hair.

"Don't be so crazy, Mari-Jen. He is only trying to trick you like he tricked me. It's Patrick, your father, they look so much alike."

I got away from her and ran towards the house but I could only see a blur in the doorway. I went back home and looked out the upstairs window. Again, I could see him. He was holding up a picture he had taken out of a paper bag. It was the picture of the dancing girls old Zeppie had given me before he died.

I told Mama about the dream. She was very annoyed.

"That'll be the day or night you'd get anything from the government, Mari-Jen—anything of value."

"I like him, Mama. That taxman had a kind face."

She went into her room and closed the door behind her. There was something about him she didn't want questioned. I knew what it was. I had known since I was a child. He was my uncle, James McGrath, fiery red hair, blue eyes. Old Zeppie had been wrong: "Only God knows for sure who owns that girl and her brothers," he had said. I knew. I knew who my father was by name, and I knew that he'd never be coming into my world, but I felt luckier than my brothers. I knew that I liked my uncle and possibly could have loved my father—if only he had wished like I did on his birthdays.

I wondered if Mama and my father did it the same way as Aqua and Wave. Did they smile afterwards? Maybe that would take the sin from it—the smile—that would take the sin right out of it. I wondered what people who didn't smoke Black Cat cigarettes did afterwards. Maybe they just sang or prayed like Aunt Clara did.

I dug up old conversations between Mrs. Landry and my mother. Hushed conversations after storms. "He doesn't even know their names," I heard Mama say. Alfred and Albert were sleeping. They were tired from hanging from the rafters like spider-monkeys, by their hands and feet. I lay awake looking at the shadows that streaked through the upstairs window after a storm.

Mrs. Landry and Mama were having a cup of tea. "I should have married him. I would have saved myself a lot of misery." My mother's voice was heavy as she spoke. "He wanted to marry me but he'd of never been happy if he had to stop doing what he liked. He was a good man when he wasn't drinking. I knew he'd never be around when I needed him." Mrs. Landry's voice cut in. "He was happy enough to put you in the family way, Adele, but you were wise not to marry him. Good men, if you ask me, like good times and leave the rest for the women." Her shoulders shook as she spoke. "You were too good for those men, Adele. You put up with a lot to rear your kids on your own." I heard my mother crying softly as Mrs. Landry made another pot of tea.

They were only words then, unlike now. Unravelled and put into place. My brothers didn't have this information. They didn't gather words like I did. They had asked who their father was at one time. "He's dead." Maybe he was dead at that time. Maybe Daniel Peter had asked them not to question these things.

I remember Daniel Peter saying in his quiet voice, "The mind hide so very much for you. Sometime no answer come." This may have satisfied them. They never asked her again.

I asked Mama what labour felt like. "It's like the rest of your life. You ask the stupidest questions." I did not think it was a stupid question.

"They're not stupid, Mama," I said, "just things every girl wants to know."

"The less you know about them things, the less you'll find out," she answered, and went outside. Mama never knew how much I knew about "them things."

I went upstairs and took Alfred and Albert from their bed. I opened the window for them, the one facing the road. A cool breeze ruffled their wool hair. We could hear

Daniel Peter calling to Tolstoy. "Come, Tolstoy. Now for eat. Come now." He threw a handful of seed from his open hand. The rooster ran out from behind the barn, followed by a scattering of hens. Tolstoy chased a couple of the hens away but they returned as soon as he started to eat again.

My brothers laughed and I laughed with them. "Tolstoy is getting bigger," said Alfred.

My brothers laughed to themselves. I didn't know why they laughed. I pulled them from the window and sat them by their bed.

"We wanted to stay by the window, Mari-Jen," said Albert.

"You can't," I snapped. "I hate people laughing at me. Always laughing at me. I hate it. I hate it, I hate it."

I told them to keep quiet, that I didn't want to hear voices for a while. My head was pounding with pain. *"Mari-Jen is going crazy,"* I whispered. *Mari-Jen (proper noun) is going...is going (verb...verb). I thought I could hear the voices of dead Margaret and her friends out on the porch singing to me. "Red Rover, Red Rover, let crazy Mari-Jen come over."*

I wanted to go and talk to Daniel Peter. He would know who was crazy. He knew everything. He read everything. But Mama said I was too pretty. Men go crazy around pretty girls. I would have to stay away from him. He did not have a girlfriend. He kept telling me that I didn't look good.

My pounding headache was hurting my eyes. I tied a rag around my head and crawled over to my cot to lie down. I heard Alfred and Albert whispering. "You look like a pirate." I heard another voice. The voice of Uncle Jule, crawling along the rafters. "You're crazy, Mari-Jen. Just like the rest of the family."

"Go away!" I screamed. "You hurt women."

His harsh laughter filled the air and stopped near my feet. I could feel his hot breath sneaking along my legs. I tucked my skirt under my feet until he went away. "He's gone now, Mari-Jen," I heard my brothers whisper. "We took care of him."

I looked around and crawled towards them. "We took care of him," said Alfred. "We took care of Uncle Jule."

I looked over at the spot where I had been sitting earlier. A stain of red blood marked the spot. They were not lying to me—they had taken care of him.

I didn't want to come downstairs when Mama called. I felt safer upstairs with my brothers. "Mari-Jen, get down here. You know how hard the stairs are on me."

When I went down, she was sitting by the stove. "I need some yeast cakes. I can't make bread from the wind."

I turned to get my coat.

"Mari-Jen, change your skirt. You got blood on that one. There's enough rags around here to stop that from happening." Her eyes were full of sad things.

I walked slowly to the store. My belly was aching and my head hurt. I heard Daniel Peter call to me from his field but I didn't stop. I was afraid of him. Afraid of the strange looks he was giving me.

The two brothers were at the store. I didn't see them until I walked in the door. They were talking to a group of older men. They stopped talking, then turned to the men and whispered. They all laughed out loud. I ran from the store. I knew what they were saying. They were going to get me. I knew it without even hearing the words. I waited until they'd left and went in the store again.

The store owner was annoyed. "You ran off like a scared rabbit, Mari-Jen. Your mother didn't send you here to play games." I got what I needed and left without answering her.

I went straight to bed when I got home. My body was shivering. I told my brothers about the people who were after me, including Daniel Peter. "You should see the way he looks at me," I said. "He just stares at me."

"Mari-Jen, Daniel Peter is your friend. You can't turn on him," they insisted.

"He's not," I sobbed. "He keeps asking about my body, and how thin I look."

"He's worried about you, Mari-Jen," said Alfred. "You look sick."

"He's after me, and those brothers are after me," I protested. "I'm going to have to stay upstairs."

I let Mama call to me until her voice cracked. There was danger everywhere. I couldn't go too far from my brothers.

She called to me again an hour later. I went down the stairs. "Are ya going deaf, Mari-Jen? I've been calling like a damn banshee for over an hour."

"I fell asleep. My ears don't work when I'm asleep."

"I need ya to help me get the bread in the pans. I'll be up all night baking it. You took so long coming home with the yeast."

I punched the white dough with my fists. It rose slowly. I punched it again. It rose again like a slow swelling, like the swelling in Marcel's sister's belly before her dead baby was born. She had two babies now, hanging from her arms like torn rags. Her husband never carried the babies. I saw them walking along the road when I went to church. He always walked ahead of them. Yvonne followed behind with the babies. Their legs dangled as if their limbs were disconnected from their joints.

Her husband was short and fat. His face was blank, always empty. He walked as if he let the wind make directions for him. "Look at that," someone said. "How did that man know where to put it? He wouldn't know tits from turnips." People made fun of them and praised Marcel.

Father Benoit said that Marcel was getting along well. He was enjoying his new surroundings, his new joy.

Mama went to bed before the last loaves of bread were baked. "Keep an eye on them, Mari-Jen. I'm worn out."

I put the last pan in the oven. I turned the radio on while I waited for the bread to bake. I kept turning the dial until I got a voice. It was crystal clear. And warning. "They'll fill your belly up for you, just wait, just wait until they catch you." Uncle Jule's voice screamed from every station. "Just wait, Mari-Jen. Those brothers will fill you up when they get you."

I pulled out the plug and ran up the stairs. I pulled on the light above my cot. I took Alfred and Albert and put them beside me. I thought I heard them singing before I fell asleep.

# twenty

My mother was very angry in the morning. "Sweet Jesus, Mari-Jen. Look at that loaf of bread! You could choke a horse with it!" The loaf was burned black. I had left it in the oven.

"I can't afford to throw bread out!" she screamed, as she threw it in the stove.

I sat by the table. I didn't bother to answer her. My head was aching.

"You're just like them. They don't worry about anything or anyone."

"They are in Europe," I said, without thinking.

"That's good. I'm sure ya can burn bread in Europe too."

"I forgot about it. I thought it was all baked."

"Ya never even closed the damper on the stove. Are ya trying to turn us into ashes?"

I got up and went upstairs. I could hear Mama ranting in the kitchen. "Ya better be up there getting ready for mass, Mari-Jen. Ya can't be left alone near a flame."

I threw my clothes on. "You two stay near the window," I said to Alfred and Albert. "I don't want you going downstairs when I'm gone."

Mama and I walked to the crossing in silence to meet the truck. It was later than usual before it came. I heard it coming over the hill. The Co-op man had put the tarpaulin over the back. He put it on in the fall and removed it in the spring of the year. We sat with four or five women on the bench near the cab of the truck.

"There's not much kick in this rig for a new truck," said one of the women.

"You can be sure it would happen on a Sunday," said another. "I tell you, it's the devil himself frigging with the motor so people can't get to church on time."

They all agreed. They all believed that the devil had landed in Ste. Noire and possessed the motor of the Co-op truck so it was hard to start.

I looked into the faces of these women nearing middle age. They were unmasked, with pale and uneven skin caught in the change. They didn't wear any makeup or lipstick—on their way to worship in a truck with a possessed motor. They had had their children; pushed them from their wombs with such brutal force that the strain had stayed with them. They talked about childbirth, about the complications that it brought. One woman had been ripped wide open, they had said. There was no way she could go back to being a woman again for her husband. The poor woman went strange after that. She didn't even want to look into the crib and see the fruit of her labour, a healthy twelve-pound boy with a full head of hair. The child was raised by her sister, and every time he came near his real mother, she screamed like she was in labour all over again. They had seen nothing like it—a woman being so affected by childbirth.

She was not to blame, they believed, for her strange ways after that, and they couldn't really blame her husband for taking his relief elsewhere when the strangeness of his wife didn't pass away. After all, he was a young healthy man with his church dues paid in full.

I saw Sister Thérèse walking up the hill from the convent with Mother Superior. She held Mother Superior by her left arm; Mother Superior balanced herself with a cane in her right hand.

I stayed in the back of the truck until they passed. I could hear Mother Superior's voice. She was complaining about the slant of the hill. Sister Thérèse didn't speak a word. I wondered if she had ever regretted her vows of obedience and silence. I had seen the broken look in her eyes more than once—the aftermath of obedience and silence. She was very delicate, almost childlike. Under the robe, I imagined she looked like a woman. Her eyes were grey, like soft mist, rushing into blue, then green with certain moods, like the sea. I used to love watching her hands, the way they moved, finding the correct page without even looking in the book.

She would have been a beautiful wife and mother. I could picture her walking into church with her blond, grey-eyed children, directing them orderly into pews. Her husband would follow in a dark suit and kneel quietly beside them, and then she would open her prayer book without looking at it and find the correct page.

She had told a group of children at recess one day about her calling in the convent. "It was so special," she beamed, "that inner voice that called to me one day when I was walking through my grandfather's field. The hay was so high. I thought someone was playing tricks on me. But when it returned the next day, while I was inside, I knew God was calling me and why."

Alfred and Albert were in the group listening to Sister Thérèse. I saw them look at each other and smile. "Where was Mother Superior," asked Alfred, "when she was called? In a tornado? Did she ever tell you what the voice called her?"

Sister Thérèse's face flushed. I saw her put her hands to her lips to cover her smile.

I watched her and Mother Superior walk up to the church door. Mother Superior was still complaining. I wanted to run up to Sister Thérèse and ask her about my inner voices. Would they disappear with obedience and silence? But Mother Superior turned suddenly and saw me walking up behind them. I turned and ran in another direction.

I heard the church bells ringing as I leaned up against the old graveyard fence. They didn't bury anyone in this graveyard any more. "It's filled up," Mama said. "Half the parish is sleeping there now."

She said this when Uncle Jule died and was buried in the new graveyard beyond the hill. His grave, outside the fence, in unconsecrated grounds, for lost souls. There were about a dozen graves there in the lost souls section. One of the graves belonged to a young woman named Hattie Deluxe. Her real name was Deloupe, but they called her Deluxe. People said Hattie would drop her drawers for a dime and drink any man under the table. Her brothers made moonshine, they said, and Hattie drank it.

Mrs. Landry said that Hattie gave the nuns a hard go at school. These were the nuns in the old school. She used words and slang like "Go fry in hell" and "Bite my arse close to my hole." She was put in a home for wayward girls on the mainland and thrown out when she was caught drinking with the caretaker in the toolshed, bare-naked. There was one thing that they never mentioned about Hattie. Her bold courage. It must have taken some kind of courage to do what she did. Something drove her to unconsecrated grounds at thirty-two years of age.

I went into church and sat beside Mama. Father Benoit was complaining about the conditions of the village. He moaned in an old-woman voice, "The conditions of the roads are parallel to the conditions of the politicians."

Ste. Noire was made up of Conservatives and Liberals. Alfred and Albert would take me with them outside the polling station to wait for the results. And the fights. We hid in the grass below the bank of the road until the horns started blowing. This was the signal that the victory had been announced. Men in dark suits mingled with men without them, and a few women kept their distance and their eyes on the men. Voices soared and fists were raised and then a suit-coat went flying in the air and the men stepped back and the women screamed. The thump of flesh pounding flesh filled the air. Blood roamed in uneven directions out of open wounds. Alfred and Albert jumped with excitement.

"What does this mean?" I cried in fear.

"It means the Liberals must have lost again," said Alfred, as we headed for home when things grew quiet.

I thought about Hattie that day after we came from church. Alone in her unmarked grave. What would Mother Superior say if I'd used Hattie's language on her?

*May the souls of the faithfully departed, through the mercy of God, rest in peace. Amen. Rest, dear Hattie, rest.*

I heard Mama's voice calling to me to take in some wood. "You better fill up the woodbox, Mari-Jen. It calls for snow tonight."

I put on an old jacket and scarf and went downstairs. Mama was sitting by the stove.

"What are you doing upstairs all afternoon? You'd think you had company up there or something."

"I was thinking about that young woman, Hattie, who's buried outside the fence."

"She doesn't need to worry about heat," Mama said. "There's plenty where she's at."

"I believe Hattie is in heaven. Just where she belongs," I said.

Mama shook her head and poked at the fire.

It was getting dark when I carried in the last armload of firewood. Christmas was four weeks away. I wasn't anxious for the holidays. I hated them. People at church spoke to me and Mama at the midnight mass. "Peace to you, Mari-Jen, and happiness," they offered. They waited for me to reply but I would not.

The rest of the year they passed us by like a bad smell. I did not want their Christmas charity. I knew they pitied me because they thought I was slow and stupid.

"Why don't ya answer people, Mari-Jen?" snapped Mama. "Ya got a tongue."

I knew my withdrawal from people bothered her. She lapped up the Christmas chatter like a gift.

I went into the church and sat at the far end of the back

pew. I was very angry at my mother and my brothers in Europe who didn't send me a gift this year. I expected something different this Christmas, something that would have Paris or London engraved on it. I was set to let it dangle for people to see and read the name, and make some remark like, "My, aren't them two landing in high places."

Once Margaret had worn to school a chain and medal sent to her from her aunt in Quebec. The aunt had visited Rome and sent Margaret a medal blessed by Pope Pius XII. Margaret's neck was exposed for the rest of the day. Mother Superior brought her around to each and every class to show off the gift. Nobody was allowed to touch it. The class was allowed to walk up to Margaret and look at her neck, then go back to their seats. "Touch with your eyes only," warned Mother Superior, "or I will strap you raw." Margaret stuck out her tongue when I looked at her neck.

On the way home from church, I took off my red gloves and put them in my coat pocket. I didn't need anything from them. A cold, stiff wind played with my fingers. My hands were numb when we reached the house. I soaked them in a pan of cold water to ease out the frost.

I didn't realize I was crying until Mama spoke. "Sit down, Mari-Jen, and have some meat pie." She had cut a piece of the pie and put it on a plate.

"I can't eat that at this hour. It would rip my insides clean out of me," she lamented.

"They could have sent a card," I sniffed. "Even a card."

I didn't look at her face when she replied. "They are men, Mari-Jen. How can you trust them to do anything for you when you need them?" I could sense the hurt in her voice. I looked at my mother and saw what was smashing her beautiful face. There were wrinkles in the corner of her eyes and around her mouth. Dark circles under her eyes like shadows. Her hair was turning grey. It was only when she smiled at me, with all that wreckage in her eyes, did I see some of the beautiful Mama return. Albert and Alfred had her smile. I had her high cheekbones and full mouth. Mama had given herself away piece by piece and she had nothing left. I wanted to tell Mama what I knew. How I was feeling. But I knew it would make her sad. I knew the voices that I heard would frighten her. They frightened me.

We sat by the fire and drank cocoa with marshmallows. It was an extra treat around Christmas time. We said our beads in French before we went to bed.

I went upstairs when Mama went to bed. She said she was very tired. I wanted to tell her that I loved her, when she hugged me, but I didn't, because I knew that love always frightened Mama.

Alfred and Albert were sitting by the window. I left them there and went to my cot and covered my head. They didn't deserve to be treated kindly, even though I could hear them crying softly by the dark window.

# twenty-one

It is January of 1967. The calendar on the kitchen wall is new. There is a glossy picture of the Sacred Heart of Jesus above the months. The heart is exposed, flaming red. In bold, black lettering on the bottom of the calendar is written:

Clovis' General Store
Gas, Feed, and Groceries
Fishing Supplies
Ste. Noire—Cape Breton

I am reading this in my bare feet. The house is very cold. My feet are stinging. I do not remember bringing this calendar home from the store.

There is no fire in the stove. It is bright outside. Ten minutes to ten, says the face on the old alarm clock on the shelf.

My mother will not answer me. I go to her bedroom door and call out to her. She does not answer me. I know she's in there. I can see her. She is wearing the nightgown that Alfred and Albert sent her. One of her arms is covering her face. The other is resting on her chest. Her hands are cold because they are blue. I want to warm her up so I am in the kitchen making a fire. I take the kindling out of the oven and wrap it in paper. But I cannot find the matches.

The matchbox is empty. My mother will know where the matches are.

She is still in her bed. She has not moved. This time I can see her rosary in her hand. It is dangling from the hand that's covering her face. She will not answer me. I will have to look for the matches myself.

They are in the drawer of the porch cupboard. I light two of them before the paper catches. My hands are trembling. They are turning blue like Mama's hands.

The kindling is crackling under the paper. I can hear the sizzle. I will let it burn for a while, then add a piece of wood to the flame. Mama adds a handful of sugar to get the fire to catch sometimes, so I do the same. I throw in a handful of sugar on the piece of wood. The fire is roaring now. It will warm her up soon. She will feel the heat and get up for her tea.

I move the kettle over the flame. In no time the steam is rising. I empty the old tea leaves from the pot. I put them in the can on the back of the stove. Mama saves them for her plants. Her plants grow like weeds, she says, because of the tea leaves.

I call to her again, this time from the kitchen. "Your tea is almost ready." But she won't answer me.

I go back to her bedroom. She still hasn't moved. I notice this time that her mouth is partially open, as if she is going to call out to me. But she doesn't. She doesn't move. She must have one of her bad headaches and she is sleeping it off, as she calls it.

I go back to the kitchen and pour myself a cup of tea. I drink it black because my feet are too cold to go out in the porch for the milk.

It is eleven o'clock now and the mass will start at twelve noon. My mother will not be late for church. We have not missed one mass this year because the snow has been light. We have not been snowed in.

I go upstairs and get dressed. I am not mad at my brothers any more. Their Christmas card arrived after the holidays. They are going to send a parcel soon. The card was mailed from London. I hung the card above my cot with a nail.

I look at it as I get dressed to go to church. We will have to walk quickly to the crossing to meet the Co-op truck.

I call out to Mama as I walk down the stairs. She still does not answer me.

I go into the kitchen and put more wood in the stove. It will burn slowly until we get back from church. The house will be as warm as toast. It's the kind of warmth that I like.

The sun is shining brightly. There is some kind of bird perched on the clothesline. It is kind of bunched up as if it is trying to crawl within itself. Its eyes are half closed.

I don't know what type of bird it is. I have never seen one like it before. I will ask Mama when she gets up. She knows more about these things than I do. She knows a lot more than she lets on.

She uses a special sewing needle to make our quilts. She does not own a sewing machine. She says she is going to get one sometime, maybe a second-hand machine, because of the swelling in her hands. Sometimes I thread the needle for her and finish off the straight stitching. I'm getting better at it, but I don't like to knit. The wool makes my hands too itchy.

It is eleven-thirty. I will not wake Mama to go to church. It is too cold for her to go out with her bad headache. I will tell her that when she gets up.

I stay home too, in case she calls me to bring her a cold cloth and an aspirin.

The kitchen is rosy warm now. I fill up the kettle and put it on the back of the stove. I take some sticks from the woodbox and put them in the oven. They will be good and dry for tomorrow's fire.

It is afternoon now, exactly twelve minutes after twelve. The old alarm clock keeps perfect time. Mama wound it last night before she went to bed. She went to bed early because she wasn't feeling too good. She hugged me good-night. I didn't hug her back, but I smiled at her. She said I was starting to look like my brothers. That made her face smile.

I go and check on her again. She hasn't stirred. Her hands are so blue. Her mouth is still partially opened.

I want to go in and cover her with another quilt. But I am scared. I do not want to wake her up if she is sick.

I go back upstairs and sit on my cot. Alfred and Albert are still in their bed. I take them out and sit them by the chimney.

It's warm upstairs. I tell them that Mama is still asleep and not to make a noise. They whisper to me and to themselves. I tell them about the funny bird on the clothesline. They want to know what colour it is. It tell them that it is black—a bluish black. It resembles a crow, but yet it is different. They want to look out the window to see the bird for themselves. I take Albert to the window first. But the bird has vanished. He is very disappointed and tells me that I don't know a bird from a clothespin. Alfred wants to look out. He wants his turn, but he cannot see the bird either. It has not returned.

I put them back by the chimney and tell them to be quiet. I go back downstairs to check on the fire.

It is one-thirty now. Mama is still in bed. She has not moved and her rosary is still in her hand—her blue hand. If she knows how late it is, she will be annoyed that she stayed in bed so long.

*It's one-thirty, Mama,* I tell her, but she doesn't seem to hear me.

I go back upstairs to Alfred and Albert. I tell them that Mama is still in bed and not to make a racket. They ask me to take them downstairs so they can look in at her.

I hold on to them tightly as I walk down the stairs. The three of us stare in at her. I can feel Alfred and Albert stiffen in my arms. They tell me to walk closer to the bed so they can get a better look at Mama.

One of her eyes is open, but without colour. The other is hidden under her arm. We can see the colourless eye. It is staring at us. We can see inside her mouth. A bead from the rosary has fallen in there. I had not noticed that her rosary was broken. I had not noticed it before.

Alfred and Albert are telling me to leave the room. "She's dead, Mari-Jen," Albert says. "Mama is dead." I scream at him to shut his mouth. I will not let him play tricks on me now, so I drag the two of them up the stairs and sit with them on the floor.

She will be up soon, I tell them. She will be up soon.

The upstairs is getting cold. I'm glad I got dressed and put on my boots.

I am holding Alfred and Albert in my arms. It is getting dark. I don't know what time it is and I can't go downstairs. I don't know why, but I can't go downstairs. My brothers don't want to go down either. They have been very quiet since we came back upstairs. I can hear them praying.

It is getting very dark now. I hold Alfred and Albert closer. I feel warmer with them in my arms. The floor is wet where I am sitting. Alfred scolds me for wetting my pants. He says, "You could have used the pot, Mari-Jen. It's not that far from your cot."

The house is so cold and dark.

I tell Alfred to be quiet and listen. There is someone moving downstairs. I can hear footsteps. They are getting closer to us, coming up the stairs with a light. "Mama is awake," I whisper to them.

A voice is calling my name over and over. "Mari-Jen—you say answer for me."

I feel the light in my eyes and then it flashes on Alfred and Albert. I can hear Daniel Peter's voice. He is crying. Loud sobs, as if his body is breaking in two. He finds the string and turns on the light.

He takes Alfred and Albert from my arms and puts them on my cot. And then he grabs their quilt and wraps it around me and carries me down the stairs and out to his truck. There is a full moon. In its light, people move like naked shadows in and out of the house.

I can hear Father Benoit's voice. The woman from the store gets into the truck with me and then Daniel Peter drives us to her house. Daniel Peter carries me into her kitchen. The woman is washing me and puts one of her nightgowns on me and dry underwear. She brushes my hair and ties it back with a ribbon.

I can hear her telling Daniel Peter that it was lucky he checked up on us when there was no smoke early in the afternoon. "Mari-Jen could have frozen to death. How long do you think Adele has been dead?" she asks.

Daniel Peter does not say too much. He replies, "I have no answer for this." He is asking the woman about some hospital, about the conditions of the road.

"It's such a shame," the woman is saying, "her being like she is. No wonder she hid upstairs. And the boys so far from home."

Daniel Peter's voice is agitated. "I go now and take my Mari-Jen." We are back in his truck. I lean against the side of the window. The drive is so long.

Daniel Peter speaks in intervals, in his own language, but not to me. He is asking someone else for answers, as the full moon follows us out of Ste. Noire.

# twenty-two

Spring 1970. My mother's house is empty now except for the ghosts that keep me away from the door. The curtains are drawn on the windows in dusty, delicate folds. They have not tasted the wind in the years I have been away from Ste. Noire. Three years, three months, and six days.

At twenty-two years of age, I am back and living with Daniel Peter and his new wife, Anna, a Polish immigrant.

From the hilltop where I am standing, our old house is blooming like a flower coaxed out by the sun. The upstairs window, facing the road, is full of warm sunshine bursting to get in. The dolls once lived behind this flame of spring sun. Or so I believed. I gave them images of Ste. Noire through this pane. They took long, slow, colourful stares like prisoners watching a live parade. Curtains drawn, they recoiled like smiling snakes snarled around each other's limbs.

In the winter, they lay against the frosted curtain until I tasted its lace, and Tolstoy appeared at the end of my tongue. Their roommate, Lizzie, still lives among the ghosts. She once roamed freely throughout this house. A pale, soft moth with my arms for wings.

There is a shadow in Mama's bedroom window. Walk into this darkness and you will find her bed. Cold and clean, without a wrinkle of body form having ever been present. The ghost in this room is very neat. Disinfected. She washed everything that touched her skin. Clothes and shoes. Men and children. We slipped into her life between scrubbings, I do believe. Albert told me once that we were baptized in creolin. I was ten years old. He said the priest insisted on it. The church wouldn't let him waste holy oil on babies without fathers. He said Father Benoit kept a jug of creolin in the vestry with "bastard oil" written on it in ink.

I believed him because that's what Uncle Jule called us. Bastards of the womb. He is the ghost I still fear above all others. Death reduced him to a whisper, but still his gravel voice crawls along my skin at times. A worm in an open grave. Waiting for the corpse.

These are the images and voices I surrendered to the doctors. I started to speak again after three months of silence, when my brothers returned from Europe. But oh, silence is a noun. I was always aware of that. The doctors took notes.

I watched their black pens spilling nouns and verbs onto their white paper. My memory became sharper with each spill.

I shared a room, for six months, with an older woman named Evelyn. A duet of muted forms in 214-C. I never did hear her word voice. She howled like a lonely wolf when the nurses opened the curtains. "Oaaaah," she cried, as her sprawled fingers crawled towards the light like white spiders. We lay hidden in a room that didn't like the sun or moon to drop by. But there were the smells to contend with day and night. The eau de cologne they anointed her wavy skin with. Evelyn's three daughters, dabbing at their ghostly mother like a wilted flower in need of fertilizer.

Behind her ears, in the folds of her large breasts, on her blue ankles, their hands busied themselves in the flesh that had created and moulded their likeness to this dying bloom. They were soft and plump and in their forties. Age had not welcomed them kindly in their dreary print dresses and flat loafers.

In the fractured darkness of the night, in that hospital room, I remembered the smell of gasoline. Twice that night Daniel Peter had stopped for gas along the highway. In my mother's kitchen, I was later to hear, women busied themselves over a balsam flame, heating water in a galvanized tub. What they had to dilute was the smell of creolin on Mama's hands and the Vick's Rub on her chest. They dusted her hidden skin with talcum powder. She was wearing the blue nightdress that my brothers had sent to her the year before. It had never been worn. I would remember this myself in time.

My mother died with her daughter and her two rag-doll sons out of reach, above her head. I know that now.

I clung to the darkness like lint in that hospital. Each particle growing thicker. Tighter. Even dust became faint. What I inhaled were things I thought I would never see again. Eyes that recognized me on sight. Hands that led me safely through wild branches. Once, somewhere in the darkness, a face leaked in. I didn't recognize it for a moment, the free-flowing waves dancing off white shoulders.

Eyes as blue as the Madonna's robe. Mama, I whispered, I didn't realize how beautiful you were, even on your deathbed. I emerged from unconscious consciousness with the hand of madness churning in my stomach like hunger. My tongue as thick as pea soup drooled for familiar words. Images passed me by like young leaves. And then the dead appeared, Mama and Mrs. Landry and her husband, Zeppie; and they pushed me back into the light with their tinted ghostly white hands.

In the light that warms the ghosts in Mama's house today, in the light that plays hide and seek through the open veins in Mrs. Landry's house, I have been standing for over two hours. The sun has taken a new direction. Its flame has crept up to Mama's bedroom window and swallowed the shadow. A prism of colour explodes and bleeds upon the glass. Come closer, Mari-Jen, it beckons. Closer! Closer! But I do not move towards the house. I can do nothing this time, this day, this hour, but raise my hands to its pure light and bathe them in its stream of colours.

# twenty-three

My brothers took me to live with them when I was released from the hospital. The Victorian house I lived in with Alfred and Albert is located in the south end of Halifax. The house takes cool comfort in summer's twilight as the giant elms fan the roof. Breezes simmer through the leaves like the voices of a children's choir.

At night, from my bedroom window, I could hear the trains scream on the brow of the city. Foreign ships slid into watery paths down at the dock. The dockyard workers, on the graveyard shift, grunted until daybreak. An all-night café collected the lonely and the poets. Soft words fell on hard paper. Life and death happened between poems. Babies were born. Hearts stopped beating. Taxis came to a halt two doors from the bootlegger's door. Winked their headlights. A figure appeared, silent as a cat on blue snow. Motors purred.

I collected these sights and sounds from my bedroom window. It was directly across from Alfred's room. Thick crown moulding, as wide as footboards, ran along the dropped ceiling. Flaming red poppies, on the stained glass window, danced shadows on the walls. The double bed is from an antique shop on Barrington Street. Its heavy pine heading is Gothic shaped with a crack down the left side.

Albert painted the walls a pale blue. We hung long, white curtains on the windows. I had a dream about my mother in this room. She was laid out in her coffin in her Sunday dress. Her eyes were wide open as if she were watching someone. But her lips were sealed like old Zeppie's had been. Alfred and Albert said Zeppie's lips were glued together with balsam when he died, but my mother's lips appeared to be held together by thick red lipstick in my dream. The parish women were crying more for the circumstances of her death, rather than her death itself. In between prayers the women cried out my name like a chorus of bloodhounds. They were searching Mama's room for the picture she kept hidden. I called out to Mama that Alfred and Albert and I were not far away. I knew she was waiting for us to touch her goodbye.

There were no relatives under Adele Delene's roof to give her the final touch. I reached out and felt her flesh. It was hot in my hands. Felt the shape of her mouth that left the word "pretty" on my skin.

I felt the arch of her brow. And then a light came on, and Alfred took my hands from his face. We went downstairs and drank tea until dawn. Alfred told me it was okay to dream of the dead when you miss them. "It's part of the grief, Mari-Jen, part of the grief."

Alfred and Albert headed out west the day they left Ste. Noire. That was the morning my grief began. Daniel Peter drove them to the bus station in Antigonish. They stopped in Toronto long enough for a hamburger and headed out to Vancouver. They got jobs as hired hands on a freighter. They roamed through the ancient ruins of Europe and South

America. Tried to coax a roar from a zoo lion. Collected the names of the dead like poor Amos and found their future etched in stone in an old cemetery. They marvelled at the marble angels that stood higher than grown men and studied the smooth faces with the round sightless eyes. Albert filled a notebook with sketches and said, "Why not?" They would design and sell tombstones. Alfred would throw in an epitaph at no extra cost. "Here lies Cassie Smith: Drove too fast when she was lit." They were joking about the epitaph to hear me laugh again. They own and operate a monument business. Their business cards read: Delene Brothers' Monuments—We Top the Best.

They employ stone cutters and engravers. Office workers and truck drivers. Their beautiful marble stones rise above the hearts that stopped beating in the dark.

They told me the story of their return. The freighter docked in Halifax at 2:45 p.m. The March ice under their feet was a winter grey Above their heads a pleat of white clouds folded into one. Several pigeons busied themselves a few feet away from the pier. They were pecking at a crack in the ice. Inside the ice lay a crust of bread.

In his hand, Alfred carried a brown leather bag. Inside a pair of black, fluffy slippers and a glass dome were wrapped in a green flannel shirt. Beside the dock, Daniel Peter turned up his collar against the March wind. Alfred and Albert embraced him with hardy handshakes and ready smiles. They had written to him to tell Mama and me that they were on their way back to Nova Scotia. Daniel Peter told them in a quiet and compassionate manner. "Your mother she run out of life, and your sister she run out of words."

Albert entered room 214-C first. Alfred followed. He had removed the slippers and the dome from the bag and held them firmly in his hands. They had turned into sturdy grown men. Unshaven and sea-whipped. Their bronze faces gaunt as they stood at the foot of my bed. Daniel Peter had waited downstairs. They whispered my name in unison.

"Mari-Jen. Mari-Jen."

I looked at the two figures standing by my bed. They didn't speak a word to each other as they stood there as awkward as two schoolboys reciting poetry. Evelyn groaned and pulled her quilt up over her face. Two of her daughters came into the room. They didn't take their eyes off Alfred and Albert.

"She don't talk to anybody, the poor little thing," said the older daughter. Alfred and Albert looked at each other and whispered something in low voices. Alfred put my slippers and dome on my bed. I heard them talking about speaking to the doctor before they left. They grabbed my big toes and tapped my feet before they went out. I drifted into sleep. I woke to an empty room. It was evening. A dim light from under the bathroom door flickered on and off. Evelyn rocked her head back and forth on her pillow. A sly smile cracked her lips. I knew that she was dreaming again. Whatever she was planning fermented behind her smiles. She had a life of her own behind the silence.

I felt a sudden sting in the air. It swiped at my feet and ran up my legs. It pulled at my tongue. I sat upright in my bed. The light continued to flicker. OFF-ON. OFF-ON.

My tongue felt as thick as pea soup as my mouth began to drool. My hands played frantically in the slow spill.

Something was leaking out that I wanted desperately to hold onto. Words. OFF-ON. And then they slid warmly off my tongue and into the palms of my open hands.

OFF-ON-OUT.

"Alfred. Albert."

Sixty-four days, three hours, and twelve minutes. That's how long it took to unravel my tongue. I would ask for the count myself. That's how long it took for Anna and Daniel Peter to fall in love. That's how long it took my brothers to say they would never leave me again. My favourite doctor smiled. A warm March smile when my voice returned. It was the same smile he used as he stood over me as I lay on that white table. Under white lights. Six white hands held me down. A river of eels ran through my body. From head to toe. They swam at leisure. Taking bites, electric bites. They would not taste my flesh again because I fought the shock therapy off with words, in March, when my brothers returned.

Daniel Peter waited beside the door that first time. It was February. Above his head, the black hands on the white face of time rippled one minute past noon, he remembered.

There is no silence in being silent. Silence is a sharp spear pecking holes into your skull. Everything crawls in. Voices in hymns. Voices in anger. Voices too loud. Too soft. I have since made a bargain with silence. I will not bruise its energy nor awaken its humilities, but tap gently upon its doors when the time is right.

My mother's face lingered at the opening and closing of my internal dialogue. "Why did you leave me alone?" I wailed inside my head. My words buzzed around and around like a fly trapped in a jar. I could not remember the sound of my mother's voice until I realized that I was angry at her for leaving without a goodbye. The day that I was able to let my mother rise from her deathbed was the day I knew she was gone forever. I led her along the trail of warm rooms by the hand and sat her by the fire. There with her blue hands around her cup of tea, her half-opened mouth offering up her crystal bead, I let her say her goodbyes. Her words fell like daisies on my skin.

"Daisy, daisy, give me your answer please!"

"I loved Mari-Jen, I loved her not, I loved her, I loved her not, I loved her. I loved Alfred and Albert. I loved them not. I loved them. I loved them not. I loved them."

My mother never meant to make me bleed on purpose that day in early summer. I was ten or eleven then. She meant to hit Albert instead. But she missed and hit me on the foot with the stick. The cut bled openly all over her clean kitchen floor. She didn't make me clean it up. She realized her mistake. I could see the sorry in her eyes but she didn't say anything. I sat by the stove after she cleaned my foot and covered it with a clean cloth. She never said sorry with words. She made me cocoa instead. She went outside and picked a handful of daisies and set them on the table in a holy water bottle. I sat beside the flowers and drank my cocoa. She had thrown Alfred and Albert out of the house that day. They stayed out until late into the night, but Mama stayed up and made them a pot of fudge. Mama always let us know that she loved us with cocoa and fudge and a handful of daisies.

# twenty-four

The daisies had not yet bloomed when I returned to Ste. Noire, along the same moon-dusted road that had escorted me away from it. In broad April daylight.

A warm sun dozed on patches of green grass in the long empty fields. Tulips started a colour guard along the pole fences, then bowed out of sight. Clotheslines full of white sheets flew at full mast, like majestic ships ready for destinies a long way from Ste. Noire. Grey wood smoke spiralled above the masts. Waves waltzed up on the shore.

In Ste. Noire's kitchens, stews simmered. Bread baked. Pies cooled on window ledges. Schoolbooks lay forgotten on chairs. And amid this domestic symmetry, weary housewives took long glances from behind their starched curtains as Daniel Peter's truck rode by on the day of my return.

In the graveyard, a fresh mound of clay rose to a peak covered in a blur of red, pink, and white carnations. This vagrant trail of light settled over a corpse I did not know. My mother had set a wreath on Uncle Jule's coffin. Its sickly sweet smell curled my insides. On the card, the words were as toxic as the smell. "In dear and loving memory of Jule." I wondered if someone had gotten a wreath for her grave. She had died out of flower season. January does not bloom in Ste. Noire. The housewives would be watching for fresh blooms on my mother's grave with my return.

I had visions of my mother's grave blooming with daisies, her favourite flowers. I will plant the seeds and watch them grow.

Alfred and Albert placed the stone on her grave last year. They said that they think Mama would be pleased. And that I will be too when I visit her grave. They have learned more about her in death than they ever knew about Mama in life. Alfred smiled when I told him about her favourite flower.

I want to leave her my touch when I visit her grave. My final goodbye. I know my mother would want this.

I am drawn to Ste. Noire, as Anna and Daniel Peter were drawn together. Daniel Peter had brought Anna to my hospital room to introduce her to me just before I was released. Anna worked as a cook in the cafeteria where they met.

Her voice drifted from one corner of the room to another as she paced the floor like someone at a wake trying to build up enough courage to face the corpse. At times, it sounded much larger than the voice of the petite woman with the luminous dark eyes trying to avoid mine.

Daniel Peter's voice cut in softly. He talked about Tolstoy, his wise old rooster. All his roosters retained the name Tolstoy. At six a.m., Tolstoy calls out to the new morning. The dawn responds with puffs of smoke. Children's voices. The thrust of an axe. Cow bells ringing. All this the wise old bird sets in motion. Then stands on his perch and listens. The morning bugler then struts out and pecks at the earth. The first kiss at dawn for Ste. Noire.

Before Daniel Peter and Anna left my room, he tapped me gently on the head. Anna stood in the middle of the room pushing hairpins into her neatly tucked bun. She resembled an angel with outstretched wings mending her halo. She looked up and caught my smile. Pecked my cheek. The first kiss of friendship for us both. Six months later they became man and wife. They went down to Pier 21 in the fog to retrace their footsteps for good fortune and a long life together in Nova Scotia, on their wedding day in 1968.

Anna and I had become very close friends when she and Daniel Peter came to visit. It was she who offered their home in Ste. Noire to me when I was ready to leave the city.

"I teach for cook and sew," she said with a glint in her eye. Later she would tell me that she loved the patter of another woman's voice in her home. Behind her footsteps. In her secrets. Trying her recipes. The scent of freshly washed hair and cold cream vanishing beneath our skin. The wind whistling up our skirts. Women need these things, Anna believes. They need connections to words and smells and touches.

"The heart have no age," says Anna, who is fifteen years younger than Daniel Peter. "You, Mari-Jen, get good man for love." Anna laughs. "You know love when he look for you straight in nose and he say this for you."

Women stare at the open affection Anna and Daniel Peter share with each other. Many of these housewives have not been held by their husbands for a long time. They secretly marvel at the way urges swell up in Anna and Daniel Peter.

"Some kind of Jesus foreign custom, in that relationship, the way they claw at each other in broad daylight," the women joke.

Anna's long hair hangs like a black wave over his shoulder. Daniel Peter's smile trembles on her skin as they enter the house. The sun is set on high noon. The moon will have to await its turn.

"What is pain, but knowledge learned backwards?" declared Olivia McKenna, the retired schoolteacher my brothers had hired to be my tutor while I lived away.

Olivia McKenna sat across from me in a dark grey suit and blouse. She wore pink teardrop earrings clasped to her lobes. She reminded me of a large mouse. Her red cheeks flooded her face when she smiled. I stared at her for some time and imagined her in a confession box, exhaling her sins. Inhaling her penance. She both frightened and excited me at the same time, like a circus clown a child has to be coaxed to shake hands with for the prize balloon. She referred to me always as Miss Delene.

"There is one rule, Miss Delene," said Olivia McKenna, pausing before continuing, "whatever knowledge you acquire must be passed on or you will have learned nothing at all."

She passed me a sheet of paper with a printed sentence in black ink written across the page. My dog is fat. My cat is white. "Dog–noun. Cat–noun. Is–verb," I said, quietly threading the world of words cautiously with a fat dog and a white cat.

"Bravo," shouted Olivia McKenna. "Do the cat and dog get along?" I did not answer. She leaned over the desk. "Miss

Delene, these silly questions force one to think as well as read. Add flesh to the imagination. One cannot dance without music or else the feet go lame." She heaved a great sigh and dropped her hands at her sides.

"Yes, I believe the cat and dog get along," I answered in a louder voice. Olivia McKenna smiled. "Then you and I shall get along as well."

Olivia McKenna said a learning disability was responsible for the words that tumbled off my pages in Ste. Noire school.

"Why in the name of God did no one question it?" She asked herself that question in an angry voice.

"My friend Daniel Peter helped me," I informed her.

"Indeed he did, Miss Delene, you are very lucky to have met him." She stood up beside her desk, her weighty flesh smelling of cake powder and mild soap as she mumbled something I could not make out. She cleared her throat. "You possess a keen memory and a love for knowledge." Her voice rose. "You can read words, Miss Delene, but one must read victory into every syllable. God knows how you've spliced sentences together from nouns and verbs."

She sat down again and swiped at her brow with a starched hankie. Sweat bubbled up like large transparent pimples on her forehead as she stared at me.

"You, Miss Delene..." her voice cracked "...are capable of learning." Her face was flushed and sweaty as if she had just completed a race. "I can see the disbelief marooned in your eyes. You have had the misfortune of letting others think for you." Olivia McKenna shoved the damp hankie into her purse. She glanced around the room slowly as if invisible enemies were lurching forward and were about to pounce on her. Her large fist thumped the small desk. "Incapable of learning what."

My first lesson ended on that note. What followed were pages of lines filled with red dots. I had to print on the red dots only. I connected all the words together and began to read in full sentences.

"The brain, oh how I love thee, how I love thee," shouted Olivia McKenna, clutching at her heart.

"The dot at the end of the sentence," Olivia McKenna said hesitantly, "is referred to as the period, a rather boring climax to end on. No doubt it was concocted by the British." She smiled bravely. "You can make it more interesting, Miss Delene, by referring to it as a ball, and by drawing two ears on the ball. You may call it a rabbit." She took a deep breath before she continued. "This exercise will teach you that the rabbit comes to a full stop at the end of a sentence." She fumbled in her purse as if she had spotted something crawling at the bottom of it and then eyed me directly.

"Now we shall go to the beginning of the sentence, Miss Delene. Should you be wondering why I started at the end of the sentence, rather than the beginning, it is quite simple. Some people have to know where to stop before they begin."

Olivia McKenna removed a package of McDonald's Export A cigarettes from her pocket and asked, "Would you mind if I fed my lungs?" I shook my head no. Her voice seemed to come from behind a cloud of smoke. She inhaled deeply once again and in a raspy voice announced, "The beginning of a sentence always requires a capital letter." She passed me a sheet of paper and asked me read aloud. *My lungs are black.* Smoke advanced to the ceiling. Hacking and coughing, she asked me to colour the capital letter with a green pencil. "Very good, very good, but there is more, Miss Delene." She smiled as a puff of smoke whistled out of her mouth. "Proper nouns such as names and places require capital letters as well as the pronoun I. Language has a law unto its own. It is riddled with rules." She wrote another sentence and passed it to me. *The city of Paris is located in France.* "Colour the beginning of the sentence green and the proper nouns red, Miss Delene!" I coloured correctly.

Olivia McKenna's grey face appeared from behind a cloud of smoke. A butt clung to the end of her lip like a cold sore.

"You have begun to colour your world, Miss Delene. Amen. Amen," she declared passionately.

Marriage has filled Daniel Peter's life with colour. Their bedroom walls, papered in pale blue, explode with butterflies from sheaves of tall grass. The pantry is a yellow meadow of buttercups and navy blue shelves, displaying hand-painted glass jars and old china plates. Anna has braided a rug for the living room with swirls of red and green and blue running together like children playing tag. Two white tulips, open-faced and snappy, sip from the morning dew beside the house. The bulbs were tucked into the Cape Breton soil by Anna in the fall. She had purchased them from the Vesey Seed Catalogue in Prince Edward Island. They were a new breed from Holland.

"A piece of Europe again for love," beamed Anna. She plans to nurture them with spoonfuls of showers and two good knees.

# twenty-five

There is a secret I want to take into my mother's house. It is the secret that started when I answered the phone to a soft-spoken male voice. The voice asked to speak to either Alfred or Albert Delene. The man left a number for one of them to phone as soon as possible. Albert made the call. It was answered by a priest in St. Mary's Parish. A man named Jack McCluskey had asked the priest to phone Ste. Noire Parish. He informed the priest that it was urgent that he contact my brothers.

Two days later, as thunder rolled over the city like a runaway boulder, Alfred and Albert faced the dying Jack McCluskey in his hospital bed. He looked up at them with eyes that edited the last of life's struggles and said simply, "I am your father. For what it's worth to you, I've lived and loved most of my life on the waves. Delivering small cargo to big ports to keep sailing. One woman anchored my conscience and that was your mother. I didn't track you down to ask for your forgiveness, but for you to forgive yourselves for knowing the truth."

And then he fell asleep. The sixty-year-old, one-hundred-pound speck of a man as brown as a raisin from too many suns called out to Alfred and Albert from his dreams.

They took me with them to visit Jack on their next visit. Jack, in his delirium, called me Adele. He begged my forgiveness.

"You were too good for me," he cried out. My brothers turned their eyes from the dying man, from the stranger leaking out his heart to Mama's ghost. A heart machine hummed. I watched as they looked solemnly around the room.

The dying man rambled on. "I should have followed you. I knew where you were going, and what you'd given up. That job..."

The room had the aroma of a salt wave. He was delirious as he pleaded with heaven to follow its course, as if he were out on the sea and had seen something coming to meet him. An old priest came in to give him the last rites. Jack opened his eyes. Reaching for my hand, he cried out, "Jesus Christ, woman, can you forgive a dying fool?"

The priest whispered in Latin between our hands. Jack never finished his sentence about "that job" until two days later. We learned that Mama had enrolled in a dress designer class. Her work was so impressive she was asked to go to New York to work for some big company.

"The seasons should have been fairer for you, dear woman. You could have fashioned an angel's wing," whispered Jack, in a weary voice.

I remember my mother running her hands along material she had laid out on the kitchen table. It was the colour of a milky white moon. She kept pulling threads along the edges until it was perfectly even. And then she cut it in three pieces. Without a pattern, she stored them all in her head. A day later, she wrapped a full skirt around my waist. I stood still as she pinned the sleeveless bodice to the skirt.

She sewed it by hand that evening. The next morning a woman picked up the beautiful dress for her niece in California. With the scraps, she made the same dress for Lizzie.

These are the abilities of Adele Delene that would have impressed New York. But she had traded these abilities in when she returned to Ste. Noire with her identical visible sins. The hands that could have fashioned an angel's wing took up belts and kindling and handfuls of sugar to sweeten the wounds in her life.

Jack lived on for a few more weeks, sipping on black tea and soft pudding, my brothers feeding him from a spoon. What he fed them were his failings and their mother's strengths.

At night, after I went to bed, I could hear them going over things Jack McCluskey had brought into the light. They whispered Mama's name in soft tones. Walked through old storms. Remembered the two cowboy vests she had made them, on their eighth birthday. The Carnation Milk cans she saved for hooves. And the fudge faces, cut in a circle with coconut for hair and raisins for the eyes, that always appeared on cold winter nights.

Together, for the first time, Alfred and Albert were grieving for Mama's life and death. I pulled my blanket up over my head and wept along with them.

A week later, at Jack's bedside, he reached for my hand. Then something yielded. Jack's hand fell out of mine, releasing it gently on the sheet. His lungs gave the death whistle. That's what Albert had said the dying always save for the finale. Jack whistled hard.

He had to with all that sea air in his lungs. We left the hospital shortly afterwards and went out for something to eat. There was not much for my brothers to do. Jack's wish was to be cremated and his ashes scattered over the waves. He left nothing behind but an old wooden boat with his identity. My brothers had it hauled from the marina and set it up on planks in their backyard. They gutted its intestines and gave it new life along with a new name. They smiled as they worked on *Gulliver*. They appeared more content than I'd ever seen them as they scraped and polished the boat. Perhaps the man who had not asked for their forgiveness knew they would find it, just where he had hoped they would.

I know that this knowledge would settle my mother's nerves if she were here. She would take comfort in the fact that a dying man may always tell the truth. Mrs. Landry would go further and say that it was the last rites that hauled it out of him and shook up his soul. He should have done the honourable thing in the beginning.

I wondered if my mother would have told me about my father had she known what was to come. I could tell her that I'd liked Jack McCluskey. That as a woman today, I, too, was drawn to the rusty voice that spit words off his tongue. I looked for resemblances of my brothers in his sunken face. Traces of them appeared in his quick smile. In the rugged jawline that seemed to slice into the sheets. I watched as Alfred and Albert traced the man for similarities to take with them for private moments. I imagined

Mama in Jack McCluskey's arms, close enough to water to drown out the stains.

He had offered her whatever a wandering man could offer a woman on a blue wave, with twin boys at her breast. My own conception must have been dull compared to my brothers. My father would have waited until Jack McCluskey's sons sank into a deep sleep before he rapped on the porch door with January's crest seeping into his veins. He would have complained about the cold, standing there beside the burning spruce in the kitchen stove. She may have warmed him up with thick pea soup. It would be after he thawed out that her worries would begin. She would have washed away all traces that a man had been near her, as my father crept away a few hours later through the snow, as silent as a shooting star. He may or may not have wondered what he'd left behind.

I recall her telling Mrs. Landry that she was two months along when he took off and never returned. For a moment, I had wished that Jack McCluskey was my father, too, but then I remembered Daniel Peter as he carried me down the stairs the night my mother died. The man who always did the honourable thing, at the honourable moment, wept openly against my cold skin.

I have been tasting Ste. Noire with my tongue and the rain on my skin for a week since my return. Under a beaded, black sky, the first Tuesday of my return, I collected raindrops on my tongue. I swallowed them slowly like a host, Corpus Christi, Body of Christ, coating my insides. I went down under the wharf, where years before, kids had fastened an old plank for a diving board. What remains of the plank belongs to the ants and spiders of Ste.

Noire for their own feasts. I took off my shoes and pulled up my skirt. My legs turned red. The seagulls flew over the plank and squawked in threatening voices.

"It is me, Mari-Jen. I have come to dance under the wharf," I shouted.

In the distance, the faint sound of music rippled in with the tide. Of musical waves. It was coming from a fishing boat a few miles offshore. I listened to it for a while before walking back towards the road. A dog barked farther up the shore road, wagging its tail and following behind two young children. They turned and spoke to the barking head. "Be quiet, Spooky, we're only going to school!"

The disciplined dog bowed its head, but kept pace with the children. Black and white, Spooky sat like a stone at the bus stop as the orange school bus drove out of sight. The dog turned its head in my direction as I walked along the road. I saw the milky white scalp over its eyes. Then its nose dropped to the ground as it manoeuvred its way towards me. Head still down, hunting for a scent. It beat a new black and white fear in me. The old dog lifted its head, barked, and then blinked its white eyes, as if I were guiding it in my direction with my voice. I felt its warm tongue trace my closed fist as if it were an ice-cream cone. I opened my hand and it drank from my sweat. Spooky wagged his tail and continued to taste parts of me. My wrist, my face, my eyes. I stood beside the road talking to the blind dog. The dog listened intently to my secrets, and then left with them through a path in the tall grass.

I watched as the dog reappeared on the crest of a hill, a short distance from my grandparents' old house.

# twenty-six

The American who bought my grandparents' old house turned out to be an artist born in Italy. John Mino flew the American flag alongside the Canadian flag in front of the house.

Atlantic fog sipped in the seams of Old Glory and the Maple Leaf. Seagulls flew above them and landed on top of the flagpole. Squawked at the two countries flapping beneath their feet. On windless days the flags hung like colourful scrub-rags at rest from harsh labour. He has painted the house a moss green with yellow trimmings. It resembles a fresh garden salad at a distance. Demolished the old barn.

We met as he came out of a cold May wave. Smiling. His wet hand extended. His voice a musical lilt. "I'd like to meet your friend," he shouted to Anna as we picked shells along the shore for her garden. Anna waved him over to us.

"This my friend, Mari-Jen." He smiled deeply and kissed us both on the hand. Anna pretended that she was flushed, but she laughed heartily.

John Mino had visited Anna and Daniel Peter at their home on two or three occasions. He has painted images of Poland for Daniel Peter as a gift of remembrance for Anna on her birthday. Daniel Peter believes that the true artist is privy to eternal images.

The colour of the evening came from an orange-red blister on the dying sun as Daniel Peter walked along the shore road. He knocked gently on John Mino's door. His request came out of a soft voice. "I have image of old country you bring back for my Anna eye."

Anna's village of Opole is now dozing and dreaming above their bed. It is a rather ghostly painting of empty houses, pale as a frightened heart. The only hint of colour comes from a solitary gold flame in one of the windows. There is no mistaking the terror in the eye of the moon. It is already crying. In Daniel Peter's village of Namyslow, an old house rises from the embrace of a green hill. There are no people in either painting. The lacy calligraphy of the clouds appears as an omen. Heaven was about to drop its veil.

I had not gone down to my grandparents' with my mother when she sold the house. She mentioned him briefly, the artist who was planning on coming to Ste. Noire on visits.

A week after our introduction, we met again down by the sea and sat on the breakwater spilling out our lives to each other. Between tides, I was living with friends. He wasn't. His frame was slight compared to the long copper fingers he used to stir the tides of Ste. Noire on canvas.

"What brought you here?" I asked.

"The sea, Mari-Jen," he grinned. "It's so mournful, it won't let you go. Keeps me dipping for more." His eyes kept watching the waves.

"You've come a long way for a dipping," I teased as he turned to look at me.

Sister Thérèse said I had artistic abilities when I started school at six years of age. I drew Lizzie with her button eyes.

Sometimes I coloured them blue with my crayons. Sometimes they were brown. Then grey. Then green, like the sea. I always drew Lizzie's eyes much bigger than they actually were and stuffed the pictures in my pocket and pretended that she was at school with me. I told John Mino about my drawings and about a particular school picture that I'd wanted to keep but couldn't afford to.

John Mino invited me down to see what he had done with my grandparents' old house. He said the mornings are when the house is on its best behaviour. The light is what does it. I went down on a Monday morning in early July.

A painting of a pirate ship sails merrily along the deep sea-blue walls in the kitchen. Above the long wooden table, a glass shelf displays a row of plants. Their pale leaves crawl down the wall like green spiders reaching for the sugar-bowl. The floor glistens like a puddle full of fresh spring rain. He has turned the living room into a studio. Deep forest-green walls, smooth as moss, are covered in paintings. The largest painting on the wall is of a seagull in flight. Its wings are folding from the force of the wind over the sea. A furious look is in its eyes. Two or three more gulls ride on a wave, their beaks piercing into their chests. There is no hope for survival in this painting. On the south wall, a painting of an old man hangs above the seagulls. His head is bowed, face smiling into a blue sweater. A big dog, brown as cocoa, sniffs at his heels.

In a charcoal sketch, two young boys are crossing a river in a makeshift raft. A greedy, daring look on their faces. Up the stairs and into the small landing, I stood for a moment before going into Aunt Clara's room. The blue on the walls is as silent as an even breath. The ceiling is flooded with blue-white clouds. The room is stripped of all furniture except for one wicker chair. It sits in the middle of the floor, dressed in a pale yellow cushion. The wide pine floors are smeared a forest green with warm streaks of gold. There are no paintings on the walls in this room. On the window sill lies a convoy of old seashells.

"It's my inspiration room," said John Mino, as he walked in behind me. "I've always felt that someone is watching me in here." I told him about Aunt Clara and that this room belonged to her. John Mino smiled when I told him that Aunt Clara inspired the saints to enter through the window. He told me to look around while he brewed fresh coffee. The door to Uncle Jule's room was closed. I did not want to go in. I went back down the stairs into the green room. A sketch pad filled with pencil drawings lay open on the drawing table. On the last page was a sketch of a young girl. She sits on a step holding a rag doll in her arms and wearing a dress and rubber boots. Her hair straddles her shoulders, Flips out like paper wings made for make-believe angels. Her eyes are sorrowful above a sprinkle of freckles. Large button eyes on the rag doll stare out like someone ordered into darkness. He had remembered what I had told him about my school picture. The one my mother had to return because she couldn't afford to buy it.

The rag doll resembled Lizzie, although I had not gone into much detail about the doll.

From the corner of my eye, I caught a glimpse of a painting of a young woman. It was leaning against the wall on the floor. She stared back at me with black, pensive eyes.

Her mouth a flame of fire and smiles. A snake-like braid crawling over her left shoulder. Red ribbon weaving in and out of the hair. Dripping like blood over her breasts. She was beautiful.

John Mino walked into the studio as I was admiring the painting. "She is...was my lover," he said, placing the two cups of coffee on the drawing table. "She refused to marry a travelling paintbrush. Maria is a dancer in New York, but we were born in the same village in Italy."

I stared into the dark pools made by the coffee. I could feel her presence in this room. Felt her eyes pruning my flesh. Tasted the salt from her brow. Music pumped in my head. I imagined her swirling around the studio. Letting the snake loose to smear John Mino with her blood. John Mino could feel it too. I could see it in the way he looked at the painting.

"I am working on something for you, Mari-Jen," he said as he held up the sketch book. "I will turn it into a painting. Is there something you would like me to add?" He smiled.

"Yes," I answered. "You can put a ribbon in my hair."

I walked slowly along the shore road on my way home. The tide was low. Fog swam out from the planks under the wharf. It looked like smoke. I walked along the edge of the water and down towards the planks and looked in at where I had spied on Aqua and Wave. In the sand bed were broken lobster claws, crinkled chip bags, and an empty wine bottle. Its label had been peeled away. I was either too late or too early for any kind of love under the wharf.

Anna said she suspected that John Mino was heavy in the heart. That his spirit followed him at his heels. He had chased it out of his soul and let something else move in. Something that only made him smile in his dreams. Anna swears that dreams are great matchmakers. It is in a dream that a man can truly realize that he is in love. When he wakes up, he has no one to rationalize this with but himself.

I thought about the dancer that night. Thought her into my dream. She danced her way along the wharf calling out to John Mino. He appeared in a robe of mist. She too was naked. They jumped into the sea together and swam under the wharf. Turned into Aqua and Wave. They continued their dance to music from an invisible violin. Danced her to him. Him to her. She offered the first gift. The red ribbon from her hair. He swiped a brush from mid-air. Painted bright yellow wings along her outstretched arms that carried them up and out over the deep water. They took the music with them when they fled. Left nothing behind but silence, seaweed, and sand.

I wanted the dance that lovers danced, and the music that broke their limbs and made the skin speak.

A woman doctor at that hospital had asked me if I had ever engaged in a sexual relationship with anyone. She drew circles with her pen while she waited for my answer. Her black bangs were salted with grey. She was in her forties. Some of the patients referred to her as the Old Grey Mare because she hadn't married. A dull silver cross protruded from under her blouse. She always looked distracted and hungry. I wondered why she was so thin, but then I remembered watching from my window as she nibbled her lunch on a bench beside the building. Always a carrot and a tomato.

She washed them down with something from a Thermos and then entered a side door. She was watching me watching her when she'd asked me the question about sex.

"What are you thinking about at this moment?" she'd asked.

"Were you a nun?" I blurted out.

"No, I'm not even a Catholic." She started to say something else but then paused. The cross was inside her blouse. Two of the buttons were undone. I waited for her to ask the next question.

"You didn't answer my question, Mari-Jen."

My answer was no.

"Do you have any desire to be with a man?" She was staring at me as if my answer would pass her by and she'd have to go looking for it.

"All humans have a need to bond with someone," explained the doctor as she gritted her teeth and drew more circles. "Do you understand what I am getting at, Mari-Jen?"

I knew what she was talking about. "Your getting at 'it,'" I offered slowly.

"At what, Mari-Jen?" The doctor's voice rose with agitation, but my thoughts were elsewhere. I imagined the warm breeze coming off the sand in Ste. Noire. Off Aqua and Wave after their bonding and panting beneath their desserts of Black Cat cigarettes under the wharf. I knew what this women wanted to hear. I didn't like her, but had to see her when my favourite doctor was away.

"I want to wait," I heard myself say.

"You want to wait until you are involved with someone?" she inquired from her circle.

"I want to wait for a low tide," I informed her. She stopped doodling and looked at me sharply.

"That doesn't make sense, Mari-Jen, I thought you were making progress here."

"It makes sense to me. It made sense to them when they were at it under the wharf."

She swiped the bangs from her brow. She looked like she had been hit with a mop. "Who are they?" she asked annoyingly.

"They are the couple I used to spy on under the wharf in Ste. Noire."

"Did they know you saw them?" she asked.

"No," I confessed, as if I was about to be punished.

"Did your brothers see them as well?"

"No, they were gone away. But I told the rag dolls."

"Why wouldn't you tell someone? Why would you waste such a secret on rags?" She sounded as if she didn't believe me.

"Because I couldn't tell my mother," I answered.

I was afraid to tell my mother what I had seen. She would have forbidden me to go down to the wharf. There was always danger and fear in the scenes I brought to her. The encounter with Aunt Clara and Uncle Jule. I can taste fear in my mouth, before it goes anywhere else. It idles in my throat like a piece of chewing gum that is hard to swallow. It was there, the fear, when Daniel Peter drove down the Church Road a few nights after I came home. It was dark. We drove past the convent. Most of the lights were out. I watched as a hand pulled down the shade of a window on the ground floor. Two silhouettes appeared. They moved slowly. Back and forth. Criss-crossing as they moved in the window.

She is still in there, old Mother Superior. I can taste her a mile away. I know she is no longer at the school. Someone said she is retired. I have only to hear the ringing of a school bell and she comes to me. Her eyes burning. Arms outstretched. White hands firm and ready to grip something in her path. Talons on the loose.

What scares Mari-Jen?
Black and white scares Mari-Jen.
Who scares Mari-Jen?
She scares Mari-Jen.
Who is she, who scares Mari-Jen?
She is Mother Superior, who is black and white, who
    scares Mari-Jen.
Why does she scare Mari-Jen?
Mari-Jen knows why. Mari-Jen does not want to be
    scared.

This is my secret dialogue. Nobody knows that it lives on my tongue. Sometimes I can taste it when I hear the nuns singing in the choir, and they forget to smile.

# twenty-seven

There is a scoop in the earth where my uncle Jule's fish shed once stood. A carpet of white sand under my feet, spread out like a sheet over the ghost of my past. I am shouting words into the waves and listening for their echo. I feel as if I have never left the liquid edges of Ste. Noire.

In the distance, a thin, black cloud coils the tip of the church steeple like the tail of a cat around a fence post. The church bell is ringing. Marcel told me that the bell needed repair. The trouble is in the gong, he said. It needs a good going over to get it working up to pitch.

He is no longer pale. A faint pink blush swims under his skin. He is much leaner now for his role as the new curate. The newly ordained Marcel returned to Ste. Noire a month before my return. He is no longer making believe in his father's barn. This is the real thing. The souls that come to him are bleeding from original sins and mortal confinements. Father Marcel is their fresh cloth, on loan to Ste. Noire until the old parish priest recovers from his illness.

He is a welcome host to Ste. Noire. The village people refer to him as a spiritual beacon. They believe only a saint could have been flushed from that house. His mother is safe from broken glass and whiskey insults now. His father has been put away. This means he will live out the remainder of his miserable life in striped flannel and bibs. Inside this flannel, he plays out his madness in a Home, swirling his knife like Zorro with a sword.

They can't imagine that a man like him could have ever fathered a priest. But through some miraculous intervention they know that Ste. Noire has been blessed by this mishap of whiskey and faith. And now Marcel belongs to them, the harmed parish people, like some orphaned waif returned to the flock from a storm.

People said Marcel's father cried out in fear when the young curate held his hand. He couldn't understand why Marcel called him father and then wept into his hands. They believe Marcel has the special touch. In his hands are the powers to cast out evil and sickness. On his left hand are two special scars from Mother Superior's strap.

Marcel's siblings surround their mother like dogs on a meaty bone. They are harmless married couples whose commerce comes from seasons of full traps and balsamed hands. They are not pretentious people. They save their money and their money saves them. Their homes are perched on the top of the shore hill where white waves and hurricanes come into full view.

Marcel came to dinner one Sunday evening and smiled sweetly at his surroundings. Anna spread out her best lace tablecloth. She had gathered wildflowers from the fields and arranged them in her crystal vase on the table. White, piping hot dumplings swam in a large bowl of chicken stew beneath two over-hanging daisies. Everyone bowed their heads as Anna thanked the God of Abraham for such plump Cape Breton chickens and good company. Marcel answered, "Amen," as he eyed the fat dumplings.

Anna said later that Marcel would make a good rabbi and a good husband for me. Daniel Peter smiled and shook his head. He knew that Anna was being kind, offering me what love had offered her.

"It be true," said Anna, as we walked along the shore one evening. "Your friend make good husband if he be rabbi."

I smiled at her. "He is married to God, Anna, that is all Marcel ever wanted."

"Same like rabbi, Mari-Jen, but rabbi give God break and get wife." Her hands waved in mid-air. "Maybe God sorry for this, maybe not." We laughed out loud.

There are moments in my life that will belong to Marcel alone. We were ambushed behind the school one afternoon. It had been our turn to clean the erasers, pound the white dust out of them against the school. I loved this errand with Marcel, leaving the dusty moments of our lives sealed forever in Ste. Noire. I heard the voices behind us getting closer.

"What in the hell are youse two doing, kissing?" Shouted the biggest of the group. He was a pudgy youth with dark bulging eyes. The boys were about Marcel's age.

"Ah, fuck," spoke the tallest of the three. "If it ain't the pope and the retard." Marcel remained calm. My teeth chattered. We turned to avoid our attackers, but they kept advancing towards us. "Let's pounce the pope," another voice shouted.

Their hands crawled through the chalk-filled air and pulled Marcel to the ground. Savagely they kicked at his back and legs. I knelt on the ground and cradled his face. Blood ran down his face into the open fountain of his mouth. The ringing of the school bell sent the boys scurrying down over the hill, leaving their victims to their white unfinished pleasure.

Marcel begged me not to tell Alfred and Albert. He didn't believe in revenge. "There is a reason for everything that falls, Mari-Jen, you will understand it someday."

I didn't mention a word to anyone. Not even to Sister Thérèse. I trusted whatever Marcel said.

I will miss my friend when he leaves Ste. Noire. I see reflections of our past life in the glass dome that Alfred brought to me from Europe. I shake it to watch the two swirling figures in the white flakes. They are almost invisible to the naked eye as they stumble and fall. But I know who they are. The closest I ever came to a dance is in there in the storm, tangled in white limbs and a reason for the fall.

Anna and Daniel Peter have taken to dancing in the kitchen. Her soft white arms hold him gently as they swirl past the green frills of plants on the window ledge, past the wood stove, the table dressed in daisies. Without music. Only the hum of his voice in her ear. They come to a halt under the kitchen light turned moon, and Anna takes her final bow. The people of Ste. Noire have come to like and respect the quiet, gentle man that they still refer to as the D.P. They like Anna's warm personality.

They are no trouble, they believe, not knowing what they mean by trouble themselves. Daniel Peter has helped the parish men repair the church roof, restore its stained pews, fix its old windows. And had the decency, they said, to work with his cap off the whole time. If they didn't know any better, they'd swear the man was a Catholic.

I smile when I remember Mrs. Landry telling my mother that it was a bigger sin on your soul to steal a priest and turn him into a married man than it was to marry a Protestant. She would have believed that Anna wanted to lure Marcel from the church with dumplings and daisies. But I know that he is safe in the dome where he belongs, where no one can reach him in his white pleasure.

# twenty-eight

The day my mother died she smelled of creolin and Vick's Rub, an old combination to take to your grave. The Vick's jar was visible on the window ledge, the smeared lid on the bed. Daniel Peter said it was an infection in her heart that caused the final explosion. Between the explosion and death came the hard bite. Mrs. Landry would have attributed this final act as some form of saintly knowledge, to bite into your rosary like that. Some foresight into heaven that beckoned you to swallow your prayers whole before stepping into the light. Mama would have begged for forgiveness for not finishing her prayers. The bead in her mouth was from the fourth decade of her rosary. Icy blue, it lay there in her open mouth, like a crystal host waiting to be swallowed. An appetizer for the dying.

Early evening, at this moment, balsam marinates the flames that thicken in the old wood stove of my mother's house. I am burning the kindling and wood that I found in the woodbox. It was my choice to come back to the house on my own. I am so cold my bones dance under my skin. My hands move instinctively to the orange flames of the fire. It is the end of May. The end of a muggy, warm day that turned cool at suppertime.

My mother's favourite season was fall. God lessens his warnings in the colder months. Or maybe he goes into hibernation. Except that October when I turned five and my brothers wore Carnation Milk cans on their feet when they turned into cowboys.

The paper carnations that I'd cut from the Carnation cans and glued to the stove warmer are still visible. They are faded somewhat, having been in bloom in the lost seasons of my life.

The four wooden chairs are tucked under the table, upright and proper like old maids at cards, ready to cheat. My mother's domestic commandments ruled this house. The neatly stacked firewood, the starched curtains. Sheets, pillow slips, dishtowels, and doilies—a clothesline parade of square, rectangle, and oblong remnants fluttering in Monday breezes. All bleached, then dipped into a powder that gave the wash a pale blue hue. Cleanliness was her art. Once a stranger's camera had given her the simple pleasures of the domestic artist that she was, a frame or two of our lives stolen and carted off across the border to hang in some fancy gallery. Mama believed the man who took pictures of our clothesline, one summer, was an American photographer from a big city, where, she'd laughed, "they don't hang clothes on a line with care or anything else for that matter."

There is no calendar on the wall now. Nobody keeping time any more in Adele Delene's kitchen. The storm months have vanished. The old thunder cot (that's what Alfred and Albert named it) rests along the back wall in the front room. On its cotton cover, orange marigolds poke out from behind a fence like the faces of sunburned children. Mrs. Landry had brought Mama the material to cover the cot.

"Look what my sister sent me to make curtains with," her hurried voice cried, coming over the step. "Sweet Jesus, she sent enough material to cover the windows in Buckingham Palace."

The old cot creaks and heaves as I sit on the edge. Beneath my feet, an oilcloth square blooms with red roses cropped by an edging of delicate blue-green leaves. Mama had seen this oilcloth in the store window one Sunday morning as we waited for the Co-op truck to take us to church. A gift to herself is how she described it. Something she let into her life between penances. Alfred and Albert carried the oilcloth home through the field on their shoulders, marching warriors with the prize beast.

There are few pictures on the front-room walls. Mama never did keep any of our school pictures. She could never afford them. She eyed them carefully before returning them with the message "Not buying" spelled out across the envelopes. The picture of the Last Supper, with the twelve apostles, surveying the room with dull, heavy eyes. The hungry traitor and Jesus both look full. For a moment I imagine Mrs. Landry snoring soundly under their gaze after a storm. Here on the thunder cot, she'd ease into a deep sleep and dig into her subconscious for her heaviest sins, then swat at them in mime with the sign of the cross.

Above the door, a picture of an old house rises from a wash of wildflowers. You can see the thatched roof. A dim candlelight lingers in an upstairs room. I'd turned my imagination on that flame as a teenager. I imagined a scorned, downtrodden woman behind the lace curtain who still waited in agony for her husband to return to her.

Mama said the picture belonged to her grandmother Alfreda, a women of sparse conscience who literally drove her husband to his grave with a team of oxen. Mama's bedroom door is closed. The doorknob is made of heavy glass shaped like fingerprints on the edge of a piecrust. I slide my fingers around the knob and the door opens with a slight squeak. Her bed is made up with her favourite quilt, a multitude of colours that she had hand-sewn together, beside the kitchen stove, the fall before I started school. She had scolded herself for the mistake she made with the red patch. It was larger than the others. It lay like a stain of blood in the middle of the quilt, as if she had left the imprint of her labour there for all to see. I remember once when I had the death fever, as Mrs. Landry called it, my mother had taken the quilt off her bed and wrapped it around me to sweat out the fever. I felt like a kitten must feel put in a bag to be drowned. My breath sucked in at the red patch until Mama let me loose and held me in her arms beside the fire. She sang me to sleep with a song.

My feet are soundless on the thick pine boards on the stairs. The faint smell of lye soap lingers in the wood.

I can see my cot at the top of the stairs. It has been stripped bare and is covered with a piece of clear plastic. Alfred and Albert's bed is empty. It looks worn out and forbidden like an old leaky boat. I look at the spot where Daniel Peter had found me sitting with the dolls. The dolls are gone.

There is not much space up here. I had imagined that it was wider, this open space with its ribs of two-by-fours and pine footing. The chimney is very close to my cot. It leans on a slant, this pillar of heat, blowing smoke over Adele Delene's roof once again. The heat that surrounds me tightens like a pair of old arms that will never hold again.

May has insulated the cubbyhole with cool dry air. It greets my hand like the touch of a stranger as I seek out my treasures. Out first comes my little childhood book. With their brightly coloured wings the butterflies dance out of darkness. I cannot remember having put the book in the cubbyhole. Pages of underlined nouns and verbs crinkle in my hand like dried-out leaves.

There is something else I want to find. I feel her soft, worn limbs and plunk her into the light of day. Lizzie with her button eyes stares back at me. I hold on to her like a medal. The patron saint of dusty isolation has been crowned with a halo of cobwebs. There are scraps of paper I do not recognize, dated the summer of 1964, in Alfred's handwriting. "Poems by Alfred Delene" is scrawled in ink. The first one is titled "The Confessional."

> We ran like shivers through the summer grass
> After confessing in boxes tinted black
> To moments of temporary thrills
> That amounted to nothing more than a penance.

The second poem is titled "Identity." He has separated himself from Albert in this poem.

> Je suis,
>     Je suis,
> Je suis,

I am,
I am,
I am,
Somewhere between two tongues
Without a mother.

Alfred was always the more sensitive of the two. He was the one who tucked the quilt up under my chin on winter mornings before the heat from the old stovepipe swallowed up the chill in the air. It was Alfred who knelt beside me the Sunday I made my first communion. On guard and paternal, he may have shamed Mama with all the attention he gave me. Her son, turned father, her unknown poet, Albert and I would never obtain absolution, she believed, no matter how carefully we swallowed.

The house is growing colder as I am ready to leave. I will leave behind words that I could not have spoken openly to my mother. "*Ego te absolvo*. I do absolve. You are forgiven, Mama, for all your red stains."

Outside the bare window, the day is dipping into night. Leaves are falling in drunken directions. A sudden streak of lightning breaks through the clouds. A sliver of silver silence follows as the sky seals out the day. Thunder claps. And the rain falls in all its white fury, and spits into the earth. The evergreens are full of wind and rain. Their thick green branches blunder like a wild beast without sight. I can see them through the upstairs window while listening to a loud banging coming from the porch.

Anna and Daniel have gone to Antigonish. They will not return until later. Bang . . . bang . . . bang . . .

Mari-Jen is all alone. I speak to myself out loud as I drop Lizzie and the papers at my feet and descend the stairs slowly. A song enters my head, or is it a verse? I cannot remember. My voice is light as I recite it. May showers bring up the May flowers. No, it's April showers. I correct myself at the bottom of the stairs.

A bolt of lightning is my candle as I reach for the light switch. A dim bulb comes on over my head in the hallway. I am so thankful that my brothers had the power turned on last month.

The back door is a few feet from where I am standing. It is the door Mama used to make her escape. In that storm. Bang ... bang ... bang ...

The wind is in the house. I can hear it making itself welcome in Mama's kitchen. Something falls over and crashes to the floor. The wind comes uninvited into the living room. It hides under the cot and sends out the dust. Bang ... bang ... bang ... A flash of lightning turns the room white. The walls, the pictures, the floor, the cot. I am almost blinded by its light. I walk towards the window as thunder jigs over the roof.

Mari-Jen will not go out in this storm. My voice is dry. I pull the blind up and look out. The trees, the fields, the road, and the puddles of Ste. Noire are those of my childhood. But they are safe. Mrs. Landry's house is a skeleton and its bones are breaking one by one. Bang ... bang ... bang ...

"Hot and cold, the devil's voice is bold." That's what my brothers sang in French during storms. I know that there are no voices in a storm. Mari-Jen does not hear voices. I repeat it even louder. Mari-Jen does not hear voices. Daniel Peter said it is only a collision of hot and cold air exploding. Bang...bang. God's voice is silent.

The house is very cold as I move towards the kitchen. Mari-Jen must keep warm. My words are trapped in my teeth. I am wearing a sweater over my cotton dress. Bang... bang...bang...I remember the quilt as I walk into my mother's room and pull on the overhead light. It slides off the bed with ease and I wrap myself in Adele Delene's patchwork warmth.

My muscles unwind. Free my feet as I move towards the kitchen. Switch on the light. A holy water bottle has fallen to the floor. Small pieces of glass swim in a pool of water, like silver minnows.

A small fire is still burning in the stove. I can see the porch door swaying from where I am standing in the kitchen. Lightning circles the old outhouse as I look out the open porch door. It fills the half-moon design my brothers cut out in the outhouse door. It skirts the board nailed across the door to keep it closed, flashes on the roof, and licks the boards holding down the rotting asphalt shingles. And then it leaves the old outhouse standing with its wooden Band-Aids to protect it. Bang...bang...bang...I have to pull hard on the porch door, with both hands, against the force of the wind to close it, but finally I fasten the hook securely in place.

I smile as I speak to myself in French. Mari-Jen chased the wind out of the house like a cat.

Black rain continues to assault the windows and roof. I am as safe here as anywhere in Ste. Noire. This second. This minute. This hour. Under my mother's quilt. It is six minutes past nine o'clock, and I am grounded in my old rubber boots. I found them in the porch.

Anna and Daniel Peter's house is in darkness. They have not returned home yet. I check the fire in the stove as it suffocates under a slow blue flame. At eleven minutes past ten o'clock, a quarter moon is sneaking through the storm over Ste. Noire. Moons have been in here before, in Adele Delene's house, and traced the stolen paper map above her son's heads while they slept. Adele Delene died under a full moon. Perhaps before she died, the moon gave her a glimpse of the nightgown she was wearing and highlighted the red rose appliqué against her exploding heart. She had added the rose herself.

I take light steps as I go up the stairs. My old boots are wearing thin. Even the wind that I chased out of the house is silent. Gone down to the sea with the rain. The lightning and thunder following, rumbling as it goes. I am alone, in my house, under the quilt. Without a drop of rain noise. Without a song rehearsing in the eaves. Without a full moonbeam on my cot. Without a ghost to disturb my sleep.

# twenty-nine

Mother St. Pius, a passionate mix of pranks and prayers, will be the new Mother Superior of Ste. Noire school. She will begin her duties in September. Sister Thérèse will be her assistant. Some of the village people signal this as the end of good discipline and learning. The old Mother Superior is thick with arthritis, people say, but she could still chew the hind legs off a coyote, if she had to.

I am listening to these comments on a grey day in May, in the general store. From the window, behind the counter, I can see a fishing boat that has returned to the harbour. Seagulls beg above the salty deck for their meal. The wharf protrudes like a dark hand being pulled from a white sleeve.

"Somebody said the old nun is twisted like a ram's horn," calls out a woman's voice behind me.

"Nobody has seen hide nor habit of her since she came back from the hospital," answers the storekeeper.

"Them nuns keep things to themselves," adds the voice. "Nobody knows their joys or sorrows. That's how they want things. They'd never let on if someone was shooting at them. It has something to do with that vow of suffering they swear to, the poor souls. I hear they'll be shipping her out soon to some convent place for old nuns."

"I got nothing on that Sister Thérèse," says the store-keeper, "she's different than some of them. Either praying or crying. Makes me wonder how she finds time for working."

I do not offer an opinion. I don't think they expect me to. They had stared at me when I came into the store after I returned from the city, the way one would check out a leaking roof in search of the open crack. I stared back at them, not with indifference, but with a shy smile. They lowered their eyes and mumbled something as if to a child at their feet. After a couple of weeks, they believed I had been patched up sufficiently and would not crack open in public.

They now greet me with kind eyes. "That D.P.'s wife sure does a lot of baking," says the storekeeper when I put in my order. I smile back at her. "Her name is Anna."

I listen as the two women continue to gossip. They are absorbed by the changes in the convent, in Ste. Noire, in me.

I can read their worn faces. Other women have much more interesting lives and they know it. Especially Anna, who would rather maul her man than cry or pray in public. These women have stayed their lives with gossip over tobacco and loose tea.

Sister Thérèse had met me outside the church on Sunday and told me about her new position at the school. She seemed anxious to tell me herself before the word got out. "There is something I want to discuss with you, Mari-Jen. I will call you."

I wished her well. "Pray for me, Mari-Jen," she whispered between tears. She reminded me of a patient I knew in that hospital. Her name was Patsy, but most of the people called her Pesty. Patsy wore a lace panel curtain on her head like a veil when she roamed in and out of rooms, asking for prayers and forgiveness from everyone. Nobody ever knew what she wanted to be forgiven for. One evening Patsy came into my room and whispered, "You can't talk, can you." She leaned over my bed and began to sing, then left quietly with my jelly beans and fudge hidden under her veil.

When I left the store, they both smiled my way. I had offered very few words to their conversation. Outside the door, I could hear their hushed conversation.

"She's looking more like her mother every day. I heard them twins are hauling in the dough," said the voice. "They could sell a crow to a farmer."

"There's nothing stupid about that girl," adds the storekeeper. "She was hauling in every word we said. I heard she can get through a book as quick as anyone now."

Sister Thérèse had not mentioned Mother Superior or her illness to me.


Nor had I asked. I could smell something coming from Sister Thérèse's hands on Sunday. A liniment smell. A remedy for troubled limbs. It stayed in the air long after she left. I could feel my throat tighten, my tongue thicken with musty saliva. I imagined Sister Thérèse kneading her soft white hands into Mother Superior's flesh. Along the spine. Cracking knee joints. The vows of obedience throwing shadows on the walls. (I assumed this would be a nightly ritual.) Mother Superior's bones rippling under her palms. Her twisted limbs spreading out their agony. Her thin shrill of a voice. "Where did you learn to knead a woman, Sister Thérèse, in a sawmill?" She would be hard to please. To unravel. Day or night.

Sister Thérèse would not answer, of course. The vow of silence would force her to keep kneading. She would pray in whispers and remember her vows and weep silently for the pain of obedience.

I do not know when Mother Superior is leaving Ste. Noire. Or what memories she will take with her when she leaves. If any. Someone said that she liked to walk along the shore in the early evenings before her illness. They said she could be seen standing close to the cliff overlooking the sea, like a black ghost trimmed in white.

Ste. Noire Catholic School lies in the palm of the village below the church hill. My first visit back to the school is a dusty Friday afternoon.

In early summer, the schoolyard is a dust bowl of scarred earth patches from skipping ropes and dancing feet. Hopscotch squares and alley lanes. Red Rover athletes. Tattletales and slow brawls. Year-end scars and victories left behind for Mother Earth to swallow. In winter the snow angels will rise from the ground and dust themselves off to coast on the shiny blue hills.

Three young boys are huddled together on the ball field. Their books and scribblers at their feet, the pages flapping like the wings of furious hens.

The last busload of weary children descend over the hill. A small hand unfolds a white scrap of paper from the back window of the bus. Perhaps it is a paper dove or butterfly the hand has released over Ste. Noire. There is no way of telling from where I am standing at the main door of the school. The wind has given wings to the mysterious white smudge now floating easterly towards the church steeple.

Inside the school, the smell of cleaning compounds rises up the stairs to greet me. I can hear, but not see, the janitor move his broom in slow even strides along the auditorium. There is a silent pause, and the man behind the strides appears in the open doorway. He is surprised but not startled to see me. He is not much older than my brothers. His young face is lacerated by something even sharper than pain. His name, hand-sewn above his left shirt pocket, is Jerome. The letters are pure white against his navy blue shirt.

He knows that I am remembering the last time we met face to face. It was early fall, I tell myself quietly. He and his brother delivered a load of firewood to my mother for winter. I'd walked out to the woodpile, the axe dangling behind my back like a dog with a sharp tail.

"There's nobody here," says Jerome, in a flat voice. "Sister Thérèse had to go to the convent, she won't be long." He is watching my face for a performance. For something I can deliver without an axe. Jerome's thoughts melt from him like dirty sweat. He cannot comprehend why I am here on my own. Why I am reading the name on his shirt. Dressed in a pale blue skirt and sweater, my hair rolled in a French twist. There are no visible signs of undoneness about me.

I am twenty pounds heavier than the axe-carrying waif he remembers. The weight of my silence is absorbed in his gaunt face, every line flexed into injury because he feels I am ignoring or mocking him. I wait. Jerome's hand has not left the handle of the broom. His white knuckles retreat and go fishing for something in a white plastic bucket. A spray of green skirts along the floor. Some of it hits the wall. I watch it pool in a corner.

"What is that stuff called?" I ask, without looking at him. "I love the smell of it."

"I dunno," his voice drifts. "It's like wet, green sand. Settles things down while I sweep."

"Does it have a name?" His eyes avoid the label on the bucket that is facing him, as he continues to push the broom along the floor.

"How da hell do I know?" he retorts. "The nuns tell me what's in the fucken buckets. I don't have ta read."

He is moving along now like a child thrown from a game, head and shoulders bent over the broom. He knows I have figured out that he cannot read a word.

"It's Dustbane." I offer my information lightly, turning the bucket around with my foot. "That wet, green sand you're throwing around has a name."

"Whatever ya say," he fires over his shoulder at me in a liquid voice. "My wife could read, but she died of some kinda cancer in the spring."

Jerome moves slowly around the corner and into the furnace room. He comes back out in time to hear me say, "I'm sorry." He stares at me from a distance with a blank look.

"I heard that ya were kinda busted in the head after your mother died."

"I was. I ran out of words for a while." I shrug. I will not let him get to me now.

"How in the hell do them bastards cure that?"

"They use insulin. Drugs. Something else called shock therapy on some people." I frown.

"Jesus." Jerome half whistles. "I'm glad I ain't fucken foolish. Don't they rig your head with wires and nearly electrocute ya to hell?"

"No, I didn't have to have that done to me." He looks puzzled.

"Ya don't look like crazy Amos, I don't suppose ya'll be sniffing at tombstones like a dog looking for a place to piss. Now that Amos, that should be fucken wired if ya ask me." He shifts his line of questioning to my brothers. "I hear them two brothers of yours are raking in the dough." He shakes his head.

"They have their own business selling tombstones," I tell him. "They're doing all right."

"Selling tombstones," he gasps. Jerome stands back with a dull look on his face. In his limited world, people and events bewilder him. He walks away slowly towards the furnace room, then stops suddenly and turns his head towards me.

"My wife's name was Cecile," he says. "I made a wooden cross for her grave."

Silence and scenes gather around me in the empty auditorium. I remember the mound of fresh clay sinking into the ground, decorated in carnations on its descent. I had paid particular attention to that grave driving back to Ste. Noire. I don't know if it is his wife's grave.

I walk across the auditorium and take the stairs to the first floor. Along freshly painted moss-green walls, a small handprint resembling a leaf catches my eye. The paint tester has planted his or her mark under the stair railing for safe keeping. The village of Ste. Noire shines in from east to west through two long windows at the ends of the hallway. Brightly coloured doors lead into spacious classrooms. Grades primary to five are on this floor. To my left is the door I'd entered like a ghost. Invisible Mari-Jen offering up penance wedged into a ninety-degree angle. A smiling picture of Jesus, nailed to the wall, on duty to pick up the spills of my broken prayers. I know now why Jesus bleeds in public.

The title "Principal's Office" is spelled out in bold, black letters. Like some priceless jewel that forbids the human hand a touch, a collage of old school photos are encased under glass on the wall beside this door.

In the centre of the display, Margaret looks down at me with an angry, squinting look. Under the picture, printed by old Mother Superior's hand, are the words: "In God's Precious Garden There Blooms A Sweet Margaret Rose." Every word is capitalized. Sweet Margaret Rose is dressed in a pleated orange dress. A matching ribbon dangles from her straight hair like a dried orange peeling. She looks unsure whether to smile or look mysterious. I had caught her and her friends in the washroom mirror practising the "mysterious look," as she'd referred to it. "You just have to tilt your head and slant your eyes and slump one shoulder like the models do in magazines to get it right," I'd heard her say as I stood outside the door. The photographer may have thought she was falling asleep and bolted her back to an upright position for the picture.

Sister Thérèse has left the door to her office unlocked. Perhaps she assumes I will wait for her here. "Meet me at the school on Friday afternoon" was the phone message she'd left with Anna.

The door knob to the office turns without a sound. I enter a powder-blue haven. The off-white ceiling, twelve feet above my head, has the stark beauty of an ancient desert. I stand beside the door for a few minutes. The old lock has been removed from the door, to my relief. For a moment I imagine the click it made when old Mother Superior locked the door behind me. The trap-like bolt crying, "Bang." I'd stood half-naked and half-bloomed like a spring flower growing in snow as she stretched out the white cloth when she bound my breasts. I've always remembered the look in her eyes when she pinned it in place, her face awash in sweat, her mouth drooling, spit and half sentences sliding out. "Fires of hell for you, girl," she had hissed.

The afternoon sun traces the leaves of the plants on the window sills. Joseph's Coat was what my mother called these plants. Deep luscious layers of burgundy and rose, toasted with green down the centre. I wonder what kind of fashion statement Joseph would make today with these colours on his back.

On the far wall, the smiling Jesus has been moved and reframed. In gold. The old desk has been refinished in a lighter varnish, behind it the chair with a deep blue cushion and needlepoint people out for a stroll. There is a chair in front of the desk. Someone has painted flowers on the seat and back of the chair—bright, plump daisies with their long stems tied in a bow. On the top of the desk is a box of old pictures marked "To Be Discarded." I reach in and pick up a handful. Albert is standing behind Margaret in a class picture. A nervous look is stamped on her face. They are standing on the wooden platforms that were constructed for picture taking and concerts. I am absent in most of the class pictures, except for the one taken of the "Misfit Class," as old Mother Superior referred to it. I am standing at a distance from the others, in my cotton dress, a silhouette of altered puberty, my chest flattened. I remember now that this picture had been taken a few days before Cletis poked the pencil in my back. Cletis is standing at the end of the back row in a ragged sweater. His thin lips are stretched over a row of broken teeth.

The girl the boys had made fun of is at the other end of the row, her arms folded across her large breasts. They called her Rosie Knockers. The others look wayward or ambushed in some way. The next picture, of a bride and groom, has been hand-painted. The bride is wearing a mid-calf wedding dress and long veil. A bouquet of roses and baby's breath firmly shields her waist. The groom on the left is dressed in a pin-striped suit. His boutonniere, a white rose, is slightly tilted. The bride is not really pretty but has a borrowed attractiveness about her, satin and lace her cosmetic for the day. The groom is a head taller than the bride. Nobody is smiling on this bliss. He looks misplaced and nervous, like the students in the Misfit Class. Something about the picture makes me smile. It's the bride's red hair. On the back of the picture two names are scrawled in black ink. Madeline and Urbain.

Sister Thérèse taps me on the shoulder. "Mari-Jen, I see you have been entertaining yourself." She smiles. "I hope you weren't too bored. You can see that I have been house-cleaning before Mother St. Pius arrives. She wanted a fresh new office." I ask her about the picture I am holding.

"There's a story and a half about that picture." She hesitates. "But Mari-Jen, this is for your ears alone." Her face is more serious now. "That woman is Mother Superior's sister. Her husband was Mother Superior's beau at one time. The secret is still on their tongue," she sighs, "as to why her sister ended up in the white veil and Mother Superior in the black."

Neither one of us speaks for a moment. She knows I have unlocked the secret on my own. She buries the picture in the "To Be Discarded" box. Poor St. Urbain, you are finally put to rest. I can now ask Jesus to take you out of hiding. There is something funny about this, but I cannot laugh.

Sister Thérèse exhaled. "Mon Dieu, I was going to give you a pastel tour of the old place in its new colours." Her hand swiped her brow. "Look at the time, I received a phone call before I left the convent," she apologizes. "I have a meeting later with a new English teacher—his relatives were from Ste. Noire—who will be starting here in the fall." I remind her that I can come back anytime.

"No, no, no, Mari-Jen," she exhales, "you will come to the convent where I can speak to you about the job at the school I hope you will take. I will let you know." She smiles me a good-day as I leave the office.

In the hall, I pause and take another look at Margaret's picture that will soon make it to the discard box. Behind the anger in her eyes there is something else—a vulnerable dried-up seed. She may have known then what lay in wait.

She would never get another chance to get it right. Poor Margaret Rose, she had given it her best shot. I imagine her in the garden, not as a rose, but as a wilted French marigold, clinging to a vine.

I linger beside the long window facing west on my way down the stairs. The sun is a red ball on the flat sea, waiting to dissolve.

Outside the day is cooling. On the tall church steeple seagulls cry out like children in immediate danger. Thin lines of grey smoke hurry out of the chimneys of the surrounding houses. The young boys have gone home to fish suppers boiling in pots. Abstinence is on the Friday menu. A brown paper bag flaps on the front step. Inside the bag is a jam bottle full of Dustbane. I remove the lid and settle the dust of Ste. Noire that is gathering at my feet. An aroma of dust and Dustbane circles over my head before being taken by the wind around the corner.

# thirty

The *Gulliver* arrived like a ghost in Ste. Noire, in mid-August, after the dust settled along the roads and the night sky etched out a milky pasture of stars and a slim white moon. The boat trailed like a silver shadow behind Alfred's truck. In the stern of the boat, the dust of Jack McCluskey lay compact and sealed in a black seashell-shaped urn.

My brothers had waited until mid-August, Jack's birthday, to scatter their father's ashes over the Atlantic. Keeping company with the urn was a bottle of old Teacher's Highland Cream. The date on the shiny label read 1954. Someone had given them the whiskey in gratitude for a finely cut stone. They had stored it away for a special occasion. Albert said they wanted to bury their father and christen the *Gulliver* with Jack's ashes and a few gulps of the old liquid.

We set sail from Fog Harbour on a blue-green canvas of Atlantic waves and ripples and small swells, my brothers and I, the following morning. The quiet radiance of the new day dropped the sun's warmth on the village and shook sleeping children from their beds. Four or five small boys had gathered on the wharf for a rock-throwing competition.

Jack's urn rattled close to the whiskey bottle until we reached Seagull's Point, a few miles from shore. The lighthouse keeper stood on the upper deck dressed in a yellow oilslick. His full attention rested on something on the ground. Behind him the fishing huts looked like smudges on a dirty window. A few fishing boats were in dry-dock for repair. Fishermen, pooled in small dark groups as they worked, waved us good-day. Brightly coloured dories rocked gently like cradles full of sleeping babies. The wharf served as a runway for a dozen or more seagulls keeping a close watch on our journey. They hovered over the boat, cried out an obscenity, and then flew back to the wharf with a safe landing.

I could see the church steeple to the west of the *Gulliver*, coming in and out of grey clouds that burst and fell away like balloons pierced by a sharp object. Alfred had taken along his Kodak camera.

With its new outboard motor purring like a kitten over a smooth bowl of cream, the *Gulliver* ran long and lean towards Cape Laround.

It was somewhere beyond the cape that Albert said Ireland still sang lonely ballads for her ancestors who had made the crossing long ago. My brothers said Jack's family came from County Clare, in Ireland. His parents had sailed to Halifax when Jack had not more than an ounce of wind in his lungs, at two weeks of age.

We neared the edge of Cape Laround, and the swells began to thicken and swallow the *Gulliver* from stem to stern. The sea turned grey and the day that had had a setting of radiance and warmth disappeared under a black sky. Rain, wind, and thunder take on different voices upon the sea, as though they are part of its vast magnitude and must do their part in harmony, like voices in a mass choir. White streaks of lightning announced each rumbling note. I had put on my new rubber boots and a pair of heavy socks that Anna insisted must be worn for emergencies.

"It's only a squall," Albert shouted as he turned off the engine. We wore life jackets, yet I imagined that should we drown, our bodies would float in different directions. Perhaps one of my brothers would reach the coast of Ireland at the edge of a ballad. Or I would float ashore in Ste. Noire and be given a full Christian burial by Marcel, in my emergency socks. Or Albert might never be found.

I had heard stories of fishermen lost at sea. Alfred and Albert had told them to me themselves when we were kids. How fishermen were found bound together by rope and bones. They could identify them only by the rope that bound them, and sometimes widows got the bones of each other's husbands when the dead were untangled, and buried them as their own.

I looked at my brothers. Terror starched their voices and scarred their faces like the day Mama had beaten them with a stick for starting the fire in the field. I put my arms around them and felt them as light as rag dolls, and watched their lips move in a way only the desperate can pray. Albert reached for the bottle of whiskey and opened it with his teeth. He passed it to me and I swallowed it and a mouthful of prayers in one gulp. My throat shivered from the bitter taste of whiskey and salt and circumstances. I felt as though we were toasting our own death. Alfred drank slowly with a trembling hand, as he watched for a break in the storm.

"I am certain," Alfred said, "that the fishermen are waiting in a boat to come and haul us back to shore. They know exactly where we are," his voice choked, "as all fishermen know the sea like the back of their hands."

*Gulliver* rode the swells and sipped from the sea the angry foam that turned to water on the bottom of the boat. Albert removed the galvanized bucket hanging on a hook. None of us spoke for a time, as if we were suspended in the first moments of waking from a nightmare. Alfred's voice broke the silence. "I wonder what Jack would have done out here." His voice sounded tired and hoarse.

"He'd ride her out, Alfred," Albert answered angrily, "he'd ride her out."

And just as suddenly as it had disappeared, the sun broke through the clouds and we peeled out from under the tarpaulin and stood up, clinging to one another. I stroked the water with my hand as the swells became tranquil and spread the sea out long and smooth. We saw a fishing boat approaching near Seagull's Point as we emptied the *Gulliver*. Three fisherman called out to us as they pulled up beside us.

"You're damn lucky ya hadden got too far out beyond the cape," called the oldest of the three. "It's much worse out there, these winds come up like leftover hurricanes. The thunder and lightning rile 'em up, but we knew yer boat could handle this guff."

Alfred thanked the fishermen and offered them money and whiskey for their concern as Albert started up the engine, and we headed back to Fog Harbour. Jack McCluskey's ashes lay dry and compact in their shell.

Jack had done just what Alfred believed he would do. He rode her out.

We were approaching the harbour when Alfred said he had seen the ideal spot to scatter Jack's ashes. We walked to the end of the wharf after anchoring the *Gulliver*. A parade of gulls squawked at us for trespassing on their weather-beaten runway. They followed us at a safe distance above our heads with their majestic wings flapping like arms soft with lace.

We sat on the edge of the wharf facing what we believed was Ireland in the faraway distance, and dangled our feet into the sea that supposedly had carried Jack and his small lungs to Nova Scotia years before. Alfred and Albert opened the shell and returned their father to the sea. Six white speckled gulls stood side by side, like honorary pallbearers, on a large rock jutting out of the water. They waited as we did, until Jack McCluskey floated from our lives towards Seagull's Point on a smooth wave, and we all departed in silence.

# thirty-one

A ghostly bright August moon hung over Ste. Noire on the evening of Jack's burial, and spread like a blueprint over the village. Its sober eye, with one cool wink, rested on the warped windowsills of the Landry house, caught in the stillness of decay, its once-upon-a-time occupants long gone. Yet the moon lingered on the step like an old acquaintance dropping by for a visit.

The occupants left nothing to offer their visitors but cobwebs and rain-patterned walls in the still, empty rooms. There are seams in the floorboards for the moon to shine through. What it might find is a scurrying field mouse, on his way in, or his way out. It will be startled as all intruders are for a moment, at the invasion, the journey interrupted. But the mouse will continue his journey when the moon leaves. Will poke his furry head and vacuum with its nose along the floorboards. There is always something left behind for the living.

The moon's light will trace my mother's gravestone and warm her full name. She may or may not have welcomed a stone in the shape of an open book. The final page of her life exposed for passersby and moons to smear for eternity like some Greek tragedy. Margaret at fourteen years of age will get her swipe of the moon. It is Hattie who would long to linger under it. Let it drink from the dew of her new estate.

Hattie and Uncle Jule's remains, now part of the conse-crated grounds, ferment under crooked, wooden crosses. Someone has moved the fence back several feet to let the unconsecrated in. There was probably very little ceremony for the dozen or more souls waiting to reach consecrated grounds. Perhaps a fresh blessing is what they received. It would have caused more of a stir to be buried outside the fence before the new law. Like a public lynching. People remembered your name and your sins for years, as I have remembered the stories of Hattie Deloupe.

Hattie's cross rises from the ground like a stake driven in a blind fury, as if she herself had laid claim to what was rightly hers. Uncle Jule's cross is a few feet away from Hattie's. Private Jule Delene was the last of the lost to make the cross-over.

Amos continues to outwit the living. His impulses drive him to new and old graves like an agent for mortality. He kneels on the graves with news and weather reports and fresh prayers daily. He believes the dead have a right to be informed. They should be told which way the wind blows and if the sea is too moody to tamper with some days. Since his mother's death, he avoids soap and water. He smells like wind and rain. His cloudy eyes peer out from a tangle of greying hair like a strange sea-creature lost on land. His clothes are shapeless on his slight frame, knitted into the contours of his body, left melting and peeling like skin in salt water. People leave food at his door. He is well fed.

Nobody tries to have him committed to the "Home" any more. What would be the use, they shrug, he'd die without the dead to keep him alive.

My brothers had placed the marker on Mama's grave before I returned to Ste. Noire. Alfred designed her marker, using a pinkish stone and design he'd seen in an old English graveyard. Her full name is written out in calligraphy style. On the edges of the stone run a frill of chiselled leaves, each leaf identical in size, each leaf tinted a pale green. The effect is stunning. It took me a few minutes to remember the square of oilcloth Mama had bought for herself, the one she had seen in the store window while we waited for the Co-op truck to come and take us to church. Its edges were trimmed in leaves. Every Saturday she washed and paste-waxed the square. I would put on a pair of old wool socks and slide across it when the wax had dried. It never lost its shine from one week to the next.

I made my first visit to Mama's grave in May. I went up on my own. Alfred and Albert and I went to visit the graveyard after we left the wharf. They stood behind me as I knelt beside her grave. Clouds matted like old grey wool overhead. Mud spit up my skirt. Raindrops fell light as snowflakes.

I reached down and rubbed the stone with the hem of my skirt.

"There, Mama," I whispered low. I had something else I wanted to do on her grave. In that hospital, it had grieved me more than anything else, not knowing if anyone had given Mama the final touch.

On a decaying wooden cross, a few rows up from Mama's grave, a black crow pecked feverishly at the splinters in the rotting wood. The cross leaned over the bones of its tenant in one solemn and final bow. I walked up to it as the crow took flight, flew east in a mad flurry under a woolly cloud. The name on the cross was fading away. Half-decayed, half-eaten, an *e* and an *s* left of his or her identify.

Alfred and Albert were checking out the stone markers. I walked up the path a little farther. A spray of brightly coloured pansies caught my eye, spread out like a row of young girls in colourful flared skirts, dancing on Margaret's grave. A stone-white lamb lies on top of the marker. It looked asleep or drugged. Her parents have placed her picture in a glass-like box cemented against the stone. There is a door that slides on the front of the box. Margaret is in her teens in this picture, dressed in red, white hands cupped into a knot. Her bushy hair is flattened to her head with Brylcreem and bobby pins. A heavy rubberized cloth is tucked under the picture frame. On their daily visits to the grave, her parents protect Margaret's picture from inclement weather and the sun. They have made a ritual of keeping Margaret shining in their lives.

Margaret's frightened, wild eyes seemed to follow me as I stood over her grave. They had the look that comes to sheep during their slaughter. I had not realized how much fear she carried in her eyes. I plucked a pansy. The glass door slid open with a mouse-like squeak. I placed the pansy under her white hands and closed the door. The flower was yellow, the colour of the sun that no longer shines on her.

It had started to rain heavily before we left the graveyard, falling like breaking twigs on the back of Margaret's lamb.

I called Alfred and Albert over to Mama's grave. I left my handprints on the green, shiny grass of her grave. "It's your turn," I said to them. Alfred spread out his open palms beside mine. Albert shuffled his feet as if to take flight.

"Mari-Jen, would you like for me to jump on all the graves and give them a weather report while I'm here?" I knew he was joking with me.

"No, just leave her your touch," I said. He knelt down and placed his handprints beside Alfred's. I traced Mama's name with my finger as they ran back to the truck. *Adele Marie Delene (proper noun),* I whispered, *your sons are crying too.*

# thirty-two

A steady, silent rain fell the day I went to the convent to visit with Sister Thérèse. I was led into the front hall by an elderly nun robed in white, and starched like a doily, forbidden to wrinkle. Her round face was widened by a quick smile.

"Sister Thérèse is engaged on the telephone," she said, offering me a chair. I remembered her from the choir full of Sunday hymns.

I had never been this deep inside the convent. Alfred and Albert had referred to it always as the cave. "They hibernate in there," Albert said, "they keel over from saying the rosary and fall off to sleep in their prayers, their last amen hitting them like a stone."

The air was immaculately crisp. I felt guilty for entering in my damp condition. I had imagined the walls of the convent would be all dark, oak-stained wood to embellish their durability. But they were gyproc, painted a pure white. A seamless triangle of walls gave way to a large stained-glass window at the end of the hall. A white dove with an olive branch in its mouth descends upon the ark in the glass. Noah looks spellbound. He has yet to drink from the fruit of the vine. The animals stand two by two, ready for duty. Noah's wife is not in the picture.

A statue of St. Theresa is elevated on a wooden stand in the corner, a spray of rose petals at her feet. Her pink mouth is tinted by a shy smile like a bride whose bouquet has just come undone.

From behind the closed double doors to my left, I heard a laboured moan, the clearing of a throat. I listened closely to what was coming from behind the chapel doors, to a lone rattle of pain. The polished door handles fit snugly into my hands. The red vigil candle on the white altar gave the chapel the blush of a setting sun. A wooden cross hung above the altar, suspended on a colourless wire. The crucified Christ dozed off into death, waiting for His final hour. There were a dozen or more pews in the chapel, polished and empty like waiting boats beside a stream. The slow ceiling fan above my head provided the only voice. A low hum of distant thunder.

The moaning voice rose again from behind a pillar. I walked slowly towards the altar and watched as a diminutive bag of criss-crossed bones fought with the beast in her throat. She was unaware that I was behind her wheelchair until she turned slightly. Face to face with me, old Mother Superior's black eyes exploded with the expansion of disbelief, as her cruel fingers sketched in the air.

"Ahhh," her voice croaked. She had recognized me and now watched me suspiciously as one would watch a predator. It was she who was bound this day, her coiled limbs melting into the steel bar that hugged her in place. I felt my fear melt from me.

A Saint Christopher medal dangled from the back of the chair. Did he believe she would run someone down? She raised a locked fist awkwardly as I moved in closer to her and got down on my knees. Her face was the colour of a grey pigeon, her forehead as damp as a swamp. Beneath the pallor a slow flame rose, its fire catching in her veins. I watched her mouth twist out her words slowly.

"Why…are…you…?"

I finished her question for her. "Why am I here?" I looked directly into her eyes. "I am here because I was invited."

Mother Superior turned her gaze towards the window. I released the brake on the chair and moved her directly under the fan. The crucified Christ watched in slow agony as I circled the chair. She was armed only with old victories paralyzed in her bones.

"You do remember me." My voice quivered as I faced her again. I knew she could hear me as her eyes answered with a blink and she sucked in her stomach. I am the last of the spent sacraments she expected to see. She may have believed I would be soft and silent forever.

My voice steadied as I continued to speak. She continued to stare at me. "I am back. I have entered your convent and heaven has not even bothered to interfere." She looked so small against this heavenly setting, so shrivelled at its altar. The fan's silver wings scooped up her misery and spread it around the chapel. The open side window ushered in a melody of sea noises.

"I have survived," my voice said, but she had turned her gaze to the man on the wire. What fell from her lips could not be heard, but I knew she was praying. For my damage or her own? I had her cornered. She had been caught so abruptly off guard. I knew in my heart that if she expected brutal force from me it had already been served by my presence. I had not expected to ever see her again. Some people believed that she had already left Ste. Noire.

I watched her closely as her lip began to tremble.

"You have not changed...very much...Mari-Jen."

"What is it you wanted to change in me?" I quizzed.

"You were too...vulnerable." Her voice was uneven and surprisingly soft. The colour drained from her face. "You never put...up a...fight," she whispered. "Your brothers... fought your...battles."

"How was I supposed to fight with you—I didn't have a chance."

"But you had...the words, Mari-Jen, I...realized that too late." Her head slumped as if she were falling asleep. "You knew them better...than any student I...have...ever... taught."

"What words? My collection of nouns and verbs. How did you know about them?"

"I...didn't." She closed her eyes and began to mumble as if she had summoned sleep to her rescue. "Nought's...had, all's...spent, where our...desire is...got...without... content...." Her mouth began to drool and she swiped at it with a closed fist. "The Jew taught you...well; he took that...power from...me."

"Daniel Peter is a good teacher." My voice cut in on hers.

"And you must remain...a good...student...Mari-Jen." She eyed me directly. "One must not put their head...on the block just to let the axe win." Her body trembled as she spoke. "I have...always detested...weakness...in women," she scowled. The old fire and brimstone was back and she was fighting hard. I remembered the day she had put me in her grade twelve class and she had read from Shakespeare. But now the lesson was for me only and she wanted desperately for me to learn it. I wanted to question this bitter old woman, but she was getting weary.

I was unprepared for what was to follow as she turned her drowning eyes on me with the starved sadness of defeat. Her head slumped to one side as her hand wandered like that of a young child in search of something in the dark. She looked very tired. Her body reeked of liniment. Her skin was shrivelled and flaking like a fish washed up on the shore. She had not planned to be seen like this. I moved her chair back slowly beside the pillar near the open window and tucked her white quilt securely in place.

She seemed to enjoy the choir of wind and rain and hostile waves beyond the window. Someone had removed her black robe and veil and dressed her in white. A gust of brutal wind sent her thin veil flying. It floated in mid-air before landing at the foot of the altar. Wisps of white hair clung like frost to the back of her neck as I pinned the veil back in place.

Mother Superior did not know that I had seen the wedding picture of her sister and her one-time beau. That I had seen the satin, swelling bride behind the rose bouquet. And the pin-striped groom beside the swell. I would never know who helped Madeline pin her bridal veil in place over her red hair, but when I placed the veil on old Mother Superior's head, the words "Now you look like the bride" slipped from my mouth unintentionally. She stared at me for a time like a dog about to be whipped.

"You have…always reminded me of my…sister." Her voice broke.

"I saw her picture at the school," I said.

"A good person...I reared her when...our mother... died. She would...jump over a...dandelion for affection." Her voice crawled to a whisper. "I gave her...everything that I had, and she married him." Her voice faltered. "I have...my ...own...weakness....Memories can be a weakness, a noose around the heart....I...have...never forgotten him."

I stood beside her and watched her eyes cloud over, become colourless, escape somewhere back inside her head as they drowned in a pool of darkness. She reminded me of a blind dog, head bent, sniffing for something that had once been very clear. She opened her eyes again and stared at me.

An olive branch of spread-out bones reached out to me. They were surprisingly warm.

In a glossy room, fresh as a lemon, Sister Thérèse apologized for making me wait. "I hope you have found something to satisfy the wait." She smiled over a cup of tea. She reached over and touched my hand.

"You are the one for the job. I've always known how smart you really are." I smiled back at her. She described the job as we finished our tea. "The children will love you, Mari-Jen, you can help them off and on the bus." She laughed. "You can read to them, Mari-Jen, I know you can." Sister Thérèse crossed her hands. "Mon Dieu, Mari-Jen, I would love to have you as a helper for the beginners at the school."

Sister Thérèse studied my face, the place where all good teachers start. "Winter can be such a penance, Mari-Jen, a season of scarfs and mittens and boots and jackets. Not to mention a sea of red glorious faces and frozen smiles."

A snow-white image came into my head. I, Mari-Jen Delene, am in the lead. The Pied Piper of Ste. Noire school, sliding down the hill path, past the sturdy snow figures and rising snow-castles with a convoy of wind-whipped children in tow, their heads full of fresh sums and nouns and verbs and bright stars. My answer is yes.

# thirty-three

September rapped boldly on Ste. Noire's doors, escorting sharp winds through mesh screens and open windows. A parade of black ants lingered on the border in and out, moved slowly along the window sill. People were getting ready to bank their houses for the coming winter, piling seaweed and sawdust up as high as woodpiles.

*The Farmer's Almanac* was calling for a harsh winter. People believed that Ste. Noire would mole under a blanket of snow until the spring of 1971. They know these things because nature has a way of predicting the future as early as August, they say. The wasps had built their nests high in the trees, a sure sign of a white fury.

The evening before my first day at work, in my mother's house where I decided to spend the night, a string of white moonlight wiggled across my quilt, slipped over the edge of my cot. I followed it to my window and looked out over a sleeping Ste. Noire.

I imagined Amos at rest. Scrambling in and out of dreams. Alone but for the moonlight that hung over him like a mother.

Margaret's aging parents drifting into each other sometime through the night. Rib to rib. The contact will be made and abandoned. They are separate beings in their grief and their pain. They cannot let but one light shine through.

The old parish priest stirring in his dreams under a twenty-watt bulb. It is never turned out. It dangles above his head like a dull crown that he has outgrown, like Ste. Noire. He is weary of erasing the mortal slate. The venial sins that will amount to nothing more than a penance. He is envious of the young curate who is now in France flexing his young mind. Things can't get much better for a man like Marcel, with Ste. Noire's white pleasure still in his soul.

Daniel Peter sedating himself to sleep with his four Polish sonnets. It is a privileged comfort to him now to release them on Anna's pillow. He has waited so long to read them out loud to someone.

The light that glowed in the upstairs window of John Mino's house after he returned to New York to marry the dancer, people believed it could have started the fire that burned my old grandparent's house to the ground one evening. Nobody could understand how that black and white dog sat on the crest of the hill and waited for the last flame to go out, as if it knew a terrible secret was gone forever.

Sister Thérèse retiring when everyone else is at rest. Whatever she will hear at the foot of silent beds will be returned to her vows. With a smile.

Hattie Deloupe's grandson, the new English teacher, turning the pages of Faulkner or Hardy under a Ste. Noire moon.

I had met the new teacher on his second appearance in Ste. Noire, during the last week of August. He sat in the seat in front of me at church. A missionary priest from Quebec had been invited to the parish. He looked like a man damned by his own virtues. A candelabra of light winked behind his back and danced backwards. His right hand slummed over a wrinkled brow, as if to quiet his thoughts before his lips would open up. He had to part with what he was asked to deliver, but not before he could gauge the people. Like a searchlight in a drowning wave. Years of celibacy had taught him to recognize those who were not, someone said.

His sermon to the congregation on the ill effects of fornication began with a loud, raspy cough. The young were the unmarried, the soon to be, the hoping to be, the may never be of Ste. Noire. Some of the couples sat together, being very careful not to rub shoulders. Others twitched. Scratched their chins. Checked their watches. Buttoned already buttoned buttons.

"Temptation is everywhere," the priest began. "It is beside you. It is behind you. It is in front of you, and it is in you." He looked around. "It is always eager to offer its vile touch, its superficial tongue, its temporary thrill, its..." He turned to where old Father Benoit sat as if to ask, What else? But old Father Benoit had fallen off to sleep. His head hung like someone who had just fainted and didn't care to be revived. The mission priest's voice took on a sharper edge. "Fornication is Satan's password. His illicit fiction."

Hattie Deloupe's grandson turned to me. Winked a wicked green eye and smiled deeply.

I had never seen a picture of Hattie Deloupe but the one I had printed in my mind—pulped skin, sharp hawked nose, eyes crusted and red from more liquor than sleep. Lonely as a Sunday morning dog as she lay dying, with no one around. Someone has said her grandson is her spitting image. How wrong I had been. Hattie Deloupe would have been a blond. Eyes as green as clovers. A borrowed red mouth perhaps, when she danced on Saturday nights. She would have been to light what my mother was to dark. Vulnerable, distracted, and beautiful, with years of sorrow to tempt them into fiction.

Light rain turned into mist as I walked along the road the next morning towards Anna and Daniel Peter's house. Babel the bull was out in the pasture. Babel preferred rain to flies. It rolled down his back in soft layers like an invisible hand spraying water from a black vein. The ring in his nose was beaded with raindrops. A string of dull grey pearls breaking one by one fell to the ground. He turned his massive head towards me as I passed by. Daniel Peter was in the barn.

Inside Anna's kitchen it was oven warm as I sat down to breakfast. A rippling sound rapped at the door. Anna opened it. A gift of the wind lay on the step: a small shore bird. Its quivering feathers were its only sign of life. Anna scooped up the bird like a coin, felt the rhythm of its heartbeat under her thumb. The bird was too frightened of the human hand to seek combat. Its black eyes blinked furiously. It had no voice. No one to answer to, but Anna and I asking each other if it was wounded.

I knew that these birds rarely left the shore. The fishermen called them the vagabonds of the sea, the sleepers of the waves. I could not remember the name of the birds. "It be okay," said Anna, "you see, you hold bird." We walked down to the shore to return it to the waves.

The bird felt like a ball of thorn lace in my hands, waiting to be unravelled. Seagulls were grouped in private conversations along the wharf. They paid no attention to our arrival. Yet they were the only witnesses that day who saw the bird take flight, waver slightly under a breaking blue sky. They could hear the waves beckon it home to freedom, as the sun rode on its wings.

Anna and Daniel Peter drove me to school at eight o'clock sharp. My lunch (packed by Anna at her insistence) contained Polish sausage, homemade bread, apple strudel and poppy-seed cake, one apple, one orange, a bunch of grapes, and two blocks of cheese.

Anna worried that I might be late. She insisted that her husband drive faster. Daniel Peter smiled. Sister Thérèse was standing in the schoolyard. She smiled broadly.

"Mari-Jen, you are early. Come and meet some of the children!" A chorus of small voices cried out, "Hello, Mari-Jen."

Two small boys wore yellow raincoats. They stretched open their pockets to show me the mist they had collected before the sun came out. They laughed when I told them I could see it. Their laughter was pure and unrehearsed. The pealing of the bell cut into their act. They ran to the front of the line. A parade of brightly clad beginners moved slowly towards the open door, past the nun with the dimpled smile, past the veteran teacher with a tear in her eye, past the new English teacher (who came to the wrong door; the high school classes went in the side door), past the janitor who would collect their first footprints with his broom, they followed the leaders with the pockets full of mist.

I turned to see if Anna and Daniel Peter had left. That's when I saw her, the leftover child. Her small white hand curled around the wire, a rabbit-in-a-snare image, a fairytale-gone-wrong ending, crouched on the other side of the fence. She didn't move as I walked over to her. A trickle of blood ran out from under her fingers. I knelt down beside the golden-haired wire child, already broken. The hem of her dirty blue coat sipped up the morning dew. A brown paper bag, cracked like a turtle shell, lay beside her on the grass.

I curled one of my hands around the fence. She eyed me cautiously.

"My name is Mari-Jen," I offered, "but I don't know your name." No answer. "Is your name Mari-Jen, too?"

She eyed me directly. "No, me is Isabel." Her body trembled as she spoke.

"That's a pretty name, Isabel, I'll bet you can spell it."

"No, me can't."

"I'll bet you can print it."

"No, me can't."

"Why don't you come into the school with Mari-Jen and I will teach you to spell your pretty name."

Her voice began to quiver. "Me is scared of the big school."

"Mari-Jen will stay with Isabel until the scared goes away." She did not move. "Mari-Jen and Isabel can wash their hands, then go with the other kids and colour pictures."

She moved her hand, with its small break, slowly from the wire but did not get up.

"Do you like crayons, Isabel?"

"Me got crayons," she answered, as she picked up the paper bag. Three or four broken crayons fell to the ground.

"Mari-Jen has lots of crayons, lots and lots of crayons. I will give them all to Isabel."

"What colour are them?"

"They are the colours of a rainbow."

"Now, me can have them?" Her voice pleaded.

"Tomorrow, Isabel. Tomorrow."

She put out her wire hand for me to hold. We walked slowly towards the school under a Sistine-blue sky, under a yellow-egg-yoke sun, under the wings of a white seagull, under the song of a brown sparrow, towards tomorrow and two pockets full of mist. We entered as one.